ON THE RUN WITH LOVE

By *J.M.Benjamin*

Cover Design by Mike Rush
Interior design by Brian Holscher
Edited by Sonja Brown

First A New Quality Publishing L.L.C. trade paperback printing 2008

For more information, or to contact author or publisher, send correspondence to:

A New Quality Publishing
P.O.Box 589
Plainfield, New Jersey 07061
www.anewqualitypublishing.com
anewqualitypublishing@yahoo.com
jmbenjamin.author@yahoo.com
myspace.com/jmbenjamin_author

ISBN: 978-0-9817756-0-9

10 9 8 7 6 5 4 3 2
First Paperback Edition

Printed in Missouri

Acknowledgements

As always, To The Most Merciful, for continuing to spare my life and keeping me both focused and safe on my journey in this literary game as well as in this cruel world. You've blessed me with the sight and allowed me to see things and others for what and who they really are. In You and You alone I trust. You are indeed The Greatest and the Best of Planners.

To my supporters, I appreciate those who have followed me thus far, from Down In The Dirty, to My Manz And 'Em, and Ride Or Die Chick, on down to the anthology's I contributed to. Without your genuine love and support their would be no J.M. Benjamin the author. Thanks Again. And for the haters, I can't leave you out. The more you do-the more I do! Get ya weight up-not ya hate up!

Unconditional and undying love goes out to my family and loved ones, my number one ridah, moms you already know, there's no word in existence that can express the love. My father, I've watched you come along way, keep coming, I love you. My son, Jameel, nothing or no one can come in between the love I have for you, I wish you to be the man I never was. My daughters, Yaseena & Jamillah, Congratulations! I've never been more prouder as a father then when we went prom dress shopping, you are and will always be, without a doubt, daddy's little girls. My brother, As Salaamu Alaikum, this shit about to get serious in "08", I got us.

iii

My sisters, I love you, take care of my niece and nephews.

The White Family, Kev, how you stepped up to the plate when no one else would will never be forgotten, Real Edutainment Publishing will always be the house that J.M.Benjamin & K.R.White built for My Manz And 'Em, love is love. The Benito Family, Don, Muzik N Motion & Real Edutainment Books (New Location: 144 East Front Street Plfd NJ 07060) was the best thing we could've ever done, bonded for life, my best to you and your family.

To my friends and new family of A New Quality Publishing, J-Rod Nider, (New Projects Stand Up!) Your time is coming my dude, soon the world will know why "Diamonds Are Forever". Nyema, "Back Stabbers" gonna be your one, threes a charm, remember I told you that. FiFi Cureton, your joint "Have You Ever" is gonna have a lot of sisters asking themselves that million dollar question, especially when the sequel "Would You Ever Again" drops. Caleb Alexander, they saw what you could do in "Deadly Reigns" and True II The Game 2, now let's showin' what you can do when you hungry, "Belly Of The Beast" is a problem.

Lastly, I want to acknowledge a brother, my brother in Faith and in heart, who took a stand in this industry and changed the game in the ninth inning when it seemed the game was over for him, Kwame Teague aka Dutch, author of The Dutch series, including Dutch: The Finale. Akhi, Allah protects the Believers and does not place anymore on us then He knows we can bare, for He is The All Knowing. The things that have been done have been because we were built, born, and raised to do it, no one can take that away from us. May Allah return you back to this side of the world in one peace and mind, As

Salaamu Alaikum. Oh yeah, Thug Politics by Dutch due out July 19, 2008, you don't wanna miss that! Ride Or Die Chick 2, (Fall 2008), Heaven & Earth (Winter 2008). We can't be moved or stopped!

If you or someone you know is an author, publisher, bookstore owner, or vendor and is in need of distribution for your titles, publishing company, establishment, or table, please visit www.alliancebookgroup.com and see what we have to offer.

Thank You

J.M.Benjamin

Dedication

Although I dedicated my first independent novel My Manz And 'Em to myself, I feel the need to dedicate yet another to me for many particular reasons. First in foremost, Independence Day has such an significance to why I chose this as a release date. Number one, the 4th of July will mark two years that I had my first official signing as a free man and as an author. It is also the date of my independent release from prison. It is the date that I came home and signed at my friends barbershop during the 4th of July parade due to the fact that my hometown had no African American book store in town. Now here it is this will be my fourth novel, and my first book signing will be at an African American book store during the 4th of July parade, a book store which I just so happened to own.

I wanted to dedicate this book to myself because I truly believe that I deserve all that has come my way. For those who may be picking up a J.M.Benjamin book for the first time, I wanted to share some things with you that I've accomplished in just a period of two years in this game so when you run into the haters who have the wrong perception or just live their lives as haters, you will be able to see them as I do.

About the Author (The Life Of a Hustler)

J.M. Benjamin is an Award Winning and Essence Best Selling author hailing from out of Plainfield, New Jersey. In 2006, he quickly emerged in the fast growing genre of Urban Literature, making his presence felt with his freshman novel Down In The Dirty, published by Flowers In Bloom Publishing. Ironically, having spent more than half his life in the streets and a substantial amount of time incarcerated, J.M. Benjamin's only credential as a street tale story teller is simply his own first hand experience and knowledge of what the streets consist of. J.M. Benjamin's upbringing provided him with the necessary tools he now uses in his work to capture and display the reality and horrors of the streets world-wide. He became a motivational speaker after numerous of articles were featured on his life story as ex-inmate turned author, sharing his experiences and knowledge of the streets at various high and junior schools, colleges, probation and religious programs for the youth, institutions for incarcerated men and women, and urban communities throughout his travels, in hopes to make a difference. His accomplishments as an author have been recognized in The New York Times, The Courier News, The Herald News, and many more. JOLIE magazine ranked J.M. s freshman novel Down in The Dirty as #2 hottest summer read. He was nominated for BEST NEW Breakout Author Of The Year and Best Street Novel Of The Year 2006 by the African American Literary Awards, which, he won for Best Street fiction of the Year. He was nominated in two categories and won for Best Street Lit at the Chicago Black Authors & Books Award hosted by Infini Promoters. His book Down in The Dirty was featured on the Wendy Williams Experience Book club as the book of the month for July and was voted the #1 Urban Book out of the Top 10 Street Lit novels sponsored by The Writer s Inn. All of this in under a years time after being released from federal prison. In Feb. 2007, J.M. Benjamin released his sophomore novel My Manz And Em independently under Real Edutainment Publishing, which he is founder and co-owner of. He was nominated for Best Street Fiction again at The AALA for his second novel. In September of 2007, he partnered up with a friend and opened a music and book store (Music N Motion & Real Edutainment Books), where his third novel, an Essence Best Seller (May 08) and Black Expression (April 08) favorite, Ride Or Die Chick book release party was held. Six months later J.M. and partner opened up a larger music and books store downtown in his hometown of Plainfield NJ (144 East Front Street). In October 2008, J.M.Benjamin ventured out into a another arena of the literary world, trying his hand at street distribution for authors and independent publishers alike, becoming responsible for some of your favorite street lit novels such as Dutch: The Finale, Deadly Reigns: The Next Generation, ShytList, Grown & Gangsta, and Ski Mask Way, just to name a few, gracing the tables and stores of your local street vendors and African American book stores. Ultimately, J.M.'s consistent and quality work ethics landed him an opportunity to become a part of a new distribution company, Alliance Book Group (www.alliancebookgroup.com) and recently launched a new independent publishing company himself, signing six new and known authors to A New Quality Publishing. He has three novels due to be released this year, On The Run With Love due out on The Fourth Of July, which marks his two year anniversary of being out of prison, Heaven & Earth due out this winter, both under A New Quality Publishing, and Ride Or Die Chick 2 due out this fall under Flowers In Bloom Publishing . Since being introduced to readers in the anthology, Menace II Society with the short story titled Keeping It Gangsta he has secured a position in the Urban Literature genre and become a major asset when it comes to making a difference in the minds of his readers. He is also a contributing author to the anthology presented by Nikki Turner, Christmas In The Hood, and a non-fiction motivational book titled Changin Your game Plan. All of this in a two years time frame. From the time he wakes up til the time he steals 3-4 hours rest, J.M.'s day consists of hustling.

You have Doers and you have Talkers...
Which one does it sound like I am?

Prologue

The first bullet whizzed through the air, shattering the bottle of Grand Cru Remy Martin on the table and piercing the soft flesh of Freddie's upper left side, separating two of his ribs. The burning sensation ignited his insides letting his intoxicated mind know he had been shot. But he wasn't surprised. How could he be when he saw it coming—saw them coming— from across the crowded club.

The second shot caught him in the neck. His blood splattered all over a screaming female beside him who was scrambling to get away.

Yes, he saw the bullets coming. He could see them in his eyes before he saw the glint of the cold steel in the shooter's hand. When their eyes first met, his instincts went into survival mode. He saw murder and knew he was the victim. As he reached for his pistol, something happened. Something just made him stop, and he accepted what was taking place. He was tired.

His whole world as he knew it had come crashing down around him. Everything was gone and the only thing that remained was the fact that he was a wanted man. Not only by the police but by everyone it seemed. They all wanted him out of the way. Freddie couldn't eat or sleep without the incessant thought that he was running out of time.

The third shot that hit him like a sledgehammer in the abdomen was the welcoming committee that told him it was all over. And he welcomed it.

On The Run With Love

Freddie embraced the warm sensation he felt creeping over his entire body. He welcomed the way everything and everyone around him began moving in slow motion.

The sound of screaming voices and the tempo of the popular club mix by Adrian Sykes warped in Freddie's ears to match the steady rhythm of his heartbeat as it slowly got drowned out. His heartbeat was pounding loudly in his eardrums over all the commotion.

Even the fourth bullet, the last shot he felt, seemed to move in slow motion. From the barrel of the gun, he followed its matrix-like trajectory as it zeroed in on him. He watched it come dangerously close to a woman's ducking head, break a glass in a man's hand, and finally lodge itself deep inside his own flesh. Simultaneously, Freddie's mind was sent to that place where pain can no longer reach.

His last sight was of those eyes and the determination in them. He knew it was coming, no one can run forever. His last thought was "Damn, why did it have to be me?"

ONE YEAR EARLIER

"Pimpin' is easy when a player looks good," old head Butch the barber remarked as he turned Freddie's chair toward the mirror.

Freddie Holmes looked into his own reflection, admiring his light brown complexion. He was half-Dominican and it showed in his features. His father, whoever he was, had left him with naturally curly brown hair and hazel eyes that took on a greenish tint in the summer. He wore his hair close with neatly shaped sideburns and a trimmed goatee. Freddie really didn't need a haircut, but because he took pride in his good looks, he made bi-weekly trips to Nu-Cuts barbershop, his old friend's establishment. Butch had been cutting Freddie's hair for almost ten years, since he was eleven. So he knew exactly how he liked his hair cut.

"Unc, touch up this sideburn a little. It looks thicker than this one." Freddie said, turning his head from side to side.

"You must be goin' blind, nephew. I know what the hell I'm doin'. When you sit in my chair, I create freakin' masterpieces," Butch boasted with a chuckle. "I'm like a got-damn Picasso in this bad boy, huhhh!" Butch added with a preacher's flair, making the other patrons laugh.

"Man, just fix my joint 'fore you make me late," Freddie replied with a smirk. Butch was like an uncle to Freddie for real. Their families went back generations, even before Freddie came into existence.

Butch's second barber, Mr. Shuttleworth, a short West Indian man, stopped the cut he was doing on another brother to glance over at Freddie. "Let meh fine out da likkle young gal

3

yuh bout to tie da knot wid wear da pants and got yuh runnin' home wid your nose open," Mr. Shuttleworth joked in his native tongue as the patrons joined in with laughter.

Freddie took it in stride. "Nah man, I got a funeral to go to."

"Oh, da wedding's today?" Mr. Shuttleworth snapped back, laughing hard. "'Cause mine damn sure was a funeral! Man!" Everybody fell out.

"Nephew," Butch said between cackles, "I ain't no gay ass joker or nuttin', and excuse my French, Mr. Shuttleworth, but if I had your hand, I'd throw mine away. What in the hell is you gettin' married fo'?"

"Yeah mon. All dem fine women I done seen yuh wid." Mr. Shuttleworth joined, as he shook his head in mock disbelief. "Yuh violatin' the player's code my youth!" Everyone in the shop just exploded in laughter.

Freddie chuckled along, "Naw, Unc, you got me twisted. See, y'all see these broads at they best. But I'm tellin' you, you ain't seen shit until they butt-ass naked bangin' at your door two in the mornin' wit' a broken heart and a butcher knife."

"Well, I don't know about the butcher knife," Butch replied, "But a butt-naked sistah can bang on my door any-time!"

"Mine, too!" someone in the peanut gallery yelled out.

Freddie just shook his head at the two old coons because he knew they didn't understand. You see, he was blessed with features that spoke for themselves. And he had developed a razor-sharp game that made females silly putty in his hands. But he wasn't a cold-hearted individual. He was a dog to some and a player to most; still he wasn't cold enough to not let females' emotions affect him once he was done with them. Money, sex—in that order. Those old coons hadn't seen what Freddie could do to or get from women. Besides, they had never been desired the way Freddie often was. Now the thrill was gone and the game had become more problems than it was worth.

"Y'all just don't understand," he stated simply.

"Understand what? Pussy? Man, the day pussy becomes a problem, I'll be the first black muthafucka in line lookin' for trouble!" the third barber Nas exclaimed, now joining in.

"Right behind me!" one of the regular customers added.

Then, as if on cue, the door busted open and in walked a problem. Everybody abruptly stopped laughing when they saw this big, black niggah standing in the door holding this fine, thick redbone firmly by the neck.

"Cream, get off me! You hurtin' me!" the redbone begged.

"Bitch, I'ma do more than that if you don't point out this Freddie muhfucka!" the big, black, monster-looking stranger thundered as he shook her real hard, ragdoll-like.

Freddie tensed up at the sound of his name. Then he recognized the girl. She was a stripper he'd met, or rather ran back into, at the new gentlemen's club on Richmond Street. He'd first met her back in the day at Club Eleganza's in Newark. He had fucked her a few times before she caught feelings. And with the cat standing in the doorway, he remembered her saying that her man had been in the county jail for a few weeks... and her trick-ass was out sucking the next man's dick.

"In the chair, Cream! Right there!" she pointed at Freddie with satisfaction. She'd gladly take her ass-whuppin' if she could see Freddie's no-good ass take one, too.

Cream shoved her aside and approached Freddie. "You know her, niggah?" Cream demanded.

Freddie silently cussed himself out for leaving his gun in the car. He eyed the goliath in front of him, realizing he was in an awkward position. He wasn't usually defending himself.

"Come on man, you can't be serious," Freddie replied,

5

checking all around for the upper hand.

"Answer the question, muhfucka! Let me hear you say you fucked my wife!"

Wife? Freddie thought and looked back at the redbone. He could see her smirk through the tears. The tension was too thick to reply verbally. It was either move or get moved on, and Freddie wasn't about to choose the latter. His next move was quick and effective. He spotted clippers in Butch's hand and, with lightning fast agility, grabbed the cord and swung the clippers as hard as he could into Cream's nose. Cream grunted and fell back, but only momentarily. As Freddie got out of the chair, Cream lunged at him, only to catch a Nike ACG boot in the nuts that folded him up. A pistol fell to the floor from Cream's waistline. Freddie caught him with a crushing left that broke the gargantuan man down, proving that he had a glass jaw.

"Bitch-ass niggah! Confrontin' me over this stankin'-ass broad!" Freddie barked as he bent down to pick up the pistol. "And—you was gonna shoot me?!" Freddie grabbed a handful of Cream's cornrows and brought the steel down hard on his jawline, making him spit out a tooth. "Don't you—ever—bring—this—shit—down the west end, niggah!" Freddie yelled, punctuating every word with a blow.

The redbone was in shock. She was sure Big Cream would beat Freddie down. She jumped on Freddie's back, all nails and teeth like a wolf protecting her young. "Get off my man, motherfucka!" she bellowed.

Freddie fought to get his arm loose from her grip. "This bitch," he chuckled in disgust. He grabbed a handful of weave and brought her face down hard on his knee as Butch begged him to stop. She doubled over and crumpled to the ground.

"Got-dammit, Freddie, I said stop!" Butch yelled and locked his sawed off shotgun for emphasis. He had been calling Freddie the whole time but Freddie was in a zone.

Freddie heard the metallic clack and froze mid-motion of pummeling Cream again with the pistol. Blood was everywhere. He stood up, breathing uncontrollably. "Now niggah, take your punk ass back to the east end," Freddie said before he spat on Cream's mangled body.

"I hate you, Freddie! You ain't shit!" the redbone screamed with her nose bleeding.

"Neither was your rotten-ass pussy! That's why I ain't givin' you what you want now!" Freddie taunted.

"Somebody get this brother out my shop," Butch ordered. Nas and another man helped Cream and the redbone out.

"It ain't over," Cream mumbled through lips that were already beginning to swell, but Freddie didn't hear him. He turned back to Butch as Cream was carried out.

Butch just shook his head. "On second thought, I'm glad yo' pretty ass is gettin' married."

"Just fix my muthafuckin' sideburns so I can go," Freddie spat, climbing back into the chair. "Actin' like you was gonna shoot some damn body." Freddie smiled.

"I was. You. I love you, but I'll kill you before I let you shut my business down, neph," Butch replied with a straight face. Freddie knew he was capable because he was an old-school gangster, but knew he could never harm a hair on him. "Just finish me up, unc."

Freddie inserted his key into the door of his apartment. He glanced down at himself and all the blood splattered all over his Polo shirt. He was still mad, but the more he thought about it, the funnier it became. Cream was a grown-ass man on some high school shit, fighting over some pussy. Now that was a violation of the player's code. If anything, he should have shaken Freddie's hand for showing him how triflin' the woman he married really was. Freddie busted out laughing as he entered the apartment.

"Freddie?" He heard a sweet voice call out from the kitchen. "Your mother said she was gonna kill you if you..."

His fiancée, Simone, came out of the kitchen wearing only a dress slip and stockings. Putting her earrings on, she stopped short when she saw her man covered in blood and quickly rushed to him.

"Freddie! Are you ok? What happened?" she asked in a quick succession, checking him for wounds. Then she noticed he was laughing. "And what's so funny?"

Freddie shook his head and kissed her lightly on the lips. "Plainfield," he replied with irony.

"What you done did, boy?" she inquired with a sigh.

"Don't sweat it, babe. This joker just had his people fucked up, yo," Freddie told her, checking his watch. "Let me take a quick shower and I'll be ready, aiight?"

He quickly stepped off to avoid any more questions. Wasn't no way he was gonna tell Simone he had to smash a brother over a piece of ass.

Freddie headed down the hallway, pulling off his Black Label jacket. He pulled his Ralph Lauren Polo shirt over his head and tossed it into the hamper. He turned on the shower and tested the temperature until it was to his liking. He got undressed, pulling off his black Nike ACG boots, Antic denim jeans, and Movado watch. Freddie climbed into the shower and held his head under the nozzle, letting the water cascade down his face. He watched the brown residue of dried blood slip down the drain, and thought about how easily the tables could have been turned. He could be somewhere stitched up and swollen right now.

His mind was brought back by the touch of a silky hand caressing his back. He turned around to find Simone in the shower with him, smiling into his eyes. Freddie took one look at Simone's deep, dark, Foxy Brown eyes; her small but pert breasts, nipples erect; her thick hips and forgot all about the fight. Freddie wrapped his arms around her waist and palmed her ass.

"Now we really gonna be late," he remarked.

Simone playfully hit him then wrapped her arms around his neck. "No, we're not. I'm just checkin' on my man. You came home covered in blood, laughing, and I ain't supposed to worry?"

Freddie took one long look into Simone's eyes and knew why he was marrying her. Love was written all over her face. There was no explanation that could put her concern to rest. So he just caressed her face and gently sucked her bottom lip. Then Freddie kissed her.

"Dig Ma, I love you, okay? And ain't nothing in the world gonna take me from you, so don't worry about Daddy. It's okay."

Simone gazed back trustingly and nodded. "It's just…it's been so crazy out there, baby. I just want you to be careful."

"Wit' all this chocolate waitin' for me, a niggah gots to be careful." Freddie grinned, making her blush. "Now…can we be a little late?" He flirted, massaging her ass and pulling her closer.

"So your mother can kill me? I don't think so," she answered, kissing him softly. "But ah, good things come to those who wait," she promised seductively, stepping out of the shower, dripping chocolate. Simone grabbed a towel and strutted out of the bathroom knowing her man was watching. She was just happy that he was home safe.

Dante looked at his man Cream in disgust. Cream was laid back on the couch with his face stitched up and his jaw wired shut. He couldn't believe his man played himself over that slut of a wife of his. Dante knew the bitch was trifling because half the click had tossed her up before Cream married her. But this was different. Freddie had washed his man out and shit had to be handled. Dante knew what had to be done.

His click of wolves was on the come up after having locked down the entire east end part of town with heroine and the best weed money can buy, leaving only coke sales to the scramblers. It wasn't a large territory but it was a lucrative one. With that money came the opportunity to expand. Dante knew his team would do whatever it took to get paper. Seeing Cream flip over a female—and a chicken at that—made Dante think. What would he do if shit got hectic and cases were caught? To be a killer in the streets was one thing, but to hold water in a storm was the test of a real gangsta. Dante planned to keep a close eye on Cream.

"Ay, yo, fam, we gonna handle this shit. But on the real, son, check yo' broad. Matter of fact, you need to check that broad out, yo. Dead ass," Dante told a wired up Cream.

Cream nodded in agreement, but deep down, wasn't nobody gonna tell him nothing about his wife. Shorty had that snapper and she had her hooks sunk deep into Cream.

"That shit won't happen no more," Cream replied, through the wire. "Believe me." Cream was naïve enough to think an ass whuppin' every now and then was enough to turn a ho into a housewife.

"You know where this niggah rest his head?" Dante inquired.

"He from the Nu Prozecks, but don thik he stay dhere."

"What?"

"The New Projects," Cream repeated with saliva running down the side of his mouth.

"The New Projects? Freddie from The New Projects?" Dante asked fighting back a laugh. "Are you serious?" The

10

only thing Dante knew of Freddie in the streets was of him being a pretty-boy, nothing remotely resembling a gangsta.

Cream nodded, relieved to be understood. Talking was painful with wires holding your grill together. Every time he winced, all he could think of was finding Freddie.

"Don't stress my dude, that joker something light."

Chapter Two

✝ *What the fuck is beyond the grave?* That was the thought in Slug's mind as he stood, watching the casket of his great aunt being lowered into the ground. He had come up with his mother from Goldsboro, North Carolina, to pay respects to a woman he had never known. In the process, he would congregate with a family he hardly ever saw.

Most of the Mitchells had stayed in Newark, New Jersey. Only Slug's mother and her brother had moved down south, where Slug was born and raised. Although his mother was from Jersey, Slug was strictly dirty south, tried and true. He wasn't one of those southern dudes who secretly admired up north dudes for their style or accent. He was proud to be from Webbtown as they called it in the dirty south.

Nothing about Jersey excited him. It stunk for one thing. The smell hit him in the face as soon as he stepped out of the car at his aunt's house. Slug looked around at all the weeping faces gathered at the grave. The only faces he knew were his mother's and his Aunt Arnez's. Some of his cousins were sho' nuff fine, which kept the service interesting, but he was searching for one face in particular—his cousin Freddie's. He hadn't seen Freddie since they were twelve, the year he stopped coming down south for the summer. And even though he and Freddie spent half of each summer fighting and the other half arguing, every winter Slug looked forward to seeing his cousin Freddie, not knowing that Freddie was in Plainfield doing the same thing. But once Freddie turned fourteen, he fell upon the game that he would eat off of: females.

Freddie started spending his summers in Newark around Hawthorne Ave. until his mom met a man and moved out to Plainfield. It was out in Plainfield, in the Second Street housing projects, that Freddie perfected his craft in macking the ladies. Slug, on the other hand, got introduced to the dope game and the two lost contact. But when Slug heard about the funeral, he decided to go check his fam out. Besides, it was getting hot in the Boro for him.

Slug checked his watch, realized the service was well underway, and wondered if Freddie was even coming. But a few minutes later, a money green Acura pulled up. Slug squinted against the sun, and once the driver emerged, he smiled to himself. It was Freddie. He knew that bop anywhere. He had gotten taller. He was almost as tall as Slug, who was 6'3". He walked around the car and opened the passenger door, helping a female out of the car. As they approached, he saw Freddie fidgeting with his tie and he laughed to himself because he knew Freddie hated ties. Whenever they had to go to church down south, Freddie's mama almost had to beat him to make him leave his tie alone. He always said it felt like a noose around his neck.

"I told you we was gonna be late, Freddie," Simone scolded through clenched but smiling teeth.

"Shit, she ain't goin' nowhere," Freddie replied playfully.

Simone nudged him hard in the ribs. "Boy! Have you any respect for the dead?" she whispered harshly.

Freddie was about to reply until he saw the brown-skinned brother in the navy blue suit. He had to fight the urge to yell "My niggah!" across the crowd. "Oh shit, Slug," he said and made his way over to where Slug was standing. He embraced his cousin like a long lost sibling.

"My niggah, what da deal?! I didn't know you was comin'."

Freddie exclaimed trying to be quiet, but the love in his voice resonated. Just then, his mother shot him a killer look.

"Ain't nuthin' cuz. I wanted to surprise you, yo," Slug replied. "Look at you niggah, got all tall and shit." Slug glanced over at Simone standing next to Freddie's mother. "Who dat? I hope she ain't fam," Slug teased.

"Not yet, but she will be. That's my fiancée," Freddie proudly boasted.

"Fiancée? Get the fuck outta here...You gettin' married?!" Slug asked full of surprise. The word married floated to his mother's ears. She turned around and whispered, "Eric." Slug cleared his throat.

"Yo, we better chill 'fore Aunt Ann have us in coffins," Freddie joked.

"We'll holla after the funeral."

After the funeral, the majority of the family went to Freddie's mother Arnez's house to eat. Her small two-story house off of Avon Avenue was packed with good food and hungry people to eat it. Not to mention drinks that flowed freely, making Freddie's Uncle Jerome say, slurring, "Now, I know somebody died, but who died?

"Great Aunt Rosa," a voice reminded him.

"Who?" Uncle Jerome stammered as he staggered.

"Great Aunt—"

"I heard what you said, but...why they call her great aunt? Old ass. She leave me any money?"

"Nah."

"Well did she ever give me any money?"

"Probably not."

"Then...what the hell was so damn great about her?" he commented, drawing a little drunken laughter as well as a little divine displeasure.

Freddie and Slug were out on the porch catching up on old times when Simone walked out onto the porch. She stood on her tiptoes to kiss Freddie. "Here you are. I've been looking all over for you."

"Aw, shit cuz. Let me find out shorty got a leash on you already," Slug joked, making Simone and Freddie laugh.

"No," Simone replied, "but your mother is looking for you to take pictures, and she said put your tie on."

Freddie looked down at the mangled tie draped over his neck. "Well, tell her you can't find me."

"No, I ain't gonna lie to your mama. Just come on."

"Well damn, can I meet your fiancée or what, cuz?" Slug asked. Simone had been busy helping out, so they still hadn't met.

"My bad, fam. Simone, this is my cousin Eric."

"Slug," he cut in.

"Niggah, your mama named you Eric. And Eric, this is Simone."

"Hello, Eric."

"Slug, shorty. And I must say, if you getting married, I'm glad you picked a sho' nuff stallion. Turn around mama, let me see what you workin' wit." Slug chuckled half jokingly.

Simone looked at Freddie with a nervous giggle, but Freddie put her at ease. "Don't pay this country-ass farmer no mind, babe." Then he turned to Slug, "Aiight niggah, don't make me whup yo' ass out this piece," he said, faking a jab.

Slug threw up his mitts in mock defense. "Just 'cause you almost as tall as me don't mean I can't still beat yo' ass, youngin'." Slug remarked.

"Still? Niggah, when?"

Simone saw that they were in their own world, so she respected her man's space. She kissed him on the cheek and said, "Don't forget your tie." Then she dipped back into the

15

house.

"Cuz, I don't know about you, but fuck a picture. Show me what this piss ant city is all about. Where the pussy at?" Slug asked. "Or do shorty got you wearin' a screw off dick." They both laughed.

"Niggah, if you only knew," Freddie replied. "Come on, let's roll out."

Chapter Three

✝ "Man, what the fuck is this?" Slug asked as he looked at the CD cases scattered between the seats of Freddie's Acura. "D-Block, D-Block, Kay Slay, Kay Slay, Kay Slay, Jay Z, Jay Z, Biggie! Niggah, where the 'Pac? Face? The real shit."

"Real? You just said it—Biggie!" Freddie answered as he drove through Newark.

"Man, fuck Biggie! Pac!"

"Aiight, watch yo' mouth, country-ass niggah. Up North is Biggie-land, yo," Freddie replied.

"Well do y'all got Thug Passion? Or are y'all still drinkin' Alize?" Slug joked.

"Niggah, I'm 'bout to take you where you can get all the passion you want. You wit' Freddie, cuzzo. Lay back."

"Then let's get it crunk then."

And crunk they got. Freddie took him to the livest clubs in the Essex County area and the rawest strip clubs. They even went out to Plainfield to The Gentlemen's Club, even though Freddie had beef with Cream, who was from the area. But he was feeling too good to give a fuck. He hadn't seen Slug in so long. It was good to see his family and catch up on the last few years.

At The Gentlemen's Club, Freddie's name rung bells like Sunday Mass so he got the V.I.P. treatment. He broke Slug off with a private lap dance in the down stairs part of the club and a side shot of head from one of the strippers from his hood on the low before they rolled out pissy drunk one in the morning. Freddie was slipping in the worse way because the liquor made him forget about Cream as they walked across the street to Jay Cee's Lounge to order what Freddie felt were some of the best dinners in town. But aside from having good food and plenty of liquor, it was also a good spot to get caught slipping, and Freddie knew that.

Fortunately, the last place Cream and Dante expected Freddie to be was on Richmond Street in their neck of the woods, so their slip made his slip irrelevant. Freddie greeted a few dudes he knew standing outside Jay Cee's and introduced Slug to his two home boys Wajdee and Dance at the door as they entered the bar.

"Yo, son," Freddie said in between bites of greasy chicken wings, "What you into down there?"

Slug sipped his fruit punch while eyeing one of the bartenders. "You know how cuz get down. Gotta trap the scrilla. Shit hectic now though. Seem like ere'body and they mama catchin' cases or snitchin' to come from under."

Freddie nodded. He understood because Jersey was the same way. That was one of the main reasons he stayed away from the dope game. "Damn, shorty down south thick," Slug chimed in reference to the bartender.

"That's Tawanna."

"Well, I wanna," Slug joked.

"You shot the fuck out cuzzo."

"If you say so. But seriously cuz, I'm tellin' you, shit is sweet down in the dirty. I just need the right connect to get it poppin' proper," Slug added, looking at Freddie with a gleam in his eye.

"What?" Freddie asked, really questioning the look while wiping the grease off his hands. "Niggah, I ain't no connect. I don't fuck around."

"But you know who do. I'm sayin', cuz, I came to see you, true. But I also came to see what you could do for me. Put a niggah down with some peeps," Slug suggested, lighting a Newport.

Freddie did know a few heavyweights, but he didn't deal with them on the regular basis, and he didn't want to run his cousin up on a snag. But he knew of one connect who was definitely straight. Only problem was, he was really trying to phase them out of his life.

"Man, wit' the right connect, I could lock the 'Boro down," Slug boasted. "I got a team of youngins, that all they do is grind sun up to dinnertime. Shit, if we had a connect..." Slug said while blowing smoke straight up in the air and savoring the taste of chicken in his mouth.

"What happened? Caught a case?"

"Nah, cuz...a cross," Slug snarled wickedly. "I put the cross down on some bitch-ass niggahs."

"And now you want me to hook you up wit' another one?" Freddie asked, thinking Slug must be crazy.

"Naw, cuz, you fam so I'll keep shit official. Just them Miami boys tried to play me, so I showed 'em how Webbtown get down."

Slug began to explain what had been going on for the last few months. Three niggahs named Mo Mo, Tyrone, and Black came from Miami on the strength of their cousin Bird, who lived in the Boro. But Bird got killed a week before they were to come through with the weight. Since Bird and Slug was tight, they stepped to Slug at the wake and asked him to hold them down. He agreed.

They started him off light, with an eighth of a kilo, and it was gone in an hour. Needless to say, they were feeling Slug's grind, so they gave him another, which he did the same thing with. They then hit him off with half a brick, which Slug got

19

rid of in three days, in straight twenties and fifties. The Miami niggahs felt they had a gold mine, so they went back to Florida and came back to hit Slug off with a whole bird. In the process of moving it, one of Slug's youngins got hit with the eighth cut up in twentys. On top of that, Slug used some of the Miami cats' money to bail him out. They grumbled, but decided to charge it to the game. But the grumbling got louder and started to get on Slug's nerves.

"Yo, Slug, this shit ain't no game. What up wit' dat paper on that big eighth?" Money growled. Slug was vexed because the niggah had jumped out the car with a gun in his belt, purposely visible, and Slug was talking to two chicks in Green Acres at the time. He was already tired of these niggahs paging him constantly, so he decided right then to dead these niggahs on their paper.

"Mo Mo, chill, dog. Slug don't even get down like that. I'ma have your paper, my word. But I do need another one of them twangs and I'll grind it for free to straighten my face on what I owe," Slug tried to sound as lame as he could in order to rock the niggah to sleep.

Mo Mo's greed and his thinking that he was a real killer made him reply, "Aiight, yo. But I'm telling you, Slug, you better not fuck this up."

"I ain't man. I got you, yo, I got you," he repeated, but Mo Mo didn't know what I got you meant in that context. It meant—you beat. The two girls, Donesha and Lil' Monica, giggled because they knew what he meant.

"You better," Mo Mo concluded before bopping back to his Navigator like he had put his gangsta down.

An hour later, Slug had another whole bird and the better half of the last kilo they had given him. That's when he stopped returning their pages and the Miami boys heard that now he was flossing paper, their paper.

"Y'all seen Slug?" Black asked in West Haven, trying to scare up a few of Slug's youngins. It wasn't like Slug was hiding either. He was everywhere, all the hot spots, saying shit like, "Fuck it, buy the bar out. It's on them Miami niggahs!" He was straight clowning them in the club.

Girls would see Slug driving around town and joke, "You better be careful, them Miami niggahs lookin' 'fo' you!"

"Here I go," Slug would smile. But he got tired of their threats.

So one night at Leo's liquor house, when he heard "There go them Miami cats, Slug," he decided to take it to them. Full of Hypnotic and Hennessey, feeling like the Incredible Hulk, he went outside with Nine-Millimeter Rugers in both hands.

"Y'all niggahs lookin' for Slug?! Here go Slug!" He commenced to dumping shells on the Black Navigator. They tried to fire back but Slug didn't take cover, he just stood square blazing until he had shot Tyrone, giving him a permanent bag, and made Swiss cheese of Black's Navi. They finally skidded away, trying to tend to their leaking friend in need of emergency medical attention.

After that, every time Slug saw them niggahs, he was headhunting. In clubs, at hotels, at the waffle place, even at red lights, until finally them niggahs bowed out.

"Fuck it, Slug. Keep that shit, yo." They sent word to Slug, and just as fast as it had begun, it ended. Slug watched them niggahs, but he saw the pussy had came out of them and let it go. That was where he was now, without a connect.

Freddie sat back and listened to Slug's story, knowing he wasn't bullshitting. Slug had always been wild, that's how he got his nickname, Slugger. In his younger days, two older cats had tried to take his bike and he beat them both into a coma and landed himself in juvenile detention for eighteen months. He was thirteen.

Freddie knew Slug was serious, but he didn't want to get involved with the dope game.

"Niggah, I ain't askin' you to get down, just put me on and I'll break you off ere' month," Slug proposed.

Freddie stared out into the club. It sounded sweet, but he wasn't sure he wanted to have his name mixed up in it period.

"Dig Slug, let me think-," he was cut off by his cell phone ringing. "Hold up," he said, answering the phone. "Yo."

"You busy?" the sultry voice inquired.

Damn, he thought. He should've known it was her. Even through the loud music he recognized her voice.

"Well?" she teased. "You must be if you ain't answerin'."

"Naw, yo," Freddie looked at Slug, who pretended not to be listening. "I'm just chillin'."

"So you pistol whippin' niggahs in barbershops now," she giggled.

Freddie chuckled and finally realized where he was. "What? You followin' me or somethin'?

"No, but they are. I was kinda worried about you so I just called to check on you," she replied. "Where you at?"

"Jay Cee's," Freddie answered.

"You got somethin' to prove?"

"Naw."

"I can't tell. You all up in they hood, like it's sweet and them negroes is vexed wit' you."

He didn't want to say he was drunk and forgot, so he explained, "My cousin up from down south, so I wanted to show him a good time."

"Hmm-hmm-hmm," she hummed knowingly. "Let me guess. You took 'im to The Gentlemen's Club. Ain't you tired of them stank heffas yet? Or are you tryin' to fuck all of 'em?"

"Naw."

"Then, are you tryin' to fuck...me?" That was what kept

Freddie open on her. She spoke her mind and pulled no punches.

"I'm sayin'..." Half of him wanted to say no—the half that was his heart and belonged to Simone. But his other half, which was his dick, was already rock hard.

She giggled. "Niggah quit frontin'. We both know what you wanna say. Tell your cousin I said hi and bye. I wanna see you, boo."

"Where you at?" Freddie glanced down at his watch seeing it was 1:25 AM.

"Where you think? Where I'm always waitin' for you." He didn't respond but she anticipated his state of mind. "I'll leave the door unlocked for you, but um...hurry up. I already started without you." She ended the conversation with the sound of her kiss that Freddie imagined on the head of his dick. Freddie hung up.

"Niggah, that ain't wifey, yo," Slug teased while laughing, then bellowed, "Booty call!"

Slug didn't know the half. She was the only female Freddie couldn't bring himself to cut off. She was the type of mistress every niggah wished they had—fine and a freak who asked no questions and had no expectations. Plus her paper was long. She was booty call heaven!

"Don't worry about Slug, cuz. I ain't no cock blocker. Go 'head. I'ma go back 'cross the street and try to get that bitch in the thong to welcome me to the city."

Thong? Freddie thought. "They all got on thongs, yo."

"Exactly. Country niggahs got horse dicks, niggah!" Slug laughed.

Freddie laughed with him but refused to leave Slug in the east end alone. "Alone?" Slug smirked then opened his suit coat to reveal a nine tucked into his shoulder holster. "But if I got my neener, then you know I'm straight trippin'," he rapped like Dr. Dre on "G Thang".

"Niggah, you brought that shit way up here?" Freddie asked full of surprise.

"Shit. Rather get caught wit' it than wit'out it," Slug replied, making Freddie think about his own beef and the fact that he had left his gun in the car.

Despite Slug's protests, Freddie wouldn't leave until Slug picked out a bowlegged chick with big titties, and slid into her silver 325i BMW. He jumped into his Audi Q7 SUV eager to make his rendezvous spot.

Chapter Four

✝ His conscience was killing him the whole ride on Route 22 East on his way to the Robert Treat Hotel in Newark. He knew he had a good woman at home, but it was like his dick was driving. He couldn't understand himself. When he was with Simone, it was all about her and it was all love. But once he hit the streets, it was money and pussy. And if a bitch ain't have both, he wasn't interested.

He told himself for the millionth time that this was the last time. After this, he'd cut her off cold. But he knew it was all a lie as he got on the elevator and rode to the Presidential Suite.

When he reached the double doors, he saw that she had kept her word. The door was cracked with a "Do Not Disturb" sign hanging from the knob. He entered and closed the door behind him. The spacious suite smelled just like Tiffany, her favorite fragrance, and he could hear the soft melodies of "Juicy Fruit" by Mtume, her favorite song.

Freddie looked down at his feet and found her Chanel slingback heels, one after the other, laying there. As he walked, he found her open-back, black Gucci dress on the floor near the plush couch and imagined how she had slithered her mahogany frame out of it. He approached the bedroom door and pushed it open to find her lying on the bed, completely naked, and touching herself like Tweet with the help of a long, black vibrator.

She was ghetto thick—some might say big-boned—but she

wore her weight well because she had no stomach and a small waist. It made her luscious hips curve even more into thick mahogany thighs that now were spread eagle, exposing the pink of her inner flesh to Freddie's attentive eyes. She slowly slid the sex toy in and out, taking it in as far as it would go, making her curl her beautifully pedicured toenails, then pulling it back out. She grinded her hips in small seductive circles. Her free hand massaged her large 36 Ds, pinching her nipples and placing them in her mouth, teasing them with her own tongue. The look on her gorgeous face was one of near ecstasy and sensual anticipation. It turned her on more to see Freddie standing in the door, watching her pleasure herself.

"Does it look good to you, baby?" she asked, stopping to let out a whimper and a moan. "Because it...damn sure...feels good to me."

Freddie leaned against the door, enjoying the show. She lifted one of her shapely legs and arched her back, angling the dildo upwards to hit her g-spot.

"Uhh...Say my name, Freddie."

"Gina."

"Say it like...ohhh...you want this pussy."

"Gina...but how can I want what's already mine?" he smirked, knowing it was.

Gina smiled back and sat up on her knees, putting the play toy aside. "Come show me it's yours then."

Freddie crossed the room and wrapped his arms around her waist as he began to kiss her. But she turned her face away.

"No. I don't feel like being kissed tonight. I just wanna fuck," she told him as she unbuckled his pants and slid her hand inside, grabbing his dick. She pulled his pants down, and at the same time she laid eyes on his manhood and cooed, "Damn, I missed you daddy." She slid it into her warm mouth, wrapping her full, juicy lips around the shaft, licking along the whole length. Then she took his nuts one at a time into her mouth.

I'll be your lollipop, you can lick me everywhere, Mtume played in the background.

"I wanna play a game," Gina whispered seductively.

Freddie was still feeling the sensation of her tongue on his nuts, "What kind of game?"

She replied with a smile and turned around doggy-style, bending over the bed and cocking one knee up on it. She reached between her legs and grabbed Freddie's dick, rubbing it against her clit, then stuck only the head in and tightened her muscles around him. Freddie reached to grab her ass but she abruptly stopped him.

"Uh uh, you can't touch me and you can't move," she ordered softly, slowly taking more of him inside of her. Freddie thought it would be easy until she took his whole dick and began to long dick herself, spreading her pussy lips with her fingers. His hands began to tremble trying to keep from palming her pretty, voluptous ass and ramming himself deep inside of her, but Gina was in control and she intended to keep it that way.

"Can you take this pussy, daddy? Ooh, can...can you?" She spoke in spurts between moans. She placed both her feet on the floor and grabbed her ankles, grinding Freddie until he couldn't take it anymore.

The sensation of a woman's body to a man's hand is underestimated, until he's deprived of it. He cuffed her thighs in desperation making her gasp and giggle as he took control.

"I knew you couldn't handle this pussy...damn..."

Freddie tried to bang Gina's back out, making her scream until she damn near lost her voice.

"Let me be daddy's freak!...If...I can't be...daddy's girl,...let me be daddy's freak!" she groaned.

"You are my freak," Freddie replied.

"You promise?"

"I promise."

"Make your freak cum...Freddie, make me," Gina shuddered and her knees got weak. She stretched out on the bed with Freddie still inside her, banging until he couldn't hold it anymore and nutting deep inside of her. Then he collapsed on top of her.

"Damn, baby, what you do to me?" she asked more of herself than of him.

"Whatever you want," he responded, and kissed her between the shoulder blades, causing a shiver to run along her spine.

"Don't do that or that young girl won't ever see you again," she joked to hide the tear rolling down her cheek. "Get up and get on your stomach. Let me massage you."

Freddie rolled over, pants still around his ankles and turned onto his stomach. Gina sat on his ass and began to massage his shoulders. She could tell he was tense.

"So you gonna tell me what happened?"

Freddie shrugged slightly, feeling the massage. "Some chickenhead stripper and her man caught feelin's. That dude Cream."

"Yeah, I know Cream. He one of Tay's people," Gina sighed, "You want me to get somebody to holla at' 'im?"

Freddie knew what Gina meant by her question because her family was heavy in the game all over Jersey, as deep as Atlantic City. The Peterson clan was well known and well respected. None of the women in the family worked unless they wanted to, or they had their own business. Gina, herself, had never worked a day in her life, but she lived a lavish life. Her only official source of income was a foreign car lot in Montclair, New Jersey, that she hardly ever visited and that was run by two Jews in her name. The business had been a gift from her uncle, Lou Peterson, who doted on her. All she had to do was say the word and Dante and his whole clique would be marked for death. But Freddie's manhood wouldn't allow him to let a woman handle his beef.

"Holla for what? Fuck them jokers. I can handle me, yo," he boasted.

"I knew you was gonna say some ol' fly bullshit like that." Gina climbed off his back and pushed him onto his side. "Freddie, listen to me. These niggahs is not playin' wit' you. Yeah, it's stupid, but since when you known niggahs wit' guns for hearts to think smart? What you gonna do when Tay and them come at you?" she asked with clear concern.

Freddie raised up on his elbows, agitated because his young mind thought she was questioning his manhood. "Yo, you talkin' to me like I'm some coward or something! 'Fuck you mean 'what I'ma do'?! I'ma do me! Niggahs bleed just like me!" he spat.

"Thank you, Biggie Smalls," Gina remarked sarcastically, rolling her eyes to the ceiling. She framed his face with her hands, admiring his beauty and loving his warmth but loathing his youthful ego. "Did I say you were a coward, Freddie? Did I? What? You think being a man is so-called 'doin' you'? Baby...my sweet, sweet baby. The measure of a man is not this," she said, grabbing his dick, "or how bad he can be. It's this," she said, tapping his forehead. "I know you got it in you, Freddie. You smarter than that. Don't let these people drag you down. Think, young brother. I see so much in you. That's why I...," she stopped short, hoping he didn't know what she'd started to say, but he did.

"You what?"

Gina palmed her head, then ran her hand through her microbraids and waved him off, "Just...go home, Freddie. Do you, like you said. Go on home to your little girlfriend and do you...Shit, I'm a grown-ass woman, I ain't got time for all this high school bullshit," she stated, fighting to sound strong and not let any tears flow.

"Aiight, yo," was all he replied and got up, pulling up his pants.

Once he was dressed, he looked at Gina who had her back to him, looking out the window. He knew what she was feeling and he couldn't front—he was glad she felt that way about him. Gina was a jewel and he was glad she was his jewel, even if it was only on the low.

"Can I have a kiss before I go?" Freddie teased.

"I thought I told you I ain't wanna be kissed tonight," she answered.

"It ain't night no more," he said, referring to the rising sun.

"Still no."

"Please," he begged with a smile.

"No."

He crept up on the bed and tried to kiss her but she turned away. "Oh, you gonna kiss me!" he demanded, tickling her along her sides, knowing that drove her crazy.

She laughed until she stuttered, "Fr-f-reddie, stop! I'll kiss you! I'll kiss you!"

"Aiight then," he said triumphantly, and stuck his tongue in her mouth, which she caught firmly between her teeth.

"I'll bite it off if you tickle me one more time," she warned playfully.

"Zoo gaa a winna!"

"I got a winner?"

"Yeah!"

She released his tongue, caressed it with her own, then broke the kiss and looked him in the eyes. "Then act like one."

Freddie held her gaze a moment, then said, "I'll call you."

He walked out.

"And I don't care what you say, I'ma take care of that for you!" she yelled after him. After she didn't get a reply and heard the door close, she breathed a sigh of relief, glad she had made her point.

Driving home, Freddie thought about the knowledge Gina had dropped on him about the measure of a man. She had seen right through him and she knew his pride was definitely running away with his reason. He had fixed his mind to go to war; whatever happened, happened. And for what? If he was faced with kill or be killed situation, Freddie wouldn't hesitate to kill. But then what? He wasn't tryin' to see prison for a murder rap. Then there was the flipside…if Cream killed him.

He shook off that thought. Kill him over a piece of pussy they both knew was no good? With all this pussy in the world, Freddie wasn't tryin' to die over no piece, regardless of who it was. So yeah, let Gina's fam squash the beef. He had nothing to prove and niggahs knew he wasn't no sucka, so fuck it, get on with life.

Thinking of the situation and Gina's support drew him that much closer to her, even though he tried repeatedly to convince himself that there wasn't anything to their relationship and that he could cut her off at will—like a chain smoker who claimed he could quit anytime he wanted. Cats knew cigarettes were killing them, but that puff…Gina was like that puff to him. She was what he craved after every meal, and his meal was Simone. Just thinking of his fiancée and watching the sunrise made his heart sink. Of course he had an alibi—Slug. They had hung out all night. But if he claimed he loved her, why was it so easy to lie to her over and over again? Who was he fooling—her or himself?

Chapter Five

✝ Freddie pulled up to his apartment in Bound Brook. He quietly turned the key, planning to jump into the shower, then slide into bed next to a sleeping Simone like he had done so many times before. But what he smelled made his guilt turn into sickness—pancakes and turkey sausage. He could clearly hear the sizzle of the sausage as the buttery smell of pancakes wafted through the air. Damn.

"Hey, baby. I'm in the kitchen," she called out sweetly.

All he could think about was the song "It's a Thin Line Between Love and Hate"...*Are you hungry, honey? Did you eat yet?* Freddie walked into the kitchen to find Simone at the stove in his t-shirt. He felt like shit to see the smile she flashed him as he quickly kissed her, hoping Gina's fragrance wasn't clinging to his clothes.

"Where's Slug?" she asked, looking over his shoulder.

"I, uh, dropped him off at mama's. He ain't wanna cock block a brotha," he flirted, only because a lie is best swallowed with laughter, and Simone did laugh.

"I thought y'all would be hungry so I fixed y'all some pancakes," she said, gesturing to a stack of eight golden brown cakes next to the stove as she worked on the ninth. He gently pushed her shoulder-length hair away from her face and caressed her cheek. "Damn, girl. Will you marry me?" he smiled.

Simone held up her left hand and wiggled the two carats on her finger. "I'm sorry, I'm already engaged."

"I hope that niggah appreciate what he got."

She blushed. "I think he does."

"Yeah?" he asked, inching closer for her kiss.

"Yeah," she replied and met him halfway for his.

Simone was his heart, and not once did he regret asking her to marry him. He pulled her close to him and pressed his body up against hers, running his hands up her shirt and tickling her nipples. She could feel herself going there, so she floated back to say, "I hope I didn't slave over this hot stove for nothin'," she smiled.

"Oh yeah, the pancakes. I almost forgot," Freddie replied. "Damn let me get my plate." He reached up in the cupboard, took out a plate, and sat it on the table. Then he poured syrup all over the plate.

"What are you doing?" Simone asked, thinking he forgot the pancakes.

"Getting ready to eat," he replied picking her up as he lifted the t-shirt to reveal that she was panty-less. Then he sat her in the sticky syrup.

"Freddie!" she screamed tickled, trying to squirm out of the plate, "You got me all sticky!"

"Not yet," he grinned, laying her back across the table as he rubbed her inner thighs until they were coated with syrup.

"Freddie," she purred, "This is craz—"

The feeling of his tongue tracing along her walls caught her words in her throat. He gently rubbed her clit with his thumb until it stood perky then he began to suck on it and Simone grabbed the back of his head trying to direct his tongue while running her fingers through his short curly hair.

"Ooh, I love you, Freddie, I love youuuu," she moaned, allowing Freddie's tongue to dance and flicker inside of her garden.

He cocked her legs higher and licked along the whole

length of her lips until he reached that sensitive spot near her asshole, making her gasp for air.

"Don't stop, baby, don't stop," she begged, and he didn't—licking, nibbling, and sucking her until she felt it in her stomach.

"Don't ever leave me, Freddie, please don't...I love you sooo much," she groaned passionately, rotating her hips to the rhythm of his tongue. "Right there, Freddie, right...wait...wait...," she cried out in ecstasy as her love juices flowed out, mingling with the syrup and her whole body shook and spasmed.

He tickled her along her thigh making her giggle. "Freddie, I'ma kill you if I'm stuck to this plate. Nasty-ass self. And mark this plate 'cause I ain't never eating out of it!"

"Freddie! Ay, yo, Freddie! Wake yo' ass up, niggah! This Slug!" Freddie had answered the phone in a daze. It seemed like he had just gone to sleep when Simone was shaking him and handing him the phone.

"Slug?" he croaked, "What time is it?"

"I don't know, like ten somethin'. Shit, time to get up. Come get me, niggah!" Slug yelled into the phone in his usual hyper tone.

"Come get you from where?" Freddie asked, slowly coming around.

"I'm downtown Plainfield, yo. Went on a little shoppin' spree, now I need a ride 'cause I don't know how to get to your crib."

Freddie wanted to tell him to take a cab but he was up now. Fuck it. He checked his watch: 10:11. "Aiight yo, gimme about half an hour. Meet me in front of the Music and Book store in an hour."

"I don't know where the fuck that's at, you gotta gimme a

name or address or somethin'"

"It's called Muzik N Motion & Real Edutainment Books. You can't miss it—next to a jewelry store called Bong's."

"Oh shit, I was just down that way. I brought me this platinum chain and medallion from the Asian joker, said he knew you."

"Yeah, that's my man Bong—good dude. But yeah, right next door."

"Aiight, I'll be there."

"One."

"One."

Freddie rolled out of bed still dressed in his suit. He was so tired he had just crashed. He got up and took off his clothes to take a shower. Then he got dressed in an Black Label shirt and jacket and a pair of Red Monkey jeans, finishing it off with a pair of all black high-top Prada's before grabbing his keys and heading out the door.

Chapter Six

✝ The early morning traffic was light as Freddie made his way downtown, pumping his favorite CD of all time, Redman's *Whut?! Thee Album.*

You wanna see me get smooth? Please! Save it for the breeze...

He whipped Simone's Acura through Plainfield's Front Street like only Jersey niggahs can, in and out while timing yellow lights. He got downtown ten minutes to eleven, made a right onto Park Ave, then a left on Second Street until he reached the parking lot behind downtown. Freddie fed the empty meter thinking about the meter maids who lived for writing tickets in that particular area. He had gotten caught a few times—hopping out of his whip and running into a store for a fresh fitted or pair of kicks. If he didn't know any better, he would have sworn that they hid behind cars watching and waiting for shoppers like him.

Freddie cut through the music and bookstore in search of Slug. He was not in the mood to be searching around downtown, so he hoped Slug would be where he'd told him they'd meet. As he walked through Muzik N Motion & Real Edutainment Books, he picked up the latest DJ Don Juan CD and J.M. Benjamin's last two books, *My Manz and 'Em*, which had the housing projects where he was from on the cover, and *Ride or Die Chick*. Freddie had always supported the two, who were actually the owners of the establishment. Glad to see Slug at the proper place, the two greeted.

"What the deal, cuz?" Slug said, giving him a pound. "Let me cop this best of Pac so we'll have somethin' to ride to."

"Niggah, picture you rollin' in my shit bumpin' that bullshit," Freddie joked.

Slug ran into the store and paid for the CD, then gathered up his bags.

"It's on the Miami boys, huh?" Freddie joked again, referring to all the bags and sneaker boxes.

"Naw, yo. It's on that stripper broad," Slug smoothly replied. "Shorty got that paper, yo. She damn near had a gee in tips."

Freddie stopped walking. "Come on, Slug. Don't tell me you did some petty shit like that?"

"Shit, they do it to us! Soon as that chick fell out, I hit her ass up, grabbed a cab, and told poppie drop me off down here!"

Freddie couldn't help but laugh. And Slug was right— females in the game were good for hitting a brutha's pockets and creeping out the back door. Freddie laughed it off.

"Hold up, let me go see my man Bong. He 'posed to be makin' me this sick piece in white gold. Then we out."

Chapter Seven

✝ Cream stood inside Dante's brother Mannie's bodega on 5th and Richmond Street impatiently. He couldn't stand Mannie. Mannie thought that just because he was the boss' brother, he was boss, too. Cream only tolerated his ass on the strength of Tay. "Ay Mannie! Niggah is you ready yet?"

Mannie ignored him and continued to talk on his cell. Cream sighed heavily and turned to look out the door. He was tired and his wired jaw ached, but he had to run Mannie around to make the pick-ups down on 6th Street. He glanced up the street just out of boredom and his eyes caught the gleam of a green Acura RL. He looked again because his heart leaped and pounded in his chest. It was Freddie's car!

"Hell yeah! Yeah! Ay, yo, Mannie!" Cream exclaimed, pulling his burner out and shaking Mannie's shoulder. Mannie looked up agitated.

"Niggah, can't you see I'm on the phone? And, 'fuck you doin' wit' a pistol out in my spot?"

"It's that bitch-ass nicca, Freddie!" Cream barked. "I see his car, yo! I'ma lay his ass down right now!"

Mannie knew about the situation and laughed on the inside because he, too, had fucked Cream's wife, and was still fucking her whenever the opportunity arose. But he knew Tay wanted an example made out of this niggah, Freddie. Word got around the streets how their squad rolled, so it was on.

"I'll call you back," Mannie said into the phone and hung up. "Where?"

"Up the block," Cream informed him, cocking his four pound.

"Aiight, yo. We gonna lay his ass. And when he sees your face..." Mannie let his words drift off because Cream already knew the outcome.

Freddie and Slug rounded the corner of short 3rd Street and Richmond, on their way back to the car. The two had gone into Jay Cee's and thrown back a couple of shots of Henny and Coronas, being as though Freddie had to see his man Wajdee for a minute, who worked at the spot. He knew he was pressing his luck coming back into enemy territory, but having his cousin in the area and knowing how his cousin got down had him a little carefree. Freddie chirped his alarm as they approached, and Slug went around to the passenger side.

By this time, Mannie and Cream had made their way up the block and were a short distance away from the street Freddie was parked on, locked and loaded. Had Freddie, or Slug for that matter, glanced to their left, they may have noticed Mannie and Cream.

"There he go!" Cream pointed out making his move.

Freddie inserted the key into the car door and looked up, about to answer Slug's last question, when he saw a familiar face emerge from across the street. Cream. They were already swinging out the door and raising the steel to clap.

"Slug!"

Slug took one look at Freddie's face and knew there was no time to ask what, how or where. His ghetto instincts kicked in and he knew the problem was behind him. As he reached for his pistol, dropping his bags, he dove over the hood of the car just as the passenger-side window exploded from the gun blast.

"Freddie!" Slug hollered, hoping Freddie hadn't gotten hit, too.

"I'm good!" Freddie said, pinned against the door, nervously trying to get in the car. Slug used the hood as cover and fired back at Cream and Mannie who were crouched down behind an old Buick.

Slug only had one and a half clips gone before Freddie got the door open and reached under the driver's seat. His hand fell on Cream's nine. He grabbed and cocked it, and came up firing. Short 3rd and Richmond Street erupted in gunfire, screams, and a stampede of pedestrians running for cover.

Mannie's clip gave out. "Yo, Cream, let's be out! Five-0 comin'!"

Cream heard the sirens but his focus was on Freddie. He kept firing and watched Mannie, out of his peripheral, make a dash. Freddie leaped up with a barrage of bullets, two of which found Mannie in the back of the head. Mannie met with death before he hit the pavement.

"Mannie!" Cream screamed. He wanted to keep it hot but sirens were too close, so he headed back into the hat shop looking for the back door. Slug saw him run and duck, and he tried to cut him down but missed. All of a sudden, a cop car skidded around the corner.

"Slug, let's go!" Freddie ordered, and Slug was right behind him.

One of the cops jumped out too soon and yelled, "Freeze!" But Freddie turned around and let off his last three shots, catching the cop in the chest, sending him flying back against the open car door.

Freddie's whole life flashed before his eyes. He had acted on reflex, out of fear and panic. He was making his escape and the police were the last obstacle, so he fired. "Boom. Boom. Boom," Freddie's sporadic shots ripped into the cop he'd shot at.

He tried to turn his momentum from the back peddle to forward speed as he crossed the street, but his timing was off and an old caddy skidded to a halt, landing him on top of the hood. The car hadn't run into him so much as he had run into it. The impact wasn't enough to hurt him, but it was enough force to jar the gun from his hand, making it clatter yards away.

He wanted to go back for it, but Slug hollered, "Freddie, 'fuck you doin'? C'mon!!"

More police were on the way. There was no time to go back for the gun. Freddie ran past Slug and they dipped through an old alleyway.

Police swarmed the area and quickly gained control, finding out how many gunmen there were and that they were on foot. The manhunt was on.

Twenty-Five minutes later, Freddie and Slug merged off the Newark exit off the Parkway headed toward Freddie's old neighborhood of Hawthorne Avenue. Escaping the Plainfield police dragnet out of downtown wasn't a problem, escaping the twisted fate he saw ahead of him was.

"You aiight, cuz? You ain't hit is you?" Slug queried, looking at the blood and torn fabric on the shoulder of Freddie's sweatshirt.

"Naw, that's from the car, yo," Freddie replied, huffing real hard. His adrenaline was pumping so hard, he still couldn't feel the wound.

"Cuz, what the fuck just happened? Who was—?"

Freddie waved him off. "Later, yo... Son, I shot a cop."

That made both men shudder because they both knew what it meant. Killing Mannie was one thing, but shooting a police officer? And if he died... If he wasn't dead already...

"I ain't goin' to no fuckin' prison, yo," Freddie vowed. He didn't want to die or go out guns blazing, and prison wasn't an option either.

"'Fuck you gonna do?" Slug asked.

The question was like a crossroads. The answer would determine his destiny. There was no way he could stay in Plainfield or Newark—Jersey, period, for that matter. The decision had already crossed his mind in mid-flight, and it loomed before him like the promised land.

"Yo, I gotta blow Jerze, cuzzo. I'm goin' down south wit' you."

Slug nodded solemnly. "I was thinkin' the same thing. Seem like the only thing to do, cuz. What about Simone?"

The sound of her name stirred panic in his stomach. Not because of love, but fear. The Acura was in her name! It would be no time before they traced it back to her and headed to his apartment. If he did not get her out before the police showed up, the spot would be too hot to get her and his stash out at all. It was all he had. Freddie checked for his cell, but it was gone; lost in the shuffle. He had to get to a phone.

Freddie and Slug crept out of a building and headed toward the corner store's pay phone.

"You got some change?" Slug handed him two quarters.

He inserted the coins and dialed the house number so fast he mis-dialed and had to dial again. In the distance he could hear sirens.

"Hello?" Simone picked up on the third ring.

"Simone, listen to me and don't ask questions. Empty the safe and stuff a bag full of clothes. Not much, just what you can fit in my blue duffle bag, aiight? Get out of the house now, you hear me? Now! Take a cab to JFK—not Newark Airport— JFK. Now! I'll meet you there!" Freddie talked so fast, she hardly understood him.

"Freddie, slow down! What did—"

"The money and you. Meet me at JFK, aiight? JFK, now!" he repeated, this short, firm order clarifying the first, more detailed one.

"O-okay baby. Are you ok?" she sounded close to tears.

"I will be when I see you at JFK. I love you." He hung up before she could respond. He turned to Slug, "Yo, I need you to go back to my mother's house. Tell her what happened, aiight? By the time you get back home, I'll be waiting for you. But we need to split up. Cab it up to 2418 Avon Ave., or call her to scoop you up, cool?

Slug looked around. He didn't know Newark from a can of paint. But he did know how to evade the law, and splitting up was always a good option.

"Don't worry about me, cuz, just be safe. I'm good," Slug assured him, giving him a pound and a hug. They split up like two shadows in midday, fading from the waning sun.

Chapter Eight

✝ Back at the scene of the crime, the police had Richmond Street roped off at all four corners. People milled around, gossiping and straining their necks in an attempt to satisfy their voyeuristic thirst for bloodshed and violence. Mannie's corpse lay on the sidewalk under a bloody sheet, and the officer had been rushed to the hospital where he lay in critical condition. Detective Francis Wilson and his partner, Detective Michael Woods, surveyed the scene with experienced eyes.

"You got a name on the body yet?" Wilson asked casually. He was a 15-year vet on the force and murder was his daily business. The younger Woods was just getting his feet wet, so he was more gung-ho.

He flipped open his trusty notepad and read, "Manuel Mincey, aka Mannie; 22-year-old black male with a list of priors—drug charges mostly, and some assaults."

Wilson nodded knowingly. "Now that you've read the official report, let's get down to what solves the crime. Are you familiar with Mannie?" His partner was dumbfounded.

"He has a brother, Dante, who they call Tay. He and his crew come from 6th Street. They have been making quite a name for themselves lately. Remember the double murder on 3rd and Prescott about two weeks ago?"

"Yes—two black males, 16 and 24, names—," Woods ran off like a computer, but Wilson cut him off.

"No need, I was there. That was Tay's work. Heroin beef. Remember the dead girl we found in the dumpster in the 4th

Street housing projects?"

"Yes."

"Tay again." Wilson looked at Mannie's corpse. "Whoever did it made us lucky this time. Once we run the prints and the identification on that Acura, we'll have all the answers we need to wrap up this case."

"We already did," Woods announced proudly, glad to finally know something Wilson didn't. "The car is registered to—"

"Let me guess," Wilson cut him off dryly. "It's registered to a female, correct?"

Woods' pride deflated like a balloon. Wilson could tell by his expression that he was right. "Then we don't know jack shit. These hoodlums always register their vehicles in their mama's, baby mama's, girlfriend's, or crackheads' names. Finding out who really owns the car is where our answers lie."

At that point, a uniformed officer ran up carrying a plastic bag. When he was close enough, Wilson was able to see what was in it and his heart leaped.

"Detective Wilson! We found this in the street," the officer reported, handing Wilson the gun. Wilson smiled.

"The next best thing to a scripture from heaven—a smoking gun!"

An enraged Dante had Cream pinned against the wall by the collar, nostrils flaring, eyes tearing. "He killed my brother? You let that niggah kill my fuckin' brother?"

Cream was almost a foot taller than Dante and outweighed him by almost fifty pounds, but he didn't resist because he knew that Dante's rage was really pain and grief. Besides, Dante was a bull. He stood 5'6" and had a stature like a short linebacker. He didn't work out and it showed in his gut, but he was naturally strong and had the heart to take on anybody.

"What could I do, Tay? I ain't let 'em do nothin'." Cream

tried to reason but Dante was beyond reason.

Dante released Cream from his grip and spat, "Then nig-gah, you should be in the street layin' beside him!"

Dante paced the floor. The rest of the crew was silent, like real killers. They didn't talk much and they only moved on Tay's word.

"Tell me again…tell me again, slow," Tay snarled, eyeing Cream squarely.

"We was at Mannie's store when I saw Freddie's car. I told Mannie, I told him let's follow him and find out where he lives. But you know Mannie, son, you know his heart—God bless the dead. He said 'Naw, fuck dat, we hittin' the niggah right where he stand.'" Cream lied 'cause there was no way he was telling Tay it was his idea. There was no telling how Tay would react.

Dante watched Cream closely, listening to every word. A wise man would know when a scared man is lying, but not a hysterical one. All Tay could see was blood… his brother's, and soon Freddie's.

"Fuck e'ything! Fuck money, fuck bitches, and fuck Plainfield! Until I got this niggah beggin' me to kill him, on his knees in front of me, no one eats, no one sleeps! Period! You say he from The New? Them niggahs bleed—fuck them bitch-ass project niggahs, I don't give a fuck! They can get it, too! Find this niggah!" Dante had declared war.

Chapter Nine

✝ " ...Thank you, Gary. I'm standing outside The Gentlemen's Club in Plainfield, New Jersey, on the corner of East Third Street and Richmond Street. An early morning shootout has left one man dead and a police officer in critical condition ..." the female reporter spoke into a camera and informed the inquiring public. A picture of the officer flashed on the screen.

" ...Officer Derrick Williamson was shot once in the chest, answering the call of what police believe to be a drug-related incident. The man killed has been identified as one Manuel Mincey. Mincey died on the scene. The police haven't made any arrests, but they did recover a gun that they believe to be the murder weapon. We'll have more as this story continues to unfold."

Gina sat in the bedroom of her Bound Brook, New Jersey, townhome in utter disbelief. As soon as she saw that the shooting had happened in Plainfield, she had a bad premonition. All she could think of was Freddie dead, in a pool of blood. When she heard the name of the dead man, her heart began to beat closer to normal. But when she saw the green Acura, with its doors open and police around it, she experienced a whole new set of fears.

"Freddie," she groaned as if she was in physical pain. "Freddie, what have you gotten yourself into?"

There wasn't anything she could do now. She knew Mannie, and she knew Mannie was Tay's brother. There would be no talking to Tay, and her family wouldn't go for an all-out war over a niggah she was fucking. Freddie was on his own. All she could do was sit, wait, and say a silent prayer for his safety.

"Freddie baby, where are you?"

At about the same time, Simone was standing in the middle of JFK thinking the same thing. Throngs of people moved all around her and she looked back and forth constantly, hoping to see Freddie's face coming toward her. She felt like a small child lost in the mall. Freddie's call was so urgent and his tone so intense that she couldn't help but fear the worst. She loved her fiancé and she trusted her man. She knew he was in the street doing God-knows-what because he always had money; he paid all the bills and pampered her like a queen. But she never asked questions about what it was he actually did. He never got arrested or into any serious beefs in the street, so she just went to school preparing for a career as an accountant and took care of her man.

But now, standing in the middle of an international airport with only a handful of clothes and $5,500, her heart told her their lives were about to drastically change. *Get out of the house now* she remembered him telling her, as if the house was on fire or about to be raided by the police, or ...

"Simone Simmons, Simone Simmons. Paging Simone Simmons. Please meet your brother in the waiting area of Terminal C."

She heard her name on the paging system and exhaled, knowing her brother was Freddie. She picked up the duffle bag, looked around, located the directions for Terminal C, and quickly headed off in its direction.

When she spotted Freddie, she wanted to run to him but restrained herself until she reached him. The first thing she noticed was his torn shirt and blood stained shoulder, which he was desperately trying to conceal. Her mind went back to the last time he'd shown up bloody and she automatically made the connection.

"Freddie, what—"

He silenced her with a breathtaking hug, like he was a drowning man suddenly being saved. It had been a hard trip back to New York for him, but once a car thief always a car thief. He crept from back street to back street, making it all the way to Pennsylvania Avenue before he spotted an '88 Cutlass Supreme. Being without a screwdriver or snatch bar, he had no choice but to bust out the little side window and hotwire the ignition. It was like riding a bike—you never forget.

He jumped on the highway and headed for NY, and it seemed that every few miles, he passed a trooper or a trooper passed him. One glance at the window and the jig was up. His asshole stayed tight all the way to JFK. All he could think of was Simone and never seeing her again. He thought about how his lying ways had put him in a position to lose everything. He vowed that if he made it to her, and she was waiting for him, he would change for good.

Now, holding her in his arms, he felt renewed. "Ssshhhh, boo. Everything's gonna be alright. But we gotta get out of town right away," he told her, and then held her at arm's length.

Her eyes shone like crystal because of the tears of confusion. "Out of town? Why, Freddie? Where? Why are you bleeding?" These were the questions she felt she had a right to know.

"Please, boo, trust me. I promise I'll tell you. Right now, I need a change of clothes and we need two tickets to Raleigh, North Carolina, aiight? Can you handle that while I get out of this shirt?"

She nodded and Freddie kissed her softly, "I love you, Simone." He pulled the duffel bag to him and began to rifle through it. Her clothes and his were haphazardly thrown together. He rummaged through the bag until he found a white and blue Roc-A-Wear hoodie. He dashed off to the bathroom to change.

While he was gone, Simone bought two tickets for Greensboro, North Carolina, because there were no flights leaving for Raleigh. The flight wasn't scheduled to leave for almost two hours. She prayed that wouldn't be a problem.

When Freddie returned and she broke the news, he sighed, resigned. "It's all we got," he replied.

"Freddie, please. Have I ever questioned you before? Baby, I need to know what's going on. You're acting like...like somebody's after you," she stressed, grabbing her head.

Freddie looked at his watch. With two hours to spare, there was no reason not to tell her. Besides, as much as he loved her, if she decided to leave him, it was best that she didn't know where he was going.

"Okay, yo...Let's get something to eat and we'll talk."

Simone looked down at her engagement ring, knowing it would never mean the same thing again. She and Freddie sat in a small airport coffee shop as he explained what had led up to the present situation. He was completely honest with her, but every sentence seemed to slap her love and trust in the face. She listened as Freddie explained about the stripper, and how Cream had confronted him in the barbershop. That was where the blood had come from the morning of the funeral. He explained how he had gone downtown to get Slug. That was when the shootout jumped off and he killed Mannie and shot a cop. She knew the Acura was in her name, and that the police would want to question her now. The whole thing made her look at Freddie in a whole new light.

Simone told herself that she should've known. Freddie was gorgeous. Anytime he came around, all her friends changed their attitudes and fought for his attention. She felt like she should have known—just from the way they'd met, with his smooth approach and his demeanor—that he was a dog.

Simone was working in a flower shop when Freddie walked in one day. Just looking at the niggah's soft green eyes and juicy lips made her panties wet, but she played it off and kept it professional. He had ordered a dozen yellow roses and a teddy bear when she said, "Hmm. Expensive. She must be pretty special, huh?"

"I hope she will be."

Her heart dropped. She was hoping they were for his mother, but his answer confirmed her suspicion—he had a girl.

She cleared her throat and asked, "And what would you like on the card?"

"Put...I hope to see you again real soon; 555-2345, Freddie." He smiled and made her stomach do a dance.

She processed the order and handed him the flowers, but to her surprise he handed them back. She thought something was wrong.

"Naw, everything's fine...if you'll accept my gift."

She was hooked. And from that day on, her feet never touched the ground. Now this. She felt like she had been slammed face first back into reality.

"Freddie...what do you expect me to say? You...you call me and tell me to pack up...For what? I don't know. Where? I don't know. But silly me, I'm runnin' around like crazy because I trusted you, Freddie. And now you tell me it's all because of some...bitch you couldn't keep your dick out of!" she sniffed up the tears, exasperated. "You know what? I—"

Freddie reached across the table and touched her hand, but she flinched and slowly withdrew, unable to look him in the face.

"Simone, yo…I know I fucked up, but—"

"Do you, Freddie? Did you fuck up because you fucked up or because you got caught fuckin' up? Huh? What are you sorry for?" Her voice elevated an octave, causing a few heads to turn around and tune in.

Freddie gave them a hard ghetto grill to reestablish their privacy and then turned back to Simone. "Ma, I know I'm askin' a lot of you. And right now, you don't have any reason to believe what I say, but…Simone, I love you. And I promise to spend the rest of my life makin' it up to you. I need you. If I didn't, I woulda just left without you, disappeared. But where could I go without you by my side?" He reached across the table again and took her hand in his. This time she didn't pull away. "Simone, I promise, boo. It'll never happen again."

"You promise, Freddie?" she asked incredulously. "Why would you expect me to believe that?"

"Because I ain't never promised that before."

She held her ring finger up in his face. "Oh no? Well, what is this supposed to mean?" she challenged.

"When I gave that to you, I didn't know what having a wife really meant—the woman I come home to, have babies and grow old with. But now…I know it means much more, and I hate that it took this for me to realize it. But now I know…I know it means the woman you share your life with, not just your bed or your roof. And I pledge to you, on my soul, to give you just that, boo—my life, and nothing less."

She wanted so badly to believe him. Her heart yearned to trust his soothing voice and emerald eyes, but she couldn't find a reason she should. Except the love she couldn't live without.

Freddie took her left hand and gently slid the ring off her finger, and it felt like her soul was being ripped out of her body.

"No, Freddie. I believe—"

He gently placed a finger on her lips and rubbed them with his thumb. "The ring could never mean the same. Every time you see it, what would it represent? I want our love to be pure, flawless, like a true diamond. As soon as I can, I'ma get you another one to symbolize the struggle we went through to reach the understanding we now share. You're my winner, baby. And if I die before I ever stand at the altar, God knows I've already pledged my heart to you forever."

Every word was like a healing balm to her spirit. "I love you, Freddie...Please... Don't hurt me, okay?" The tears made her look like an innocent child that he only wanted to protect. He pulled her from her chair and into his lap. She hugged him tightly.

"Now boarding for Greensboro, North Carolina. Gate forty-seven," the PA announced.

Freddie looked into Simone's eyes and asked, "So is this goodbye or will you come with me and share my life?"

She clung to him, afraid of the word goodbye. "I wanna be with you, Freddie. I wanna be with you."

Her words were music to his ears.

Chapter Ten

✝ Slug stood in his Aunt Arnez's living room silently. He didn't know what she and his mother, Caroline Ann, known to the family as Ann, would say. They both sat quietly. All you could hear was the ticking of the clock. He had told them all he knew, which wasn't much. All he knew was that they had started shooting and that he and Freddie had clapped back, a niggah dropped and a cop got hit, and now Freddie was on his way down south.

Arnez was no stranger to the streets. Freddie's absentee father was a high roller back in the early '80s—a Dominican player with long paper and a sweet dick. Arnez was young and naïve, got sucked in, ended up pregnant, and Freddie Sr. disappeared. She wouldn't acknowledge his desertion at first, even naming Freddie after him to let all them jealous bitches know who had borne his seed. But after a few months of seeing him everywhere but still being ignored, she finally got the message.

As Freddie grew up, she saw some of his father's womanizing traits in him and tried to beat it out of him, but to no avail. Arnez knew her son wasn't a murderer, just the victim of harsh circumstances.

"Well, one thing's for sure. You can't run forever," she remarked.

"Naw, but he can run for now," Slug replied.

"What does he want me to do?" Arnez asked, ready to troop out for her only child.

"He knows they'll be comin' around questioning," Slug explained, "so he—"

"I know all that, Eric, believe me. I know how to handle police. I mean, what does he want me to do? Does he need any money? I ain't got much, but Lord knows he can get my last."

Slug appreciated his aunt's devotion to her son. "Naw, Auntie, he'll be okay. I'll take care of baby boy," he assured her.

"How?" Ann questioned. "Slug, he in enough trouble already to be messin' 'round wit' you." Slug's mother was fully aware of her son's notorious reputation.

"Ma, I ain't mean it like that, I meant...get him a job or something," he lied.

"A job? Boy, how you gonna get him a job and ain't never worked a day in yo' life," Ann inquired.

"Besides, with the police lookin' for him, ain't no way he can work a regular job," Arnez added, shaking her head, "What is my baby gonna do? I should go see a lawyer."

"Good idea, Nezzie," Ann commended. "Try to work some good out of this. I mean, the way you explained it, Eric, it was self-defense."

Their dispositions brightened considerably. Slug didn't have the heart to bring them back to reality. Freddie had shot a cop. There wasn't any self-defense for that.

"Yes, the Lord works in mysterious ways," Ann said.

Slug turned to his mother. "Ma, I'm 'posed to meet Freddie in the Boro, and I don't want him down there too long without me."

Slug helped his mother to stand. "Just let me gather my things and I'll be ready. I hope Goldsboro will be ready for us."

Chapter Eleven

✝ Freddie and Simone emerged from the Piedmont Airport in Greensboro just as the sun had taken on an orange tint. They had both been in their own world, flying high above the real one. Simone thought about the decision she'd made. She didn't regret it because wherever Freddie was, she wanted to be. But she realized all she had sacrificed to do so. Because the car was in her name, she knew that if she got a job, it would just be a matter of time before the police came looking for her. And even though she had nothing to do with the shootout, it would bring heat to Freddie. The same thing with school—this hurt the most. She only had a few months to go before she would have been a certified public accountant. Now, all of that was gone, at least for the time being.

Freddie spent the flight wondering what he would do once he reached Goldsboro. He had never worked a 9 to 5 a day in his life, and he was willing to square up but he couldn't. Everything was being set up to involve him in some type of criminal enterprise. But Freddie wasn't a hustler, he was a player. All he knew was macking women—that was how he ate, how he paid bills, how he pampered Simone with everything, even the two-carat engagement ring. Still another reason to get rid of it. Simone never knew that the steak she ate, the clothes she wore and the roof that sheltered her, all came out of other women's pocketbooks. But now that he had committed himself to Simone, what would or could he do to support her?

Simone looked out over the airport parking lot and

yawned. "Boo, I'm exhausted. Let's just get a room instead of going straight to Goldsboro, okay?" Freddie looked at her and felt it was a good point. He needed to give Slug a chance to get there first.

"Yeah, no doubt ma. That's a good idea." He placed his arm around her waist and led her to one of the waiting cabs.

"Welcome to Greensboro," the cabbie drawled. "How was the flight?"

Freddie was a little taken aback by the man's southern hospitality. In Jersey, you were lucky if a cabbie didn't say "Where the fuck you goin'?"

"Uh, it was cool. Thanks for askin'," Freddie replied.

"Where to?" the cabbie asked as he pulled off.

"You know any motels you could suggest?" Freddie asked.

"Top of the line, nice, flea-bitten, or damn near condemned?" the cabbie chuckled.

"Nice."

"Comin' right up."

The cabbie drove them to the Red Roof Inn on High Point Road. "This good enough? Real nice prices, real nice people." Simone giggled because he sounded like a commercial.

"Thanks, yo," Freddie said, handing him a twenty. "Keep the change."

The meter only read $8.30. "Well, I thank ya kindly. Y'all enjoy your stay in Greensboro."

Freddie and Simone climbed out of the cab with Freddie carrying the duffle bag. "Real nice prices, real nice people," Freddie mocked, imitating a country accent. Simone hit him.

"Stop Freddie, he was nice!" she giggled. "But that did sound like a commercial."

They went in and Freddie copped a single room for three nights. Their room was on the second level. They entered the room and turned on the light because the sun had already set.

The room was immaculate and had a peach bedspread, matching curtains, and off-white walls. It was a little stuffy because it had been a warm spring day in North Carolina, so Freddie turned on the air conditioner. He tossed the duffle bag onto the bed and Simone laid across it on her back, "Ohhh, that feels good."

Freddie clicked on the TV and flipped through a few stations, caught the news and left it there, just in case.

"You hungry?" Freddie asked.

"A little. But for real for real, I just wanna take a bath and go to sleep," she said, stretching her arms over her head.

"Well, I'm about to starve, yo."

Simone was rummaging through the large duffle bag, pulling out clothes randomly. She had only managed to pack three sets of clothes for Freddie and four for herself, along with a few pairs of shoes, sneakers, and boots.

"Damn. I hope I packed some panties," she giggled, still pulling stuff out. She found a few pair of Freddie's boxers and a couple of bras. She shrugged, "I guess I'll just have to get some tomorrow."

"Dig, I'ma go get somethin' to eat," Freddie informed.

"Okay."

Freddie left the room. Simone had just pulled off her sweatshirt when she noticed that the TV had a radio on it as well. She fiddled with the remote until she figured out how to turn off the TV and turn on the radio. She turned the digital dial until she heard Avant's "Read Your Mind" on 104.3.

Simone took off her low-rider jeans, panties, and bra before entering the bathroom completely naked. She opened up the taps and sat on the toilet seat to watch the tub fill with steaming water and bubbles from the complimentary bubble bath she'd poured in. When the tub was full and the bubble level to her liking, she put her hair up in a ponytail and tested the water with the tip of her toes. Perfect.

Simone slid into the warm water like she would slide under a quilt on a cold and stormy winter night. She let the water cradle her, rocking her ever so gently whenever she moved around. She held up her left hand and looked at the light spot the ring had left on her chocolate complexion. She thought about calling her mother but didn't want to do it from the motel phone. She promised herself she'd call in the morning. What to say, she hadn't figured out yet. She couldn't picture herself saying, "Hey ma, me and Freddie on the run from the police. I'll try to stay in touch."

She laughed to herself to keep from crying because the whole situation was madness. She lathered up and washed her body to the sounds of Anita Baker, Luther, Joe, and Mary J. before she got out to dry off. As she toweled her back, she heard her song, Keith Sweat's "Right and a Wrong Way (to Love Somebody)." She opened the door to go turn it up but found the room completely dark except for several flickering candles strategically placed around the room. Freddie was straddling the sole chair in the room backwards, his chest against the back of it. Simone stopped in front of the light, right outside the bathroom, where the sink and a large mirror were.

"Stay right there, boo...Just let me look at you."

Freddie's eyes devoured his woman from head to toe; from her silky Indian mane to her slanted brown eyes, sculpted cheekbones, African nose and full pouty lips. His eyes traveled along her slender neck, which curved into small feminine shoulders. The cool air from the AC made her pretty pink nipples stick out almost a full half inch. It was like she could feel his eyes kissing her all over, because as he looked lower, her heart rate increased, her breathing shortened, and her wetness began to lubricate her thighs.

Freddie continued his visual nibbling, and as Keith began to sing, so did he, in that melodic octave that always made Simone melt. *"You may be young but you're ready, ready to learn,"* Freddie crooned, sounding a little like Jaheim. He got up and walked over to her. *"You're not a little girl, you're a woman. Take my hand,"* he continued, as he took her hand in his and kissed it.

"Damn, you beautiful, Simone." He gently turned her around to face her own reflection in the mirror. "See what I see," he whispered, running a tantalizing finger down her spine, making her jump slightly and bite her trembling bottom lip. She watched and felt his hands cup both of her breasts, pulling and teasing her nipples as he sang softly in her ear, *"I'm yours for the taking, so you can do what you please."*

Simone placed her hands on his, gripping them as he massaged her breasts. She relaxed her chocolate body against him.

You're all I, I'll ever need.

Freddie kept eye contact with her through the mirror. He slid their hands down to her belly and she watched them go lower and lower. Her eyes took on a panther-like glow, letting Freddie know his sensuality had taken her as he'd intended it to. *"Never let me go,"* he sang as he ran his finger along her pussy lips, inserting two up to the knuckle inside her. She gasped.

"I...won't."

Simone was so creamy; she milked his fingers as Freddie licked along her spine. He used his free hand to slowly push her forward, bending her over the sink.

"Freddie, I want to feel you inside me soooooo bad," she purred.

Freddie came out of his pants and slid inside her tightness, slowly; taking his time until he was all the way inside. "Look how beautiful love makes you look, boo...Look at what love looks like in your eyes," Freddie urged, long dicking her into losing control.

Simone kept steady eye contact with herself, getting more and more turned on by the expressions on her face, as she watched her own ecstasy.

Freddie gripped her around the waist and grinded her hard, making her eyes roll up in the back of her head.

"Freddie, don't stop...don't ever stop loving me, baby."

"You're so beautiful to me, Simone. So beautiful," Freddie replied. "Kiss yourself, ma." Simone kissed her own reflection on the lips as if it were her long lost twin.

"I'm beautiful," she moaned, reaching back to pull Freddie to her as she felt the quiver in her stomach build into a rumble.

"Freddie, I can feel it...I can...feel..."

Freddie knew his woman well enough to hold himself until he felt her walls flare and tighten, timing his release to match hers. The intensity of the moment damn near made Simone lose her mind.

"Freddie...I'll...kill...you...I'll kill...you," she stuttered, too low for Freddie to hear. And he was too unconscious to care to understand.

Chapter Twelve

✝ It had been a week since Mannie's murder and Tay had already sent a message to the hustlers around The New Projects. He sent a team through to wet up the buildings of 116 in the back on Elmwood, 524 in the front on Second Street, 532 in the middle, and 544 near the corner. Every day a different crew of shooters darted through the money-getting' housing projects and lit the block up like Independence Day. No one was hit because no one was meant to be, but the message was loud and clear, too loud for Power to ignore.

Power was from building 524, but he repped his stomping grounds to the fullest. He and his manz and 'em controlled the front, but it was him who played the role of enforcer, and he played his role well. He had outlasted many of his contemporaries, who were either dead or doing fed bids, so niggahs respected his longevity, Tay included. But this wasn't about respect, it was about revenge. So Power decided to go talk to Tay.

He pulled up in his classic beige Jaguar XJR with burgundy interior. Power was beyond the need to floss. He didn't have oversized tires or spinning rims like young cats. The Jag was still as-it-was off the showroom floor. There was a little league baseball game being played in Silas Field Park and he decided this was a good place to have the meeting. He came with his manz, Bash, who was also a known gunman in the town. They climbed the half-full stone bleachers and took a seat behind cheering parents and siblings. He looked around and spotted a young cat profiling along the wall.

"Yo, ock, lemme holla at you."

The young boy recognized Power's face but didn't know his name. He just knew he had paper and pushed a sick Jag. He bopped over, trying to look cooler than he was.

"What up, Unc?" the boy asked, addressing Power by the term reserved for elders.

Power pulled out a wad of money and peeled off a Benjamin. "Do me a favor, ock. Go tell Tay Power said holla at him, and tell him where I'm at, aiight?"

The boy recognized the name instantly. Power was THAT NIGGAH. Had it been anyone else, he woulda kept the hundred and dipped, but since Power was who he was...say no more.

"If I can find 'em," the boy replied.

"Yeah, you can find 'em. Hurry up for me."

The boy hurried off as the batter on the field got a hit that landed in left field, almost rolling to the fence. The crowd erupted with cheers.

"That's my baby!"

"Run, T, run!"

"Safe!" the umpire declared as the runner slid into third base.

Power laughed. "Good hit!" he yelled and clapped. He turned to Bashir. "You see this, ock? You see these pretty black mamas cheering for their man-children? Everything we do, we do for this," Power explained, gesturing with his hand, "Niggahs forget that. They forget and lose focus. But this is why we do what we do."

Bashir nodded knowingly.

Out of the corner of Power's hawk-like vision, he saw Tay enter the park, followed by the boy and another cat, looking like he didn't wanna talk.

"Bash, let me talk to Tay alone."

Bash stood up and descended the bleachers. When Tay saw Bashir coming down, he understood and told his man the same thing. Tay climbed the bleachers and Power stood up to greet him with a handshake.

"Power. What the deal, unc?" Tay greeted, a little out of breath.

Power chuckled and patted Tay's protruding belly. "Not as good as you, nephew."

Tay smiled as they sat down.

"Let me ask you something. You ever come out here and watch these games?"

"For what?" Tay was visibly perplexed.

Inside, Power shook his head because Dante was a living example of the point he was making to Bash, about losing focus.

"You ever read Akbar's book *Death of the Game*?

Baseball games, books—Tay didn't know what Power was getting at, but he wished he'd get to it. "Naw P, I don't read much. Sorry," Tay replied sarcastically.

Power detected the sarcasm in his voice. "I only asked because he said snitches killed the game. And the reason nig-gahs snitch is because they lose focus. What we do, we don't make money just to make money. We make money to provide for our family, for our people, and if niggahs was in the game for that, wouldn't be nothin' to snitch about or nobody to snitch on, because they'd know this is all we got."

Dante's young, greedy mind couldn't grasp the totality of what Power was saying. All he knew was mo' money, mo' mur-der. "I feel you, P," he said, but Power knew he didn't. "I feel you. It's about family."

Power just let it go. "That's why I understood why you did what you did, and it's why I wanted to talk to you, head up.

This Freddie cat—you got my word—none of my people got nothin' to do wit' it. I heard his name a few times, but I couldn't pick him out of a crowd. He ain't no true New Project niggah, born and raised, put work in, or got paper. You know all the real ones, ock: Tizz, Money, Chet, Pete and Squirm, Doma, Buie, Krush and 'em," Power announced, doing a quick role call of his hood. "And you know my young boys that hug the block: Wheels, Nider, and my lil' folks from 116. Dude ain't no hustler or no gangsta either, he a player.

"So you sayin' he ain't from your hood? Well, who his people? Where his mother rest?" Tay wanted to know.

Power knew Tay had totally missed his point. He looked Tay dead in the eye, "I don't know, D. But if I did, I wouldn't tell you. Point blank!"

Tay started to protest but Power continued.

"Now dig. I'll do whatever I can to help you resolve this issue. Hell, I'll murder the niggah myself and bring you the body. But I'm askin' you—no, I'm beggin' you—please don't bring that gangsta shit to me and mine no more, because I don't need that and neither do you, on some real gee shit." Power kept his tone steady, but Dante knew what he meant.

"My brother was my heart, P, and I'ma do whatever I gotta do so he don't die in vain. But I respect the fact that you came to holla at me. I appreciate it."

Die in vain? Power thought. *No matter what you do, ock, you can't change the fact that he died in vain. Look what he died for.* Power extended his hand and Dante gripped it firmly. "Anytime, nephew. Anytime. And do me a favor. Try 'n make a game or two this summer. Trust me. It'll help you focus."

Dante stood up. "I'll try, unc." But Power knew he wouldn't.

Chapter Thirteen

Never get attached to what you can't leave in thirty seconds. This is what Detective Wilson was thinking as he looked around Freddie's apartment. As soon as they'd identified the prints, they swooped down on his spot like a hoard of badged vultures, certified to pick the carcass. Wilson and several officers searched the apartment top to bottom, and from what they could see, their man had definitely left in a hurry. Big-screen TV, DVD, stereo with stacks of CDs all in tact. In fact, besides the few drawers that were pulled out and a few hangers that were strewn about, most of the clothes were still there.

"So...I see she's with him," Wilson commented to himself, but Woods had walked in behind him.

"Who? The Simmons woman?"

"Who else," Wilson stated rhetorically, strolling around the room and stopping at the dresser. The only drawer open was full of Freddie's boxers. "He must've called and told her to meet him because she did the packing."

"How do you know?"

"The two loaded pistols we found in the hall closet. If it was him, he wouldn't have left those." Wilson turned to Woods. "Mike, are you familiar with women's clothing?" He smiled.

"What do you mean 'familiar'?" Woods asked, ready to take offense because the older man had a sick sense of humor.

"I'm not askin' you if you got a thong, kid. You're young

and hip, I suppose. Do you know the styles?"

"I guess. I never really thought—"

"Step over here."

They both walked over to the closet and looked at Simone's dresses, outfits, and shoes. "Look closely and tell me what's missing—summer clothing, winter clothes, what?"

Woods surveyed the Prada, DKNY, Gucci, Chanel, BAPE and Baby Phat hanging in a rainbow of colors, fabrics, and styles.

Miller continued, "Chances are, he headed down south. I don't know a black man in New Jersey that doesn't have family down south. But where? Atlanta...South Carolina...North Carolina? We call it fugitive country." Wilson winked, "Every cat on the run usually ends up in one of those three places."

"Why not Baltimore or DC? Aren't there a lot of African Americans in these places, too?" Woods inquired.

Wilson shook it off. "Migration patterns. You'd be surprised how much like birds we are. We fly south in the winter," he smiled. "And a man usually runs to a comfort zone." Wilson closed the closet. "Keep a close eye on the Simmons woman's credit cards. From the looks of that wardrobe, she's definitely a power shopper. Chances are, they won't use 'em, if he's smart. But everybody slips up sooner or later, even the smart ones."

Chapter Fourteen

After spending a few days in the motel in Greensboro, Freddie came out to see Slug leaning against the bowling ball-painted Caddy sparkling. When they got in, Simone sat in the back seat. She was unused to the bearings. She looked at the TV screen in the rear and her eyes opened wide. She blushed when she saw that a porno was playing. She nudged Freddie's knee with hers and motioned to the screen.

Freddie looked up and saw the screen. "Yo, Slug. 'Fuck you into, dog?"

Slug looked into the rear view mirror to see what Freddie was talking about and chuckled, "My bad dog. Long night." He switched off the TV, pumped 'Pac, and began the three-hour trek to Goldsboro.

Goldsboro hadn't changed much since the last time Freddie saw it. It was still a small, sleepy town, despite the new businesses and buildings. They rode into town in Slug's tricked-out Cadillac Brougham, and it was definitely that. It was a navy blue '85 model, sporting 26-inch hundred spike Daytons. Slug had the back doors modified to open like suicide doors. He had also taken the back seat and reset it, facing it toward the rear of the car. It gave the inside a limo feel. The TV was mounted in the middle of the back of the car. The system was ear splitting, and he pumped nothing but 'Pac.

"You in the dirty dirty, cuz," Slug drawled. "We don't push Acs, we push Yacks, niggah," Slug boasted.

Once they arrived, Slug explained, "Yo, cuz, I had to move

on short notice, so I did the best I could on the apartment."

When Freddie saw his new lay-up, he understood Slug's explanation. It was a two-story apartment building on Walnut Street, diagonally across from the Piggly Wiggly supermarket on Leslie Street. It sat in the heart of Webbtown, the black ghetto of the 'Boro. Freddie remembered the building because it had been many things over the years. It had been a liquor house, a crack house, and a ho' house several times over. Now, it was owned by a closet smoker who didn't ask questions, especially of Slug, and who wanted his money in cash only, under the table. Perfect for Freddie, Slug explained. But looking at it—that didn't make him feel any better.

It was run-down and rusty on the outside, and dingy and roach-infested inside. It looked like the previous occupants had moved out as quickly as Freddie had left his apartment. Most of their broke-down furniture remained, including a dirty-ass brown couch that was sunk to the floor, a three-legged kitchen table and several soiled mattresses in each of the two bedrooms. The only good thing was that the apartment was definitely spacious with cathedral ceilings. Years earlier, it had been a prestigious office building. But as the area became more and more ghetto, the building did, too.

Simone was taken aback by the apartment as well, but she looked at it with a woman's eye. With a good house cleaning and delousing, the place had potential. The hardwood floors were covered with drug-related debris and soot, but she imagined them shined up and waxed. It wasn't the best, but it was all they had.

"Ay, yo, we'll get some heads to get all this shit out, then we'll go on and lace this shit out," Slug proposed.

"Lace?" Freddie echoed. "A niggah ain't holding' no lace paper, yo."

Slug smiled. "Niggah, gimme a gee and I'll bring you all the luxuries of home, plus a muhfuckin' computer," Slug told him.

Freddie was sold and gave him the money.

"Aiight, yo. I'll be back wit' the heads," Slug told him and left.

An hour later, Slug was commanding a small army of several heads—lift this, pull that, bring this, drop that, scrub niggah, scrub. By nightfall, they had the joint cleared out and as clean as they could get it. When crackheads worked, they did work. Slug paid them and they left.

"What up wit' the furniture?" Freddie asked.

"Tomorrow, no later than five." Slug grinned mischievously. "But tonight, it's my turn to show you around, niggah."

Freddie looked at Simone. "You wit' it?"

"In this?" she answered, referring to her soiled outfit. She had already worn everything she had brought and they hadn't been to a Laundromat.

"Naw, boo, I'm takin' you shoppin'. Matter of fact, *we* goin' shoppin'," Freddie offered, taking her by the waist.

"Freddie," she whined cautiously, as if to say, we're on a budget.

"Nothin' major, yo. Just a little sumptin' to let niggahs know how Freddie do and how he got the baddest chocolate mami in town." He smiled and she couldn't resist. He turned to Slug, "Let's go to the mall."

They didn't stay long at the mall, but the time they were there put a dent in their kitty. Freddie was used to the best and giving Simone the same. As they say: Old habits are hard to break.

They went back to Slug's apartment in Jefferson Court to get dressed. Freddie looked at himself in Slug's full-length mirror. He had copped a few pairs of Coogi and Red Monkey jeans. He threw on a black pair of Googi jeans, a pair of black on white and red number nine Jordans, an Ed Hardy hoodie, and a solid black Yankees fitted. He smoothed his curls and inspected the trim up Slug had given him very closely. Freddie was picky about who cut his hair, but he couldn't front—Slug had done a good job with just a razor and a comb.

"Razors give you a sharper line than clippers, niggah. Just chill. I got this," Slug assured him.

Simone came out of the bathroom looking irresistibly delicious in a pair of curve-hugging Seven blue jeans and a multicolored blouse that fastened at her belly button with two metallic Zs, exposing her cleavage in a dagger-like V.

"Boo, look at this, yo," Freddie said, pointing to his goatee. "Does it look even to you?"

Simone inspected the trim and gave her approval. "Yeah baby, Slug did a good job."

"You sure?"

"I'm sure, ol' pretty-ass niggah," she chuckled, "What I'm not so sure about is spending all this money. You sure you don't think we should take some of this stuff back?"

Freddie took her by the hands to reassure her. "Dig boo, regardless of our situation, we ain't gonna stop livin', you hear me? I want you to be happy, and I want you to look good bein' happy, so whatever I gotta do, it's done, feel me?"

She wrapped her arms around his neck, "You make me happy, Freddie. I understand what you're sayin' and I appreciate it, really. But boo, I'll wear Payless shoes and eat beans out of a can if that's what it'll take to stay together."

She touched Freddie down deep with her words, and all he could do was kiss her as a reply. "I love you, girl." He hugged her, adding, "Now let's forget about everything except havin' a good time. Bada boom?!"

"Bada bing!" she smiled, completing their way of saying: Understand? Understood.

Simone turned to walk out the door and Freddie couldn't help but admire her ass.

"Damn, boo, you gonna make me hurt one of these country niggahs behind them jeans."

"Shut up, boy," she blushed. "It's yours."

"Yeah? Well, walk nasty like it's mine."

Chapter Fifteen

✝ "Kiki, come get this lil' muhfucka 'fore I kill 'im!" Slug yelled, sitting on the couch.
Slug had come to pick up Kiki from her apartment in Green Acres. Kiki was his girl, his love-hate ghetto relationship. Her three-year-old son was kicking Slug in the leg, and Slug was fed up with it.

"You better leave my baby alone!" Kiki screamed back from the bedroom. "Chris! Come here, boy!"

"No!" the little brat yelled.

"I'ma kick yo' ass," Slug told him, really wishing he could.

"I'ma kick *yo'* ass," Chris replied, and kicked Slug again.

Slug shoved him, not hard but hard enough, and Chris screamed, "Mama, he hit me! I'ma tell my daddy!" He ran to his mother for safety because he could tell Slug was mad.

"Fuck yo' punk-ass daddy! Tell that niggah suck my dick!" Slug yelled back.

Kiki came into the living room carrying Chris on a curvaceous hip. She was dressed like the average chickenhead— tight spandex dress and open-toed heels from the Shoe Barn, extension braids dyed at the tips and pinned up in a bun. But she was still a real cutie. She was a redbone with light brown eyes and was bowlegged as hell. Her only flaw was a chipped tooth that she got while fighting, which she loved to do, especially with Slug.

"Boy, I know you ain't put your hands on my baby! He ain't none of your chal!" Kiki said, rolling her neck.

73

"I know he ain't," Slug said, cracking the top on a bottle of E & J, "Dat's why I'ma beat his ass, he keep fuckin' wit' me."

Kiki rolled her eyes at Slug and kissed Chris. "Don't worry, boo. He just mean," she said and shot Slug a look.

"I'ma tell my daddy," Chris played the moment through crocodile tears.

"No, no, don't tell your daddy," Kiki quickly stated. Neither she nor Slug wanted to see her baby daddy fucked up behind something so petty.

"Shit, let him tell him. I'll tell his bitch-ass," Slug boasted, serious as a heart attack. "Girl, just bring yo' ass on 'fore I leave you."

"Let me take Chris next door and I'll be ready, ol' mannish ass," Kiki huffed and left out to take Chris to her mother's.

Slug shook his head. It was a damn shame when daughter, mother, and grandmother all lived in the projects. It was like blacks were trapped in a game they didn't know was being played. He stood up and left out, locking the door behind him.

"Okay ma, damn, I heard you!" Kiki said as she slammed the door angrily. Slug was already outside. "You ready?" she snapped and stormed past him to the car. "Bitch make me sick. But let it be the 3rd and she got her nose all up my ass," she mumbled to herself. Slug chuckled.

"'Fuck you laughin' at, Slug?! It ain't funny!"

"Man, shut yo' ass up and get in the damn car," Slug replied smoothly.

Freddie and Simone sat in the back seat giggling to themselves, listening to the lovers' quarrel. Kiki opened the front door and the inside light came on. Then she ducked her head down because she damn near drooled. But it happened so quick, no one noticed except Simone. She had just nutted on herself at the sight of Freddie.

"Hey," she said, surprised.

Slug closed his door. "That's my cousin, Freddie, and his wifey, Simone. Y'all, this Kiki."

"Hello," Simone said politely, but didn't forget Kiki's reaction.

"What da deal, ma?" Freddie greeted. His accent tickled Kiki's ears.

"So where we goin'?" Kiki asked, cutting her eye at Freddie in the dark car.

"Pop Bogan's"

Pop Bogan's was the ghetto hangout for the ballers in the 'Boro. It was a club slash restaurant slash pool hall. Only the livest niggahs came through because the wannabes got clowned.

Chapter Sixteen

✝ Slug pulled his Caddy into the parking lot between a candy-apple '64 and a Benz G wagon. Freddie glanced out the window at all the sick whips and niggahs blingin'. He promised himself he'd step his game up. Doing what? He didn't know. But he was too used to ballin' to be outshined by these country niggahs.

Once he stepped inside, though, the tables turned and he outshined them all. Trick Daddy's "Thug Holiday" blared in the background, and everyone was doing their own thing. But when Freddie came through, he got the eye of damn near every female and the grill of mad hating ass-niggahs.

"Who that? Ginuwine?"

"Shit, Ginuwine wish he looked that fine!"

Kiki was so not feeling Simone at the moment, the way she was holding on to Freddie's arm, head held high. Simone had niggahs sweatin' her on the DL, but since she was with Freddie, and Freddie was with Slug, they checked their tongues.

The four of them caught a corner booth and slid in, keeping the girls next to each other in the middle. It wasn't long before a flood of familiar faces that Freddie hadn't seen in years came through. Tago Raynor, Mandrell, Scooby, and Skeet. They all came to welcome Freddie back. Freddie could tell they were all doing well and that they hadn't changed a bit. Tago was still sneaky and treacherous, Mandrell was blingin', and Scooby and Skeet were playing, but not as hard as Freddie.

The females itched to come check out the new face, but they saw Simone sitting next to Kiki, and they didn't know if she was Kiki's people. None of them really wanted problems with Kiki, so they just slithered by, asses out and eyes dancing, trying to send Freddie all kinds of messages. Simone didn't miss a beat. She watched them with one eye and Freddie with the other. She had forgiven her man but she hadn't forgotten. Freddie appeared to be taking it all in stride, laughing with the fellas and eating from the shrimp platter they had ordered.

The only female Simone didn't see was to her left: Kiki.

But Slug saw her. He wasn't sure at first, because every time he looked at Kiki to see if she was watching Freddie, she'd slyly look away. It was a cat and mouse game until Slug finally caught her looking at Freddie and plucked her hard in the face.

"Aiight. Don't get fucked up in here," Slug warned her, heated that Freddie was getting so much attention, especially from Kiki.

"Boy!" Kiki exclaimed, and mushed Slug in the head just as hard.

Slug responded by plucking her again, harder than the first time, and she lunged at him with her nails.

Simone didn't know what was going on, so she leaned away to keep from getting hit.

"Yo, Slug! Slug! 'Fuck you doin'? Watch Simone!" Freddie demanded.

Meanwhile, Slug was laughing and pulling Kiki's weave, trying to keep her hands from his throat. "Don't worry, cuz, this broad crazy. All she wanna do is fuck and fight."

"Don't hit me no more, Slug," she growled, hitting him in the chest.

Slug locked his backhand back. "Aiight now, I'm through playin'. I'ma smack the shit out of you now."

"Move then," Kiki replied, pushing his hip with hers.

"Move so I can go to the bathroom."

Slug, amused, slid out of the way. Kiki turned to Simone. "You wanna come, girl?" she offered politely.

Simone nodded and slid out of the booth behind Kiki. As the two walked away, Slug slid closer to Freddie and popped a shrimp in his mouth.

"Niggah, y'all on some Ike and Tina shit, for real," Freddie remarked.

Slug chuckled. "Me and Kiki got a crazy understanding. She the only broad I trust. There's been many a day a niggah was shootin' bad and she gave me her last to grind...She just like it rough."

Freddie nodded.

"But, yo," Slug continued, lighting a Newport, "now that you here, what's the next move? The way these chickens sweatin' you, you need to mack these hos." Slug said it with a subtle hint of bitter sarcasm, which Freddie missed. Freddie was in his own world. From the moment he stepped into the place, he felt like a former crack addict in a smokehouse. Every female's lustful gaze made Freddie think of the paper she represented. He was fien'ing to crack but he wanted with all his heart to keep it real with Simone.

"Naw, yo...Simone proved she'd ride or die when she came wit' me. Shorty gave up a lot for me and I gotta respect that."

Slug took a swig of E&J. "No doubt, no doubt. But you gotta eat. You gotta feed that pretty lil' thang. And believe me, love don't pay no bills."

He had a point there.

"Remember what we talked about up top? 'Bout the connect?" Slug reminded him. "What the deal wit' dat?"

It sounded like the move to make, but the only person Freddie knew and could trust was Gina, and he was trying to leave all that behind. He looked at Slug, "Dog, I can't trust none of them cats in my situation, yo," Freddie lied. "I'd just be askin' for trouble."

"Well, dig, cuz. Whatever whatever, you know I'm wit' you," Slug said and gave Freddie dap. "You play cee-lo?"

"No doubt."

"Feel lucky?"

"Shit, it ain't but one way to find out."

Meanwhile in the ladies room, Kiki was trying to pick Simone's brain.

"So how long y'all gonna be down here?"

Simone touched up her lipstick in the mirror and shrugged off the question. "I'm not really sure. Probably not long."

Kiki saw that Simone was being evasive and selective with her information, so she changed the subject. "I love that top, girl. I ain't never seen an Azzure like that. Where you cop that?"

"Thank you," Simone said, smoothing the material, "Just somethin' I had."

Lying, Kiki thought. They sold those at the mall. Something wasn't quite right about her and Freddie, Kiki's nosiness told her. Either Freddie was fine but broke, or...

Just then, two girls who had been eying Freddie walked into the bathroom. They looked Simone up and down and rolled their eyes as they passed. Simone was about to say something but Kiki stopped her.

"Girl, don't even sweat these no-good bitches. They just hatin' 'cause your man is fine and, believe me, in a town small as the 'Boro, that's a problem. But don't sweat it. I got your back," Kiki said.

But all Simone could think about was Kiki's own reaction to Freddie. With friends like that...

On the way over to the cee-lo game, somebody called out, "Freddie! Freddie Holmes! I know that ain't you!" It was a deep, sultry, feminine voice.

He turned around and automatically had to do a double take. She was double-dipped chocolate, a shade darker than Simone, with baby doll eyes and deep-set dimples. She was killin' 'em in her peach and white DKNY velour suit and matching, customized Air Ones. Her jewels sparkled even brighter because of her dark skin tone and she was cutting across the room with the kind of walk that made a niggah hard just watching.

"Tina? Tina Jones?" Freddie echoed, a moment before he was smothered by a full body hug and subtle grind.

She stepped back and looked him up and down. "How you gonna come home and not make Tina a priority? I thought we was better than that."

Tina had been his summer girlfriend when he was 12 and she was 13. It was little kid puppy love. Besides a few tongue-less kisses and games of Catch a Girl, Get a Girl, which sent him home with tents, it was innocent. Back then, Tina was long-legged, skinny, and taller than him. But now she was Trina thick, Luke dancer thick, and a whole head shorter than him.

Tina saw that Freddie was eying her figure, so she whirled around to slap his eyes full of ass and stood with her hands on her hips.

"Yeah, niggah, it's me. All growed up and out," she laughed, exposing his weakness—a platinum tongue ring.

"I see that," was all Freddie could get out.

Slug was definitely not feeling this. He had been trying to fuck Tina, but since she was fucking that Miami niggah, Money, she wouldn't let him smash.

"So what up, Freddie? Slug know where I live, but I bet you ain't even ask," she remarked, mock pouting.

Before Freddie could answer, Simone and Kiki came out of the bathroom and quickly approached. Simone thought all this competition was quickly getting played out but she held her composure.

"Hey baby," she cooed, wrapping her arms around Freddie's neck and giving him a quick kiss. "Did you miss me?"

"N-no doubt," Freddie stuttered, tearing his eyes away from Tina and focusing on Simone.

Simone fronted at first like Tina wasn't standing there, then acknowledged her presence. "Oh, hello, I ain't even see you. Were y'all talkin'?" Simone asked innocently, but her eyes staked claim.

Tina wanted to say something fly, but Freddie cut in. "Simone, this is Tina, an old friend. Tina, this is Simone, my fiancée."

"Humph, congratulations," she shot at Simone like a subtle accusation.

"I know," Simone smiled.

Freddie saw where this was going. "So what up, boo? You ready to bounce? I'm tired as a muthafucka."

"Tired?" Slug repeated. "I thought…" He motioned toward the cee-lo game but Freddie shot him a loaded glance.

"Sure, baby," Simone replied, letting him off the hook. For now.

He turned to Tina. "Yo, Tina, on the real, it was good seein' you, ma."

She shot Freddie a full frontal gaze that she made sure Simone caught, licking her lips, exposing his weakness. "It was good seein' you, too, Freddie. Real good."

Tina sashayed off and Freddie had to fight not to watch her ass jiggle.

"Who was she?" Simone asked as she and Freddie snuggled

81

in Slug's extra bed, relaxing in the glow of love.

"Who?" Freddie answered her question with a question, trying to play dumb.

Simone propped herself up on one elbow and looked at him like 'Niggah don't play wit' me.' But Freddie knew that if he had come right out and started talking about Tina, she would think Tina was on his mind, which she obviously was.

"I'm serious. Who?"

"Tina," Simone stated. "You used to be wit' her, didn't you?"

Freddie sucked his teeth nonchalantly, "If you call two lil' 12-year-olds bein' together, then yeah."

"Did you do it to her?" Simone asked directly.

Freddie laughed. "Do it to her? You sound like you 12, or somethin'."

"Oh, you want the grown version? Did you fuck her, Freddie?" she asked, irked.

"No, I didn't do it to her. I didn't fuck her either. I told you, we was 12. Damn." Not like he wasn't trying to fuck her at 12.

Simone sat up and wrapped her arms around her knees. "Freddie...I'm not going to compete for you. I love you with all my heart, but I don't like feeling like, everywhere we go or everything we do, I have to compete, because every time I turn around, somebody somewhere is plottin' to take what I got. It's too much..."

Her words drifted off in frustration so Freddie sat up to cradle and comfort her. "Come on, ma. You ain't never got to compete for me. What did I do tonight to make you feel like that?"

"It wasn't you, Freddie. I just saw all those girls looking and—,"

Freddie kissed her on the neck. "Simone, look at me."

She turned her head to look into Freddie's eyes and his

heart.

"Just like I can't stop niggahs from lookin' at you, I can't stop females from lookin' at me. But I can control how I handle it. So I ask you again, did I do anything tonight to make you feel like you ain't the only one for me?"

She searched his eyes for a moment and found nothing but sincerity. "You didn't do anything."

"And I won't. I promise, boo. After all we've been through, I'd be a fool to give up the best thing that ever happened to me," he assured her.

"She was pretty, though," Simone smirked.

"You're prettier," he replied.

"No...I'm beautiful, remember?" she reminded him.

Chapter Seventeen

✝ Slug kept his word. The next day, a U-Haul truck full of furnishings was delivered by a couple of crackheads who were running ghetto moves on Rent-America, flipping apartments. The crib was laced and Simone busied herself with making the house into their home.

For the next few weeks, Freddie and Simone were inseparable. They spent the type of quality time they hadn't spent in months. They went to the movies and out to dinner, or just took long walks, then watched bootleg DVDs on their jacked wide screen.

Freddie continued to spend the little money they had until it dwindled down into a no-win situation. He had to cop a half ounce and start his nickel and dime hustle with Slug as his mentor.

Slug schooled him on the ins and outs of the dope game. They set up shop in the Old Projects and Freddie stayed true to his grind. His problem was his spending habits. As soon as he made it, he spent it, determined to look like a thousand dollars even if he really couldn't afford to. Freddie didn't slack on Simone either. He kept her dipped, hair and nails done.

Simone and Kiki became running partners if not close friends. Kiki turned her on to the best hairdresser in town, Nina Simone. And Simone still got sly looks and snide comments thrown her way. Not only because Freddie was her man, and no female had been able to violate that, but because of her gear. Freddie did what he could, keeping her in new shit, but

84

his paper was too short to elevate her to diva status. But Simone didn't mind. The way things were going with Freddie and her, she'd wear rags and sweep floors to keep their love strong.

She did try to get Freddie to stack paper instead of always spending it. She pulled up in the '90 Accord Freddie had copped for $1,500. It wasn't much but it got them around. Freddie was in front of the white store shooting dice when she pulled up. He jogged over to the car, leaned through the window, and gave her a kiss.

"Freddie, I'm going to pay the bills," she informed him.

He knew the monthly tab usually came to about $700. He gave her a grand. "Take that other $300 and go to the jeweler and pay on my watch for me, boo."

"Freddie," she whined. They had been through all this before. "What about food? Hello? I need to go shopping, too," she reminded him.

"Oh, I got that. This head owe me like two and some change. I'ma get it off they welfare card," he replied.

"But still, Freddie. You know you don't need to be out here in the first place. Please, boo, we need to put somethin' up, you know?"

He gave her a shut up kiss, "After I cop my watch, okay? I gotta go, I'm killin' these niggahs!" He jogged back to the dice game and Simone pulled off.

Freddie's conversation with Slug became redundant. He constantly heard, "Cuz, I'm tellin' you, this lil' nickel-and-dime ain't shit. We need a connect." But for Freddie that was out. He was failing to see the bigger picture, that is, until the whole frame changed.

Freddie was out in front of the white store, waiting for

Mandrell to come through and sell him an ounce. He was listening to a club mix in his CD walkman, so he didn't even hear the jump-outs skid up and hop out on him.

The big, burley redneck and his even bigger black partner walked up on him and said, "Don't make us chase you; we get ugly when we're out of breath."

Freddie's heart froze. This was his first run-in with the police since he had heard freeze and fired, which is what landed him into the situation now confronting him. Fortunately, it was nighttime and he was wearing a fitted Yankee cap. But the fact remained that if he went to jail, it was a wrap. He didn't have any drugs on him and his gun was 25 feet away, under the bushes. All he had was $1,500 in his pocket. He tried to play it calm.

"Run? For what, yo? I'm chillin', waitin' on a cab," Freddie replied.

The cops picked up his northern accent so they automatically assumed he was a drug dealer. "Oh, you one of them New Yawk boys, huh? I been seein' you a lot lately. What's your name, boy?" the wannabe black officer asked, stepping toward Freddie.

Freddie weighed his options. They were too close for him to run. If he did and got caught, it was jail for sure. But if he stayed and sweated it out, maybe he could get away.

"Antoine Jackson, officer."

"Jackson, huh?" the redneck asked, frisking his pockets, "You got any drugs or guns we need to know about?"

"No, sir," Freddie answered, his hands raised.

"Any outstanding warrants?" he questioned.

"No, no sir."

"Oh! What's this?" the redneck said triumphantly, taking the wad of money from Freddie's pocket. He whistled. "Jackpot!"

JM Benjamin

If Freddie was gonna run, that would have been the time, but he hesitated, and his window of opportunity closed as quickly as it had opened.

The redneck officer handed the money to his partner, who counted it and said sarcastically, "Boy, it's over a thousand dollars here. What you doin' carryin' this kind of cash in a neighborhood like this?"

The redneck frisked Freddie again, "Take off your shoes, boy."

Freddie obliged without hesitation and they found nothing.

"Well, Mr. Jackson, unless you have some kind of check stub, we're gonna have to confiscate this legal tender here," the redneck drawled.

"Come on, yo," Freddie whined. "After I cash my check, what I look like keepin' the stub?"

"Where you work?"

"In Raleigh," Freddie shot back quickly, too quickly.

"Where in Raleigh?" the redneck drilled.

"Harlem World Styles. It's a clothing store," he lied. The store was really in Smithfield, but it was the first thing that came to Freddie's mind.

"Well, unless you got that stub..." the redneck continued.

Freddie sighed, "Man, fuck it. I ain't got it, yo. So do what you gotta do." He was sick to be losing all he had, but he'd be sicker if they tried to run him in. He was ready to get it over with.

"Just like I thought. You gave up too easy, New Yawk," the redneck smiled. "Looka here...if I drive through here and see you again, for any reason, I won't be so understanding. You got me?"

Freddie nodded.

"You got me?" the redneck repeated, firmer than before.

"Yeah, I got you."

87

The redneck flashed him a big smile, held his money up and replied, "You have a nice night, ya hear? Come on, Willie."

The two officers walked away and got into their car. Freddie's knees damn near went out. He was that close to making a break for his pistol because jail wasn't an option. When they drove away, reality set in.

He was dead broke and it was past the first of the month. Freddie walked the few blocks to the crib not knowing what to do. He could easily get money for the bills from Slug, or Mandrell could front him a pack, but he had been fingered. Now the jump-out boys knew his face, and he couldn't afford to get hit wit' murder one just because he got caught pitching.

Before he knew it, he was home and walking into the living room. Simone was making his favorite, lasagna. He could smell it, but his stomach was too sick to eat. He walked into the kitchen to a bubbly Simone. She was singing and cooking, and she turned around when he came in.

"Hey, boo!" she said like she hadn't seen him in days instead of hours. She kissed him passionately, but when he didn't return the fire, she looked him in the eyes, "Freddie...what's wrong?"

He sat down heavily at the kitchen table. "The fuckin' police, yo."

At the sound of the word police, Simone's heart skipped a beat. "Where? What happened?" She was heading for panic mode. Now was not the time for her man to go to jail. She was prepared to run to the ends of the earth before she'd let Freddie get caught. "Do we have to leave?"

"Naw, yo...The muhfuckas just took my money! All my shit!" he exclaimed angrily. He was so mad he might've cried.

Simone kneeled down in front of him. "Baby, it could've been worse. We can get the money back. Besides," she winked, "I got a little somethin' put up."

Freddie looked into her smile like a new day had dawned.

"I told you and I told you to save, so I just took my own advice. Instead of getting my hair done, I just did it myself," she said, shrugging.

He pulled her up onto his lap and hugged her tight, "Damn, you my heart, girl."

"But Freddie," she said, pulling back from the hug, "you can't go back out there. Now they know your face."

He had surmised as much, but he wasn't prepared for what Simone said next.

"Let me go."

He couldn't believe his ears. He looked up into her eyes and they were dead serious. "What?"

"I said, let me go. Let me go out there. Nobody'll bother me because they'll know I work for you and Slug. And you can be somewhere close by but out of sight."

Damn. She was a ride or die chick for real, thought Freddie. "Naw, ma. I can't let you do that," Freddie said, head hanging.

Simone put her hand under his chin and lifted it. "Well, I can't let you go back out there," and she was serious. Then she took a deep breath. "They say when it rains it pours, right? Well...right now it's stormin'." She tried to smile to lighten the mood.

"No doubt."

"No, I mean..." She stood up and walked to the stove, then turned back to Freddie, "Freddie...I got somethin' to tell you."

He looked her in the face and didn't need to hear anymore; he already knew. Freddie hopped out of his chair, joyfully. "Say word!" All the Jersey in him came out then.

Simone had been trying to figure out how to tell him all day. She didn't know how he would take it because she didn't know how she felt about it, so she planned a special evening and cooked a big dinner to break the news.

Simone nodded slowly.

"Hell, yeah!" Freddie exclaimed proudly and picked Simone up, spinning her around. "I'ma be a daddy!"

He picked her up again and kissed her like he was trying to eat her up. After a moment she spoke up.

"But, Freddie...with the way things are, do you think—"

He cut her off, firmly but sweetly. "Don't even think it, boo. I told you, regardless, we ain't gonna let nothin' stop us from living. And a baby? Yo, that's what living is all about!" He held her tight, squeezing the tears out of her eyes. "I want you to have my son, Simone. Nothing in the world will make me happier."

She had needed to hear her man say just that. There was no way she wanted to have an abortion, and she didn't know what she would have done if he had suggested it. But hearing him say what he said gave her the strength to be happy.

"Thank you, Freddie," she whispered through tears of joy. "You don't know how much it means to me to hear you say that."

He looked into her eyes. "You just take care of my little man. Let daddy worry about the rest."

"Okay...daddy," she cooed like a woman in love.

Chapter Eighteen

✝ Freddie told Slug about the police incident and he agreed with Simone. "Yo, cuz, Timmons and Jake ain't no joke. Word up, if they said it, they meant it, and you can't afford that shit."

But Slug agreed for his own reason. He thought that now Freddie would finally try and hit up a connect. Freddie had other plans. He rode out to the mall. He didn't know exactly what he was going to do but he knew what he was going for. He was dressed to kill, casual in a pair of beige Polo slacks; a black, beige and brown Polo button-up; and a pair of black Clarks. He was wearing Pleasures for men and had his short curls groomed and shining. He finished off his outfit with a pair of oval Polo frames that gave him a studious and intelligent air.

As he cruised through the mall, looking for a victim, he tried to tell himself that this was going to be a one-time thing—just to get him over the hump. But like an alcoholic deciding to have just one drink, he knew what he was doing was dangerous.

Smiling and flirting, holding doors open and warmly greeting each female's face made him think of Simone, and the guilt weighed heavily on his back. He thought of their unborn growing in her womb and the promise he'd made to be true. Still, he tried to convince himself that this was for her, that he was only looking for a woman to seduce and juice for their growing family. He finally found one at the perfume counter in

91

Belk's. She was a white woman with blonde hair who looked as if she might have been in her early 40s. He peeped the ring confirming that she was married, and he eyed the platinum Visa confirming that she was also paid.

"Excuse me," Freddie said, approaching the counter, "I noticed that you just purchased White Diamonds by Liz Taylor. I love that fragrance." He smiled.

The woman looked up into his green eyes and smiled back. "Oh, it's not for me. It's a birthday gift for my sister," she responded.

"What a coincidence, it's my mother's birthday." Freddie chuckled. "But the problem is, she hates White Diamonds. So, um…I was wondering," he began to lick his lips and made the woman watch his tongue, "if maybe you could help me pick out a nice fragrance for her."

The lady giggled. "Oh, I don't know. I'm really not an expert or anything. I just know what I like."

"But you have such good taste," Freddie said. He gently placed his hand on hers and felt a slight tremble run up her arm. "Please."

"Well…," she thought about it. "Maybe just for a minute."

Freddie eyed her closely from head to toe. She was dressed conservatively, but everything she wore was expensive. Her silk blouse clung to her ample bosom and her skirt hugged her petite waist. She stood about 5'3" but her heels made her taller.

"What about this?" she asked, showing him a bottle of Sung by Alfred Sung. She sprayed a little into the air.

"I can't tell, uh—I'm sorry, I didn't even ask your name."

"Cynthia."

"I'm Freddie, and I think I could decide better if you sprayed it here." Freddie took the bottle and sprayed a little on the inside of her wrist. Then he gently lifted her arm to his nose, making sure his lips brushed across her flesh ever so gently. He could hear the faint sigh in her throat.

"No, that's a little racy for mama. That's more of an evening, out on the town."

Freddie picked up a bottle of J-Lo, "What about this?"

Cynthia looked at the bottle. "J-Lo. I've never heard of that."

"No?" Freddie fronted like he was surprised. "J-Lo is short for Jennifer Lopez. She's a very beautiful Latina singer/actress who is known to be very hot...very sensual. In fact, if I may..." he raised the bottle and sprayed a little on her neck, making her eyelids flutter.

"May I?" Freddie flashed a charismatic smile.

Cynthia could only nod.

He leaned in close to her ear so his words could be felt. "Now this...reminds me of red...red roses...red wine...red satin sheets and sexy red toe nails in sexy red, six-inch stilettos."

Cynthia's nipples pressed against the silk of her blouse like a child pressing his or her face to the glass of a candy store, licking his or her lips.

Freddie pulled away and shrugged. "Definitely not a mommy fragrance. Maybe I should just get her a wok," he joked and Cynthia giggled.

"Thank you so much for your time, Cynthia." He shook her hand, running a finger across her palm and causing her to reflexively grip his hand as the sensation ran up her spine.

"No...no problem, umm, Freddie," she replied, slightly hoarse.

"How can I make it up to you?" He was still holding her hand.

"Oh, there's no—"

He gently cut her off. "No, there is because it would break

my heart to see you walk away."

It was a wrap. It didn't take much to convince this rich, lonely housewife to drive around the corner and meet Freddie at the Irish Inn, a seedy, secluded motel that fit Cynthia's fantasy of taboo.

Once inside the room, Freddie wasted no time putting his mack down on the squareness of Cynthia's naiveté. He pinned her against the door, snatching her skirt up to her hips, pushing past her panties and shoving three fingers inside her warm pinkness.

"Is this how you want it, huh? You want that thug shit, don't you?" Freddie woofed and Cynthia was loving it.

"Oh, yes! Yes!" She tried to kiss him but he turned away.

"I got something for you to kiss," he told her, snatching his manhood out of his pants and pushing her down on her knees. He slid the whole length into her mouth, pumping in and out, sexing her face.

"Damn! You a nasty bitch, ain't you? Ain't you?" Freddie accosted her. The only reply was the gagging in her throat. He didn't even try to hold back. He came in her mouth and watched it spill out and run down her chin. He lifted her off her knees, took her to the bed, and pushed her down onto it.

"What are you gonna do to me, Freddie?" Cynthia panted, unbuttoning her blouse and exposing her pale, white breasts and pink nipples.

"Did I tell you to speak?"

"N-no," Cynthia stuttered in mortal fear, but she was getting more turned on by the minute by the huge, black dick that was in her face.

Freddie slid on a condom, cocked her legs back until her knees damn near touched her shoulders and entered her with the force of a jackhammer. The pain and pleasure made Cynthia scream out and cum instantly, clawing Freddie's shirt.

She broke a nail.

"Oh my God!" she squealed, trying to squirm away from the incessant pounding. She felt herself coming a second time. "Oh, Freddie, not again!" she moaned as her juices flowed, soaking the bed beneath her ass.

Freddie abruptly pulled out and stood back.

"Fr-fr-freddie, why did you stop?" she huffed.

"You want this dick? Crawl to it...crawl to this dick," he commanded, and she slid off the bed onto the floor on all fours as Freddie backed away gradually.

"Oh, please, Freddie. Come—"

"Crawl yo pink ass to this dick!" Freddie repeated emphatically until his back was against the wall between the bed and the bathroom. She was all over him like a woman possessed, dragging him down to the floor and squatting on top of him. She rode him furiously, taking all of him inside of her. Freddie sat back and watched her go crazy, smiling.

"Don't cum in the condom, Freddie. Cum in my mouth again, cum in—,"

She felt him building up and hopped off his dick. She snatched the rubber off and let it explode all over her face. She licked her lips as if it were whipped cream.

After they showered together and redressed, Freddie closed the deal.

"Freddie, I can't give you my home number, but this is my cell number. Will you use it, please?" Cynthia asked, wrapping her arms and one leg around him.

"I can't...I don't know, ma. You see..." He sighed. "I feel so embarrassed telling you this."

"What?" she asked with a concern born of lust.

"I may have to leave town."

"No!" she gasped.

"I got like...this gambling habit, and I owe a few guys a lot

of money. They've been all over me and if I don't pay soon..."
Freddie shook his head then kissed her forehead. "So if I never
see you again, Cynthia, I'll—"

"But, Freddie...how much do you owe them?"

He should have been an actor. Denzel didn't have a better
method. "I don't know, like, three gees."

"Gees?" she asked, confused.

"I'm sorry, three thousand. Three thousand dollars," he
replied in sheer defeat.

"Freddie, that's a lot of money."

"I know, I know. Now you see why I have to leave—"

All she had to hear was the word leave. She couldn't imagine losing the lover of a lifetime. "I...I can give it to you."

Freddie looked at her and had to hide his laughter.
"Cynthia, I hardly know you. I can't—"

"But if you leave, I'll never be able to get to know you."

"Oh, Cynthia!" he exclaimed, hugging her and smirking
behind her back. "Thank you so much, sooo much! I promise
I'll pay you back as soon as I can!"

"Pay me back now," she said, and pushed him back toward
the bed, fire burning in her eyes. She felt that her husband's
money had never been so well spent.

3:03 AM

Freddie laid in the waterbed next to Simone, staring at
himself in the overhead mirror. *Niggah, you ain't shit*, he
thought to himself. He had brought the three gees home and
told Simone he had won it gambling, a bold-faced lie that just
rolled off his tongue like ice water. Once again, he had broken
his promise to Simone. She laid snuggled up under him, safe
and content.

Freddie felt like he had done what he had to do. If he was-
n't shit, so be it, but the bills were paid, their stomachs were

full, and both of them had new outfits. Freddie thought of Cynthia. Wasn't no way he would call her. He could see that she would get crazy. Her hormones had been bottled up too long, and now that they had been released, shit could get out of control.

But if not her, who? It would take months to build his stable up like he had back in New Jersey, and Goldsboro was entirely too small for that type of mack. Naw...he had to keep his circle small, real small. One. Gina. If he was gonna play, Gina killed two birds with one nut. It was time to give Slug the connect he'd been begging for. Why not? He couldn't resist who he was, what he was. He loved Simone, but he loved himself at the same time. Only time would tell who he loved more.

Freddie swung his feet out of bed. Simone instantly missed his warmth and stirred. "Go back to sleep, boo," he said, and she did. He threw on his pants and a tee shirt, and slid his bare feet into a pair of construction Timbs. He left the apartment and crossed the deserted street to the phone booth in front of Piggly Wiggly. He dialed the number he knew by heart. The phone rang...and rang again...and again...and again.

"Freddie this better not be you," Gina's sleepy voice warned when she picked up the phone.

He wasn't surprised that she knew it was him. Whether it was the caller ID or the late hour, Gina was always on point. "Yeah, ma. This me," Freddie confirmed.

"Well?"

"Well, what?"

"Niggah, what you want? I ain't heard from you in damn near three fuckin' months! I didn't know if you were dead, alive, where your ass was at, if you were okay...," she caught her breath, glad to hear from him and, at the same time, releasing three months worth of stress and frustration. "So I know you want something, callin' here three in the mornin'. What?

You had to wait until that little bitch went to sleep?" she barked.

She had never called Simone a bitch before, so he knew she was heated.

"What do you want, Freddie?" she demanded.

"I just called to see how you were doin', yo." He tried to sound casual.

Gina laughed in his face. "Niggah, fuck you for thinkin' I'm some lame-ass trick! 'Matter of fact, good—"

"Aiight, aiight, Gina. I don't want anything...I need to see you."

There was silence.

"Gina? You hear me, ma?" he asked, his heart sinking thinking Gina was too through with him.

"I heard you. Just gimme one reason why I shouldn't hang up in your face?"

This time he was silent.

"Uh-huh, just what I thought," Gina declared. "You know you ain't shit, don't you, Freddie?"

"I am what I am."

"What you are is a no-good little boy wit' a easy dick. And if I decide to see you, it's because I know it's killin' you to know that there's somebody who knows you for who you truly are, who you can't fool, who you ain't slicker than." She laughed. Freddie couldn't do anything but accept the painful truth.

"Gimme your number. I'll call you when I get to Raleigh."

Chapter Nineteen

✝ Four days later, Freddie drove the forty-five minutes from Goldsboro to Raleigh. It took him a few wrong turns before he found the high-rise Radisson Hotel downtown. It fit Gina's style to the tee; it was high-class, trendy and urban. The glass elevator floated up smoothly with a view of the large, sparkling water fountain down on the lobby floor. Gina's suite was located on the top floor.

Freddie was dipped in a brown, beige, and white linen outfit and a pair of brown and beige mid Gucci loafers. He had to admit to himself that he was nervous. With Gina, he never knew what to expect. She knew he was in a bind. And although he knew in his heart that she would look out, he knew she'd make him sweat it out, one way or the other.

Freddie got off the elevator, walked the hallway to her room, took a deep breath, then knocked on the door. He didn't have long to wait before Gina opened the door.

"Hello, Freddie," she said evenly, showing little emotion.

Freddie looked her up and down admiringly. Her dress was an auburn brown Versace with spaghetti straps. It had diamond-shaped cuts in the fabric on both sides that exposed the smooth mahogany tone of her firm hips. Her shoes, a pair of crystal-beaded mules with a modest heel, matched her dress. She didn't look 37, she looked 27. Her natural hair, straightened and silky, framed her face in an asymmetrical cut.

"How you, ma?" Freddie asked. "Damn, you look good."

He tried to kiss her but she turned away and replied, "I

know. Let me get my purse and I'll be ready to go." She walked over to the nightstand and grabbed her small clutch bag.

"Ready? Where we goin'?" Freddie asked.

"Oh, you ain't know? You takin' me to dinner, a show, and whatever else I can think of. Just like you do Simone. You done spent enough of my money on her, now it's time for you to spend some of her money on me," she said as she glided by him and out the door, leaving him no choice but to follow.

When they reached the parking lot, she frowned and asked, "What...is that?"

She was referring to Freddie's Accord.

"My car," he replied, now feeling a little self-conscious about the late model hooptie.

"Humph, we'll take mine," she said and tossed him the keys. Two rows away sat a platinum CLK 320 gleaming under the street lamp. The cream interior looked like pure milk. Freddie opened the door for Gina, closed it, then walked around to the driver's side. She unlocked his door and he got in. As soon as he started the car, the system blared *Devotion— someone by your side/Devotion—when things ain't goin' right/Devotion—someone to be your friend/Devotion—girl through thick and through thin.*

The Twenty Club song took him back to Jersey as he put the car in drive and whipped out like only a driver from New Jerusalem can do. Gina wasn't bullshitting, Freddie was definitely taking her out. They went to a modern dance exhibition at the Durham Arts Theatre; then to a small and very exclusive jazz club, tucked away on the outskirts of Cary; then they hit the high-class restaurant, Zakia Blue's, in Raleigh. Freddie's little stash was shrinking by the hour.

They walked in and were escorted to a cozy corner table overlooking the Raleigh skyline. Once they were seated, it wasn't long before a waitress approached and cheerfully took their order.

"Yes, we'll have the shrimp cocktail appetizer, then the grilled salmon and salad, and crème brulee for dessert...with coffee."

"Very good. And to drink?"

Gina smiled at Freddie. "Freddie, what do you suggest?"

Freddie could see it in her pores, she was loving draining his pockets.

"Water," he replied sarcastically.

Gina giggled. "He's so silly. We'll have the best red wine you have in the house. It goes well with fish."

"Very good," the waitress repeated, then left them to themselves. Gina had spent the entire evening evading his attempts to talk business, but Freddie thought the time had come to cut to the chase.

"So what's goin' on up top?"

"Later," Gina answered, quickly sipping her water. "Right now I wanna know if you enjoyed the show." She smiled at him over her glass.

"Them niggahs dance like faggots," he stated flatly.

Gina laughed. "I should've known you'd say that. I think it was sexy. You should learn how to dance like that."

"Yeah, psss...picture that."

"I am!"

The food arrived promptly and the waitress departed.

"Look, I know you're enjoying yourself, draggin' me all around town and drainin' a niggah's pockets, but you can at least tell me if the cop died, yo. That shit is driving me crazy. The other cat don't matter, but the cop..." Freddie dropped his sentence.

"No. He didn't die. Now can I enjoy my dinner?" Gina asked, cutting into her grilled salmon, taking a bite and trying to feed Freddie, too.

The look on her face made Freddie smile, then chuckle and accept the bite. "Ay, yo, word up, you somethin' else!"

"Naw, you just can't figure me out like you want to, that's all," she smirked, tasting her salad.

"What's to figure out? I thought you said we knew each other for who we truly are?"

"No, I said I know you for who you truly are. I didn't say anything about you knowing me. Eat your salmon, Freddie."

Gina sipped her wine, then asked, "So...when's the wedding?"

Freddie shrugged his shoulders and continued to dress his salad.

"Can I come?" she smiled deviously. Freddie just looked at her like, "Stop playin'," but she continued. "You should have a summer wedding. I love summer weddings. Have you set a date yet?"

"Naw."

"I know you're not having second thoughts, are you?"

Freddie wiped his mouth. "We'll probably just wait until after the baby is born," he grinned.

He could've slapped her in the face and it wouldn't have hurt as much. Freddie knew Gina couldn't have kids. He knew it was a cold way of letting her know, but if she wanted to play games, he decided not to play fair.

Gina averted her gaze, unable to meet his eyes. "That's...that's nice. I'm happy for you."

Now it was Freddie's turn to control the flow of conversation. He laughed in her face. "No you ain't, so why is you lyin'? I can see it in your face. But it's all good. Just know you ain't the only one that can play games."

"Games? You think I'm playin' games wit' you, Freddie? You think I drove 500 miles to play a fuckin' game?" she hissed, struggling to keep her voice low.

"Oh, what you call all this dinner and dance?" He mocked her voice, "'How'd you enjoy the show?' smilin' and shit, knowing you breakin' a niggah pockets. That ain't no game?" Freddie asked, matching her intensity.

"Niggah, you owe me at least this. After all the bullshit you put me through? You can't even take me to a funky lil' show and a dinner? When have you ever taken me on a date, Freddie, huh? When? Where? But as soon as your black ass is in a bind, who do you call? And you gotta have a stank-ass attitude? That's why I'm actin' like this! Cause you actin' like that!"

Shorty was right. He had never taken her out. It was either a hotel rendezvous or one of her spots—sex, maybe take-out and a movie. But he thought she was cool with their arrangement.

"Dig, yo, I'm just sayin', I—"

She cut him off. "You said it, baby, and I hear you loud and clear." She sipped her wine, wiped her mouth, and placed the napkin in her half-eaten plate, signaling that she was finished. "You wanna get down to business? Okay, let's do business."

Back at the hotel, Gina settled into the plush leather table chair that sat near the foot of the bed where Freddie sat. She crossed her thick, beautiful legs, dangling her mule off her right foot.

"Okay. Dante has a $10,000 contract on your head. It's really an open one, but Ak Kabir really the only cat on it. You know how Ak do, but nobody knows where you are, so you straight. And like I said, the cop didn't die and he's out of the hospital, so it's definitely hot, but not as hot as shit could be if he had died."

Freddie let it all sink in. He knew who Ak Kabir was—a straight murderer, dead-ass. Dante was bad enough, but Ak

Kabir? Going back to Jersey for any reason was out. But he was relieved that the cop had lived. It was still attempted murder, but that was damn sure better than murder one.

"You think there's any way I can beat it?" Freddie inquired hopefully.

"Manny? With a good lawyer, yeah. Don't nobody care about another dead niggah. But the cop? Even wit' a good lawyer you can't beat that. And even if you could, what about Dante and Ak? Either you come back ready to go all out, or stay yo' ass down here and hope them niggahs catch cases or somethin'."

"I need money for that," Freddie announced, glad to finally get to the point. She looked at him like "And?"

"I got a spot in Goldsboro—'matter of fact, a few spots. But I need a connect. Wit' the right connect I could sew shit up," Freddie explained, sounding a lot like Slug.

"A connect?" Gina smirked. "All the country pussy down here and you gonna risk gettin' trapped in some federal shit selling drugs? Fuckin' wit' cats you don't even know?"

"It ain't gonna be me. My cousin is gonna handle everything," he answered.

"Your cousin who?"

"Slug."

"Slug?" she giggled. "And I'm supposed to get you a connect for some niggah named Slug?"

Freddie waved her off. "Naw, ma. He ain't some niggah, he family."

Gina looked at Freddie for a minute before telling him what she had already decided. "I already knew what you wanted so I talked to my uncle. Straight up, he doesn't want to fuck wit' you. He doesn't know you, you're on the run, and you're desperate. So he ain't doin' it for you, he's doin' it for me. So these are my rules." She paused to make sure she had his attention.

"I don't want to meet Slug, thug, or whoever else you got on your team—that's your problem. When we meet, you come alone every time. You violate that, your ass is cut off, point-blank. Understood?"

He nodded to confirm.

"Second, I'm only comin' once a month. Not twice—once. Whatever you say bring, I'll bring, but not over 5 at a time."

"Five? Gina, we can kill five in a week! You know how much money we can make in the Boro?" Freddie was ready to get rich or die trying, 50-style.

"I'm not doing this for the money, Freddie," she stated, keeping her eye expression in check.

"Then what are you doin' it for?" he flirted, hoping he could change her mind. But she ignored the question.

"And I'm chargin' you fifteen a brick."

Freddie wasn't that familiar with cocaine in large amounts, so he didn't know the blessing he was getting. "Fifteen? Is that good?" he asked, dumbfounded.

She laughed out loud. "Damn, Freddie! How you gonna be a drug dealer if you don't know what its worth? Just ask Slug."

He took that to mean she was looking out on the price.

"I appreciate this, Gina."

"I take that to mean you accept my rules, my way."

He eyed her delicious thighs. "It's an offer I can't refuse," he smirked, licking his lips.

"We'll see."

Chapter Twenty

Freddie woke up the next morning with Gina shaking him vigorously.

"Freddie...Freddie, get up."

He blinked himself awake. The sun had barely risen but Gina was already fully dressed in a PINK sweatsuit with her hair pulled up in a ponytail. "Come on, Freddie. Drive me to the airport."

Freddie sat up. He had slept in his clothes. "Airport? I thought you drove down here?"

Gina smiled like she knew something he didn't. "You ask too many questions. Just get up and brush your teeth before you make me miss my flight."

Gina seemed to have an entirely different attitude from the night before. Last night, she had been cold and distant, business-like. She even got in the bed wearing a pair of over-sized pajamas and footies, totally closing herself off from Freddie, telling him, "You're welcome to stay, but you ain't gettin' no pussy." He was too tired to argue and just cradled her

But now she seemed lighter, her expression open and flirtatious. This always kept Freddie open on Gina because he could never figure her out. She seemed to always be one step ahead of him, and that one step kept him chasing.

He got up and went into the bathroom to use the complimentary hotel toothbrush. After getting himself together, he picked up Gina's small carry-on case and garment bag. Gina threw on her Versace sunglasses and they were out.

They drove to Raleigh-Durham International in Gina's CLK and she massaged the back of Freddie's neck singing along to her Alicia Keys CD. When they got to the airport, Gina looked at Freddie and said, "I'ma leave the car wit' you because I am not feelin' that bucket of yours. Leave it to rot."

Freddie was like a kid on Christmas morning—a brand new CLK 430! He looked at the car in a completely new light: His.

"And," Gina added, looking at her watch casually, "in the lining of the trunk is a little something to get on. After that, straight paper."

Freddie's game had nothing on Gina's expertise. Once again, she had come through like a trooper. He leaned over and kissed her like he really meant it. Gina felt herself slipping into a zone too explicit for an airport parking lot in broad daylight, so she pulled away.

"Stop, you gonna make me miss my flight," she said, checking her lipstick in the mirror.

"We can make up for last night," Freddie suggested.

She pecked him on the lips and replied, "Next time. I have some things I really need to take care of."

Freddie took the key out of the ignition and they got out to enter the terminal. Once inside, the announcement for Gina's flight echoed through the terminal. When they reached the gate, Gina threw her arms around Freddie's neck and kissed him like she hadn't eaten in days and he was her first meal.

"Oh, so you gonna tease me and just leave me wit' a hard dick, huh?" Freddie chuckled.

She sucked his bottom lip and looked into his eyes. "Just givin' you a little something to think about."

"So when you comin' back?"

"When you call."

"That's business. I'm talkin' 'bout when you comin' back?" Freddie emphasized, letting her know her kiss had made her point.

Her eyes became searching and serious. "You asked me why I'm doing this, remember?"

"I remember."

"I'm doing this because I love you, Freddie. I love you and don't say it back because you don't love me back. But I'm cool with that. I'll be here for you until I get you out of my system or you realize where you need to be. Until then, I'll do whatever I can for you. All I ask is that you don't forget who takes care of you, Freddie. Don't ever forget that. Ever."

"I won't."

"Promise me. Promise me you'll never use my love against me!"

For the first time since he had known Gina, she let her vulnerability show, and it touched him in ways he didn't understand. "I promise, ma," he repeated solemnly.

She searched his eyes for a hint of deception, and whether she saw any or not, she didn't let on. She just kissed him hard and hugged him tight.

"Call me," she whispered as she backed away.

He watched her walk away, not looking back, head held high as she disappeared from sight. He looked at the keys to the Benz in his hand, felt Gina's kiss still lingering on his lips, and wondered what he had promised and if he really could hold true to it.

Freddie whipped along I-40 feeling like the motherfuckin' man. The Benz purred like a kitten but raced like a cheetah. It was a far cry from the clanks and clunks of the Accord he left in the hotel parking lot to rot, just like Gina had told him to do. He gripped the steering wheel in a gangsta lean, feeling like the Freddie he knew himself to be. Not the scrambling, block hustling niggah he had been forced to become, but the player he was born to be.

Gina had held him down like whoa in the clutch. Whatever was in the trunk, he knew it was his jump-off, and he didn't plan to look back. As he pulled up to a light in Smithfield, heads turned and admired his profile with praise and envy. This was the life he was meant to live. He was tired of pulling up to a light or taking Simone to the movies surrounded by sick whips and having to get out of the bucket, niggahs smirking because their shit was still spinnin' while his shit was still rattling, threatening to leave him right there in the middle of the road. Now it was time to show these country niggahs a true playa for real.

Freddie opened the door to his and Simone's apartment to find Simone sitting on the couch with her arms folded across her breasts.

"Where have you been all night, Freddie?" she inquired with quiet intensity.

He wasn't used to Simone questioning him, but he knew it was justified because he hadn't called all night. Besides, he had a surprise, which was also his alibi. He kneeled down in front of her and took her hands in his, then kissed her on the cheek. "Don't be like that, boo. I made you a promise and I'ma keep it, okay? Your man been out makin' shit happen for the three of us," he explained, and caressed her stomach through her t-shirt, "Come outside. I got somethin' to show you."

He gently lifted a skeptical Simone to her feet and walked her to the door.

"Naw, naw, wait. We gotta do this right. Close your eyes."

Simone looked at him with building anticipation. "Freddie, what are you up to?"

"Just trust me. Close your eyes."

Simone closed her eyes, but Freddie covered them with his

hands anyway.

"I got 'em closed," she whined, her skepticism about his whereabouts melting away.

"Naw yo, I know you. You might peek," he chuckled.

He helped Simone out the door and down the steps, then stopped a few feet from the Benz. "Once upon a time, there was a beautiful little girl named Simone and her dime-ass man, Frederick Von Da Bomb," he joked, making her laugh before continuing. "They loved each other very much, but times got rough, and everything got dark...That's why your eyes are closed," he added, and parted his fingers just a tad to let the sunshine in. "But there's light at the end of every tunnel, and the dark past gave way to a bright future."

Freddie moved his hands. Simone gazed at the CLK in awe, slack-jawed. She gasped. "Freddie, where did you get—"

He kissed her to silence her. "I made a few calls and talked to some cats that owed me a favor. It's on, ma. No more huggin' the block and no more run-down-ass shacks. I told you we wouldn't stop livin' just because of our situation. Your man kept his word, like he always will."

Simone felt her stomach leap even though it was too early for the baby to be kicking, and threw her arms around Freddie's neck, feeling guilty for thinking what she'd been thinking about his whereabouts.

"Oh, Freddie! I'm sorry I doubted you, I just didn't hear from you, and I didn't know what to think. I love you, baby!"

Freddie allowed Simone to cover his face with kisses and tears of relief. She started jumping around like a little girl. "I wanna drive!"

"You wanna drive?"

"Yeah, c'mon!"

He held the keys above her head but moved them when she reached for them. "What you gonna give me?" he asked mischievously.

Her eyes danced flirtatiously. "Come with me and find out," she teased, taking him by the hand and damn near dragging him to the car.

"Niggah, what bank you done robbed, and why you ain't come get me?" Slug probed half jokingly when Freddie pulled up to Kiki's apartment building. Slug had been sitting on the porch in his bed shorts smoking his wake up Newport.

His pockets were thirsty and he was thinking about going back to his stick-up bag when he saw the bright, shiny, platinum Benz pull into the parking lot. He had never seen this car around before, and since it had Jersey plates, he thought it was another crew of out-of-town boys trying to trap off some of his sweet country paper.

Slug didn't know it was Freddie until he got out grinning from ear to ear like the cat that swallowed the canary. Freddie left the door open and 50 Cent's "In Da Club" flooded the parking lot. Freddie approached the porch with an exaggerated pimp and chanted, "What up blood, what up cuz, what up Slug, what up gangsta?!"

That's when Slug asked the question about what bank he'd robbed, to which Freddie replied, "Tony's."

"Who?"

Freddie lifted his Knicks throwback to reveal the kilo of cocaine stuck in his waistline next to his pearl-handled nine. "Say 'ello to my lil' fren," he answered with a Spanish accent that flowed naturally from his half-Latin lengua.

Slug's eyes got big as plates. He flicked the cigarette aside and stood up. "Connect?"

"Connected. You ready to get this paper?"

"Cuz, I been ready."

On The Run With Love

Inside, Freddie explained the situation to Slug, leaving out the who and sticking only to the what, the details of the agreement. Slug had broken out the mayonnaise jar, wasting no time in rocking up a few ounces to test its potency. The results made him smile. He lit a cigarette and sat down across from Freddie at the kitchen table.

"Fuck meetin' the connect—I don't want them to know me either—but that five a month shit..." Slug shook his head, "'Fuck? Them niggahs don't want no paper?"

"This is just the beginning," Freddie assured him. "Once they see what we can do, them cats'll come through."

"But that eighteen..." Slug drawled.

Freddie had added three gees to the real price. He figured an extra three in his pocket each month wouldn't hurt, but he hoped he hadn't gone too high. "What? That's good, ain't it?"

Slug looked at him in amazement. "Good? Niggah, you don't know?"

Freddie shrugged. "I told you I ain't fuck wit' coke like that. That's why movin' the shit is all on you and we splittin' it 50/50. Gangsta?"

"Gangsta!" Slug echoed and gave his cousin dap. "Shit, that eighteen is a blessing! Cats 'round here chargin' eighteen or better. We could kill 'em just in weight, but if we ain't gettin' but five a month, we might as well grind this shit and stretch it out."

"We?" Freddie asked as if Slug was speaking French.

"I got you, cuz. We meanin' any youngins and such. You just keep this shit hot and I'ma show you how to trap off this paper."

"Now that's wassup."

And trap it they did. All across the 'Boro, Slug's youngins were stopping cats' paper with that hard white. They were pitching chunks compared to other hustlers' pieces. Hate filled their hearts, but fear kept them in check, because they all knew how Slug was about his paper. But Slug played fair. He had youngins in every spot that was bubbling, but he called his team in every night at 8:30 to give the other hustlers the late-night rush and a chance to get their paper up. It wasn't only fair, it was smart because Slug knew that some cats wouldn't mind diming him out to the police.

Even the Miami boys came through to cop a deal. Slug cut them some slack because he felt like he owed them at least that, and besides, they turned out to be alright cats. They just had their people fucked up. Now that was straight real recognized real.

Slug flew through that package and stayed on Freddie about the 5-a-month limit. Freddie, in turn, continued to try to convince Gina. He took a lesson from her first visit, and this time had an evening planned. He took her to Atlantic Beach to enjoy the scenery, walk barefoot along the beach, and take a moonlight cruise on the Atlantic. She wouldn't relent, but along with the two he copped, she threw him a third.

Slug and Freddie were grinding their way to a lock on the 'Boro, even expanding to the small surrounding towns of Fremont and La Grange. And while they were making the money, Kiki and Simone were spending their share. No more did Simone hear the stifled giggles or get the condescending looks. Now, whenever she pulled up in Freddie's Benz, the bitches turned green. Nina Simone still did her hair and whenever she was there, she could see the other chicks studying her shoes, wishing they were in them.

The newfound wealth and Freddie's periodic absences no longer weighed as heavily on Simone. Her stomach was growing and her skin was glowing with the love of pregnancy. Freddie pampered her with all the luxuries she could want, along with the little things. He was thoughtful enough not to forget.

They spent many an evening with Freddie massaging her feet and spoon-feeding her Chinese take-out or Italian food, or listening to soft, mellow music while she read poems to him from one of her old school books (from a literature class she had taken).

Her total trust for Freddie was slowly returning. She attributed her swollen condition to the fact that Freddie had truly realized where the love was, and she felt secure in his vow to devote his life to her. She knew her man was fine, and with the paper he was checking, she knew females would try their luck. She had seen it herself, over and over.

One night at the club, Simone decided to test Freddie. She saw the chick scoping him subtly all night, but she was constantly by his side. She kissed him on the cheek. "I'll be right back. I gotta go pee," she lied. Freddie helped her out of the chair and then sat back down. But Simone didn't stay in the bathroom. She doubled back and watched Freddie from a distance. The girl finally saw her opportunity to advance and approached Freddie. Simone was too far away and the club was too loud for her to hear what was being said, but she knew her man's body language well enough to read the non-interest he displayed. It wasn't long before the girl walked off and Simone returned to the table triumphantly. She draped herself around Freddie's neck. When she caught the girl's eye this time, she winked and smiled, making the girl roll her eyes and turn away.

Simone no longer mentally questioned the overnight trips and the smells of perfume she didn't even own on Freddie. They say love is blind, so as Simone's heart and belly blossomed, her eyes fluttered shut.

Chapter Twenty-One

✟ Slug loved the way Kiki rode his dick; the way she worked her inner muscles, gripping and pulsing on the upstroke, then relaxing as he penetrated her to her deepest depths on the downstroke; the way her pretty, yellow titties jiggled in front of his face, peppered with soft red freckles, nipples like elevator buttons. Her grinding hips curled his toes and made him fight to hold back his nut with every 360 degrees she made.

He watched her face contort with different expressions of ecstasy, and all he could think about was how real she had always kept it with him. She was ghetto as hell, but she had always been there for him. When he was broke, she gave him her whole AFDC check to flip. Whenever he hit county jail, she bailed him out if she could, and if she couldn't, she held him down. He never heard a word about her creeping on him, so even if she had, she respected him enough not to let it get out.

Now that he was on, he hadn't forgotten any of it. She was the only chick he laced. Whoever else he might be fucking only got dick and a donut, meaning zero. Quiet as it was kept, Slug was grudge-fucking—all the gold-diggers who wouldn't give him the time of day before but who were sweating him now. He dogged them with a capital D. He was making them bitches feel it and he was lovin' it. But he kept it all the way live with Kiki, putting her on with all that fly shit she liked—Dolce & Gabbana, Prada, Versace, and other big-name designs. He and lil' Chris even got along better, once they got a better understanding of each other.

"Look, lil' niggah. Now I'ma take you up in this toy store, but if you keep tryin' to play me I ain't gettin' you shit else," Slug informed him outside of Kay Bee Toys in the mall.

"I'ma be good," Chris vowed.

"And you gonna stop cursin' so fuckin'—I mean so much?" Slug added.

Chris nodded his head vigorously.

"Aiight, c'mon."

He took little man inside and laced him lovely. Even Kiki noticed the way Slug had begun to step up and raise Chris. "Thank you, boo," she told him one day, giving him a big, nasty, wet kiss on the cheek as they started having sex.

"Go 'head wit' that, I ain't tryin' to hear that shit," Slug replied, but he really was.

"Ohhh, Slug, I can feel it baby! Ooooh, oooh, oooh!" she squealed, clinching up. "Slug, don't move...don't..." Her body shuddered from the force of their simultaneous orgasms and she collapsed on top of him, sucking on his neck. "Tell me you love me, Slug."

"Naw."

She sat up and looked at him. "What you mean 'naw'?"

"'Cause you already know, shit. I just said it a while ago," he answered.

"No. You said you loved this pussy. I said say you love me," she repeated and sat back on his semi-erect manhood, hard.

"Ay, yo, check this out..." Slug began, trying to find his words.

"Say it!" Kiki demanded through clenched teeth. "Right now!"

"Hold up, I'm tryin' to tell you something if you'll shut the fuck up and let me talk."

"Well, if it ain't 'I love you,' I ain't tryin' to hear it," Kiki said with an attitude and un-straddled him, laying down with

116

her back to him.

Slug ignored her attitude and continued. "Ay, yo, on the real, I ain't no romantic type muhfucka or nuthin' right, but dead-ass, you kept it gangsta when a niggah was fucked up and I respect that. But..."

Kiki looked over her shoulder. "But what?"

"Now that a niggah gettin' a little paper and I can afford to throw back...yo, I don't feel like that's enough."

Kiki didn't understand what he was getting at so she turned to face him. "Slug, what is you talkin' 'bout?"

Slug looked her in the eyes wondering if thugs were supposed to feel butterflies.

"Marry a niggah," he said quickly.

Kiki rose up on the palm of her hand, trembling. "M-Marry you?"

Slug couldn't read her reaction, so he got defensive. "Hell yeah! 'Fuck you say it like that for? And you better not say no or I'ma beat yo' ass," he said, trying to mask his nervousness with testosterone.

"Oooh, my baby does love me!" Kiki squealed like she was cumming again and threw herself all over Slug. "Yes!...Yes!...Yes!" She punctuated each yes with a kiss.

"I'm sayin', nothin' fancy. Just go down to the courthouse tomorrow, and just do it. Fuck all that other shit, yo. Be my wife, official.

"Damn, I love this niggah!"

Chapter Twenty-Two

Slug and Kiki got married quietly but the party that Saturday was anything but. The 'Boro turned out in full force to wish the happy couple a prosperous life.

"Niggah snuck and got married so we wouldn't see his whipped ass cryin' at the altar! I do!" A.B. yelled like he was crying, "Oh, baby, I do!" The fellas laughed and clowned a jovial Slug.

"Man, fuck you niggahs, yo," he replied.

"Don't sweat what these niggahs is sayin', yo. I'm proud of you," Freddie said, patting him on the back before adding, "You finally admitted to the world that Kiki got that ass wrapped around her finger!"

Slug laughed. "Oh, and Simone don't?"

"Hell no!"

They held the party at the rec center, thanks to Slug's mother who was still mad at Slug for getting married without letting her help plan the wedding. She scolded the couple good-naturedly with a smile, "Kionna, I can't believe you let Eric convince you to cheat me and your mama out of helping you plan the happiest day of your life."

"Miss Carolyn, I'm sorry, but you know Eric. Ain't no tellin' with him. So I figured I'd better take him up on his offer before he changed his mind. Now he's mine," she boasted with a girlish giggle. Even lil' Chris' father, Big Chris, showed up. He had moved to Charlotte, but when he heard that Kiki was married, he wanted to see for himself. She paid him no mind.

Even lil' Chris gave him a hard time.

"You ain't my daddy! My daddy's name is Slug!"

Slug walked up and heard lil' Chris say that to Big Chris. The man looked like all the air had been let out of his balloon, totally deflating it. Slug knew why lil' Chris said what he said—because the cat really wasn't shit—but the puppy dog look on the man's face made Slug call lil Chris to him.

"Lil' Chris! Come ere!"

Lil' Chris jumped at the sound of Slug's voice and ran over to him. Slug picked him up. "Dig, shawtie, don't play your pops like that. He came all the way down here to check you out."

"My mama said he ain't shit. You my daddy!" Lil' Chris pouted.

"What I tell you 'bout cussin'? I got to talk to yo' mama 'bout her dirty-ass mouth, too, but dig—you my lil' man, but Chris," he looked up at Big Chris, made eye contact, and spoke loudly enough for him to hear his next words, "that's your daddy. And trust me, he's gonna do better. So give him a chance. Not everybody's got a pops, shawtie."

Lil' Chris nodded as if Slug's word was law. Slug put him down and he went back over to Big Chris. Slug followed.

"What up, kinfolk?"

"What's up, Slug? Congratulations, man, you got a good girl," Chris said, extending his hand. Slug shook it.

"Yo, call me sometimes, aiight? I know it's paper in Charlotte," Slug asserted.

Chris had been looking for a job but with little success. "Good lookin', cuz."

Slug just nodded and left him to his son.

"Congratulations!" Freddie told Kiki after he hugged her. "Take care of my lil' cuz for me."

Kiki took one last look at her fantasy standing next to

119

Simone. Freddie was slap-yo-mama fine, but Slug made her happy, and that is all she really wanted.

"Thank you, I will. Now...when you gon' finish what you started with my girl right here?" Kiki asked with her hands on her hips.

Freddie looked at both Kiki's and Simone's inquiring faces. He cleared his throat. "Simone knows I marry her more and more every day in my heart," he replied, knowing that corny comment wouldn't get him off the hook with the sharpness of not one, but two like-minded black women. They both laughed.

"Hmm. That's all good, Mr. Smooth, but how about you take your heart and your ass down to the church or courthouse," Kiki chuckled.

"You really know how to put a niggah on the spot, don't you, Ki?" Freddie mused.

The party was in full swing and Simone and Freddie danced, enjoying themselves. Everything was alright until Tina caught his eye. She made eye contact with him and licked her tongue ring out at him, enticing him more than the mere sight of her did already. Slowly but surely, Freddie had gone back to his old ways, and Tina was the chief temptation on his list. As Simone got rounder, Freddie became less interested in sexing her. He still loved her, but Tina's luscious shape became more and more appealing. After Tina, more females got added to his hit list. But Freddie convinced himself he was doing nothing wrong. Home was taken care of, paper was coming like water, and the females flocked to him in droves. Once again, he was caught up.

Chapter Twenty-Three

✝ Tina nodded her head toward the bathroom, then swung ass in that direction. Freddie turned to Simone, "Be right back, boo. Let me holler at this cat."

"Okay, baby," was her easy reply, and he stepped off to the bathroom.

A few minutes later, Simone approached Slug while he was talking to A.B. and Shaq.

"Slug, Kiki is ready to take pictures. Do me a favor and find Freddie, too."

Slug knew exactly where Freddie was but said, "Tell Kiki I'll be there in a minute. Freddie's talkin' to Mandrell."

As soon as Simone walked away, Slug jogged off to the men's bathroom and found it locked. He put his ear to the door and the slurping sounds he heard confirmed what he already knew.

Slug banged on the door. "Freddie! Ay, yo, bring yo' ass on. Simone lookin' for you."

Freddie's eyes were damn near in the back of his head. Tina was giving him head and driving him crazy with the way she worked her tongue ring.

"Ai-ight-yo...tell her I'm comin'!"

"Yeah, bet you is, niggah." Slug chuckled to himself, then hit the door one last time. "Hurry up!"

Freddie cleaned himself up and rushed over to the photographer. Kiki, Slug, and Aunt Ann were taking pictures. Aunt Ann's and Freddie's eyes met and she nodded knowingly.

"Come on, cuz. Me and you gonna take a few," Slug urged. He and Freddie flicked it up, then he, Freddie, Kiki and Simone got together and posed.

Aunt Ann whispered in Freddie's ear, "I need to see you, nephew."

Freddie looked at her and replied, "Yes, ma'am?"

"Come on."

"Ma, where you goin'?" Slug called after her. "You ain't takin' no more flicks?"

"Mama tired, baby. Let me sit a spell wit' my nephew and I'll be ready."

Freddie and Aunt Ann sat in the back of the center watching the people dance and Slug take pictures.

"Freddie...I don't usually mess in you young folks' affairs, so I'll make it quick. Simone is a good girl. She come way down here wit' you after all you done did. She down here because of you, and what you doin' ain't right," Ann told him.

Freddie knew what was up, but wondered how and just how much she knew. "I'm sayin', Auntie, I ain't—"

"You ain't what? Comin' out a public bathroom with some home-wrecking heffer—I saw you, Freddie! So if I saw you, imagine who else saw you. Not only are you doing her wrong, but you disrespectin' that gal, Freddie. She's carryin' your child. Don't that mean anything to you?"

"Yes, ma'am, that's my world right there. What you saw—that don't mean nothin' to me—"

"Then why do you do it?" Ann asked, cutting him off.

Freddie couldn't answer. He had asked himself the same question repeatedly until he had just given up and accepted that it was just in him.

"Freddie, you may not want to hear this, but you gonna hear it. You actin' just like your father."

That roused his total ire. "My father?! I ain't nothin' like

122

my father!" He tried to control his tone because he was talking to his aunt. "I ain't leave my family for dead! I'ma be there for mine!"

Ann looked him in his eyes. "You think your father didn't provide? That is, until your mama got pregnant. Then he went back to his doggish ways, womanizing. You look just like your daddy, and you act like him, too. If you don't change your ways, you gonna end up just like him."

Freddie had never heard this about his father. His mother never talked about him. He didn't know his father was a womanizer, a Christianized term for what he himself was—a player. "What happened to my father?" Freddie asked.

Ann rose slowly from her seat, then looked down at him. "Stabbed to death in his own bed. His lady friend did it." She watched his expression until the story had sunk in. "It's truly a thin line between love and hate, baby."

Freddie watched his aunt as she slowly made her way back over to the photographer. Simone caught his eye and waved, then she blew him a kiss, totally unaware of the situation unfolding around her.

Kiki watched Simone with pity in her eyes. She was so caught up in the web Freddie was weaving, she couldn't see her hand in front of her face.

"Slug, come here." She called him as he was talking to the photographer.

He walked over. "What up, Ki?"

"Slug, you need to talk to Freddie."

Slug sipped his Heineken. "About?"

Kiki raised one eyebrow. "Niggah, don't play stupid. Kionna don't miss shit when it comes to these triflin' bitches. Especially—Tina—nasty—ass—in the bathroom, Slug!"

"Ay, yo, mind your business, Ki. That's on them," Slug warned her. "Don't say shit to Simone."

"Oh, trust me. I dig my girl, but I done seen too many bitches blame the one who told 'em, thinkin' they want they man. You right, that is on them, but what I'm talkin' about is Tina. You know she known to set a brother up—that's what I'm talkin' about holler at him for."

Kiki was on point and Slug had to acknowledge that. He had been meaning to talk to Freddie but kept putting it off. Freddie was a grown man. And even though niggahs was gritting their teeth, he could pull his own weight. But what Kiki had reminded him about threatened him as well as Freddie, and he damn sure wasn't gonna let Freddie's dick knock him in the dirt.

The only thing that came out of his talk with his Aunt was another lavish gift for Simone, provided by his guilt. He copped her a 2003 forest green 325i BMW with peanut butter interior. Simone couldn't believe it. She failed to see that the gifts always seemed to come after some unexplained absence, an act of infidelity that Freddie foolishly thought he could compensate for with material things. In reality, it was just creating a bigger void in their world.

But Simone was getting caught up herself. Subconsciously, she began to isolate herself. Freddie's transparent lies weren't the only blame, because for a lie to manifest itself there must be someone willing to believe it. Simone wanted to believe. She needed to believe, no matter what that tiny voice inside her head whispered. So she continued to ignore the obvious, until the day the obvious refused to be ignored.

Simone went to Nina Simone's hair salon for her weekly touch up. There were a few females there, including Tina who was getting her nails done. Tina eyed Simone evilly when she came in, but Simone only smiled at her hate. Nina could feel the tension in the room so she tried to keep Simone occupied with chitchat and idle talk.

"Didn't Slug and Kiki go to Cancun for their honeymoon?" Nina asked, as she streaked Simone's ebony mane with subtle red highlights.

"Cancun? Try Cancun and Hawaii," Simone replied. Nina hummed with envy. "Damn! Slug doin' it up big, huh? It's good though. I'm glad they got married 'cause they been together like forever, yo," Nina said.

"And don't they look good together?" Simone commented. "Almost as good as me and my Freddie." She giggled, directing that last comment to Tina.

Tina sucked her teeth loudly at the mentioning of Freddie's name, so Nina tried to find a safer topic.

"Simone, didn't you say you were from Jersey? I got family in Jersey," Nina informed her.

"For real? What part?" Simone inquired.

"She need to take her ass back to Jersey," Tina huffed, and her voice carried across the salon.

Simone turned her head in Tina's direction. "Excuse me?"

Nina could see it coming and tried to head off the collision. "She wasn't talking—"

"'She' has a name, and yes, I was talking about her," Tina hissed with much attitude.

"Tina, chill!" Nina told her. "Don't start no shit up in here, now!"

"Who startin' shit, Nina? I said what's on my mind and I don't bite my tongue for no damn body."

By now, the whole salon was all ears. Both girls were itching to put the other in her place. They didn't like each other from jump because they looked too much alike. Both were dark chocolate, Simone being only a shade lighter than Tina's Brazilian midnight complexion. Tina was easily the thicker of the two, but Simone's facial features complimented her more,

125

giving each the ups in the beauty department. But that wasn't why Simone wanted to put Tina in her place. Simone felt like she had what Tina wanted. But she was about to find out, Tina had already had it.

"Tina, you got a problem wit' me or something? You don't know me, so wassup? My car? My jewelry?...My man?" she stated firmly, an obvious question seeking an answer.

Nina's heart dropped. She liked Simone but knew she had bitten off more than she could chew. It seemed like everybody knew about Freddie except her. But now that she had asked for it, she was about to get it.

"*Your* man?!" Tina said, laughing as she stood up. She had been waiting for a moment like this. To her, Simone was a square bitch who thought she was all that and needed to be checked. "Your man, bitch? I don't have to want Freddie—I got Freddie, I had Freddie, and I can have him whenever I want!" Tina stood in the middle of the floor. "Simone, just leave girl. You ain't even gotta stoop to her level," Nina tried to convince her. She hated for Simone to find out about Freddie like this. She could see how much she loved him, so she knew what was coming would hurt her badly.

"Naw, Nina. It's cool 'cause this bitch lyin'! You a sad bitch!" Simone spat.

"Sad? No, you sad and dumb! Everybody knows I'm fuckin' Freddie. That's why Nina tryin' to get yo' dumb ass outta here before your heart get broke. What? You think you the only bitch pregnant by Freddie?! You better ask somebody!"

The word pregnant hit Simone like a hammer. The idea of another woman carrying Freddie's child enraged her. She quickly leaped up from her chair. Nina was surprised a woman four months pregnant could move that fast. She just barely got to Simone before she reached Tina.

Tina never moved. She just got into her bitch-stomping stance and held fort. "Naw, Nina. Let her go. I'ma beat the baby out her dumb ass!"

"Let me go!" Simone struggled against Nina.

"Tina, you need to leave for real! The nails are on me. You gotsta bounce up outta here!" Nina commanded, taking control in her shop.

"Ask Freddie, bitch!" Tina continued. "Ask him where he at when you call him talkin' 'bout, 'Bring me some rocky road.' Ain't that your favorite ice cream?! When he comes home smelling like Pink, ask him about them scratches on his back, that 'T' I scratched in his back! Ask him!"

"Tina!" Nina thundered, now mad 'cause she hadn't left yet. "Fuck all that other shit! You in my spot and I said leave!"

Tina had said all she needed to, she could tell by the expression on Simone's face. Simone was no longer struggling to get at Tina. Every one of Tina's words had been like a fist, and it had knocked all the fight out of her.

"Yeah, bitch, who sad now? Tell our babies' daddy I said hello." And with that, Tina was out the door.

Simone didn't move. She didn't speak. She felt humiliated and couldn't believe Freddie had put her in a position to be humiliated in front of strangers.

"You okay, girl?" Nina consoled her. "I'm sorry you had to hear it this way."

Simone felt like a fool. The pain was too deep for tears, the anger too fierce for words. All she wanted to do was get out. Get out of the salon, out of Goldsboro, out of the clothes on her back—just OUT.

She didn't respond to Nina because she barely heard her. She just pulled away from her, grabbed her purse, and headed for the door.

Her first intent was to confront Freddie, but just the

thought of seeing his face, hearing his voice, smelling his scent made her sick, physically sick to her stomach. She had to stop the car at a green light and quickly open her car door to vomit. "How could you, Freddie?!" she begged into thin air. "How could you?!"

The child she was carrying, which up until that point had made her feel so warm inside, now just made her feel full. Cheap and meaningless. He had given his seed to another woman. She couldn't face him. She felt like, if she saw him, she wouldn't be able to restrain herself from doing something she'd regret for the rest of her life. *Go home*, the little voice inside her urged. *Go home.* She knew the voice wasn't referring to the apartment she and Freddie shared, it was referring to Jersey, and she obeyed it without hesitation.

Chapter Twenty-Four

✝ Freddie pulled up to their townhouse off Wayne Memorial Drive. It was a ritzy spot tucked away on the outskirts of Goldsboro, very different from the shack they'd occupied when they first arrived. He liked the apartment, but his extravagant taste that always stayed one step ahead of his pockets had him thinking about an eighteen-room mansion, and pushing a Maybach or an Azure. The money was good, but he wanted more.

He looked at Simone's empty parking space and checked his watch. He knew she had gone to the salon, but she was usually back by now. And since Kiki was on her honeymoon with Slug, he wondered where she could be.

Freddie came and went erratically, but Simone was like clockwork. He went inside to fix himself a bite to eat and get some sleep. While Slug was away, he was handling the operation, a fact he definitely wasn't feeling. It wasn't like he was on the block scrambling, but he hated handling packages, and delivering and picking up money. That was Slug's job according to their agreement, and he intended to check Slug about it when he returned.

Inside, Freddie browsed through the refrigerator. Everything in it that he wanted needed to be cooked, and Simone had him so lazy he didn't feel like cooking. So he went into the living room, sat down on the couch, and called Simone on her cell phone. It rang four times before she answered it.

"Hello," she stated flatly.

"Ay, Sim—"

Click.

Freddie looked at the phone strangely thinking they must have had a bad connection. He pressed the speed dial again. This time the phone rang eight times, and Simone didn't answer at all. Something was wrong. He knew he'd heard Simone's voice, and he knew he had dialed right because he was using the speed dial. This time he dialed the number himself.

Simone had driven in circles for almost half an hour before finding her way to Wilson to get on I-95 North. The first time her phone rang, she knew it was Freddie, and she was all set to flip on him until she heard his voice. She felt that same sickness from before, but she felt something else, too—weakness. She felt like her heart was dangling like a puppet on a string, and hearing Freddie's voice made it jerk and spasm so she hung up. The second time, she refused to answer the phone. Instead she counted every ring until it stopped and she could breathe again. The third time it rang, she didn't want to answer and she refused in her mind to answer. But she answered anyway, she just didn't speak.

"Hello?" Freddie spoke into the phone, but she still didn't say anything. "Simone? Yo, Simone...You there?"

"What...do you want, Freddie." Her voice was ice cold and Freddie could feel the chill through the fiber optics.

"Whoa, what the deal? You okay?" he asked, but knew she wasn't.

"I'm leaving, Freddie," was all she replied.

Freddie jumped off the couch. "Leaving?! What are you talkin' about?! Where you goin'?! Why you leavin,' boo?! What the hell is—"

"I'm leaving you, Freddie!" she screamed into the mouthpiece, cutting him off. "Don't worry about where I'm going!"

"Hold up, hold up!" Freddie's head was spinning and he felt sick. Despite his foolish behavior and player ways, Simone truly was his heart. He was crazy with fear not knowing where she was and having no way to see her at that point. "Please, baby, let's talk! Please! Where you at?!"

"Congratulations."

"Huh?"

"I said...congratulations. I saw Tina and it turns out that I'm not the only one that's..." She couldn't even say the word. Just thinking about it clouded her vision so badly she had to pull over on the side of the road. "Freddie, why are you doing this to me?" she asked with so much pain and anguish, it brought tears to Freddie's eyes. "What did I do to deserve this, Freddie? Didn't I love you? Didn't I?"

"Boo..." *Damn*, he thought. *This was definitely serious.* "Simone, listen to me. I swear to you, ma—Tina is a fuckin' liar! I ain't fuckin' her, boo, I swear." Freddie was lying through his teeth. But if a lie was going to keep the only true thing in his life, so be it.

"Freddie, you're lying!" she cried, but wanted desperately to believe him.

"Simone, I swear to you, baby! That bitch see what we got—all those bitches see what we got, and they'll do anything to break up our home, boo, to ruin what we've worked so hard to build! Together! Don't let them succeed, baby, don't let them succeed! We a family, and I don't want my son to grow up without a father like we did!" Freddie persuaded. Neither he nor Simone ever knew their fathers, and they had vowed that when they had a child, they wouldn't let that happen. He thought about what his aunt had said about his father and felt a sickening sense of déjà vu, wondering if his father had gone through this same thing with his mother.

"And I don't want my baby growing up with a triflin'-ass

niggah for a daddy!" Simone retorted between sobs.

"Come back, Simone!"

"No!"

"Please, baby! Don't let it end this way!"

"It's over, Freddie!" she said, not even convincing herself.

"Then I'm comin' to Jersey! I know that's where you're going and I'm coming, come what may! Even if I gotta sleep on your porch!" Freddie said.

"Then you going to jail!"

"What else I got, if I lose you?" It was the only real thing he had said during the whole conversation.

Simone looked at the blue interstate sign beckoning her: I-95 North. *Home.*

"Please, Simone! Come back!...Please!"

The strings to her heart jerked and twisted, and reluctantly she gave in.

As soon as Freddie hung up the phone, his pain turned to rage. He was too far gone to try and convince himself that he'd try and change his ways, but he was gonna check these bitches.

Tina saw Freddie's number on her caller ID. She picked up, already talking, "Freddie, listen, I—"

"What the fuck you tell Simone you pregnant by me for?!" If Tina had been standing in front of him, he would have choked her.

"I am!" Tina yelled.

"That shit ain't mine!" he cussed her.

His comment kinda hurt Tina. "It could be! And why my baby gotta be shit, Freddie?!"

Freddie laughed. "'Cause you don't even want it! Ain't you posed to be havin' an abortion?!" he reminded her.

"I don't know now! I might just keep it!" she said, wishing

she hadn't told Freddie she might not keep it and hating even more that he had thrown it in her face.

"Word up, Tina, don't get this shit twisted. Either play your position or leave it for somebody who can. Simone is my wife and we just got a beautiful understanding. Don't let your feelings fuck that up!" Freddie warned.

"Whatever," she replied, sucking her teeth.

"So what you gonna do? 'Cause I ain't for all this drama, yo," Freddie said, laying it down.

"I said whatever. You just better check that bitch, 'cause if she come in my face again—"

"Look, fuck all that! I gotta handle some shit, yo. You got some money?"

Tina didn't respond.

"Tina!"

"I ain't cash my check yet," she said, sucking her teeth again.

Freddie checked his watch, trying to time Simone's return. "I'll be through there, aiight?"

"When?"

"Just be there."

Freddie hung up. Her little short-ass check wasn't nothing to Freddie, but it was the principle. She had violated, and she had to get broke, literally. One of them trick-ass niggahs she was fucking was gonna have to pay her bills this month because Freddie was going to claim every dime she had.

Simone walked into the house an hour later to find it full of flowers and balloons. The sweet fragrance of the assorted blooms filled the air, but she smelled nothing. Freddie came out of the bedroom, smiling as he approached, but Simone felt nothing. She was just numb, drained of what once seemed utterly important. Even the glow of her pregnancy had diminished, like the sun hiding behind thick, grey clouds.

Freddie took her left hand and produced a black ring box. He opened it to reveal a five thousand-dollar diamond ring. Its sparkle hit the dead iris of her eye; she didn't react at all. Freddie gently slid the huge rock on her finger.

"I know you confused, baby, but I swear you all I need, all I want. I told you I'd get you another ring, and I pray you know it comes from my heart."

Freddie placed his hand on the back of Simone's neck and kissed her. Her tongue tangled with his out of reflex, not desire. He slid her shirt up and kissed her swollen belly, his tongue probing her belly button. Then he carried her to the bedroom where he'd covered the bed with rose petals. He got undressed and took Simone into his embrace, but she felt nothing. She wasn't even wet. Freddie had to use his tongue to lubricate her, and while he was inside her, she remained numb.

He collapsed on top of her, kissing her gently, "I love you, Simone."

Chapter Twenty-Five

✝ The next morning, Freddie awoke to the strange feeling that he was being watched. He rolled his head around and saw Simone sitting on the bed watching him. She was wearing a white nightgown, and was leaning against the headboard with a pillow in her lap. Her face wore no expression.

"Good mornin', ma," he greeted her, and kissed her on the knee because it was the closest part of her to him.

"'Morning."

"You okay? You sick or something?" Freddie asked, not feeling quite right.

She shook her head but kept looking at him.

Yo, shorty buggin', he thought to himself. "Then why you lookin' at me like that?

"Does it make you nervous or something? I can't look at you? I can't look at my man?" she inquired sarcastically, the timbre of her voice a little cracked.

She need some space, he thought. He raised up and kissed her on the nose. "Nervous? For what? Yo, you hungry? I'ma fix you something to eat, aiight?" Freddie offered, finding a reason to get out of the room.

He got up, brushed the rose petals from his naked body, threw on a pair of shorts, and exited the room.

Simone sat back against the headboard and sighed. She slid her hand from under the pillow and looked down at the large chef's knife in her grip. She examined her own reflection in it.

She had been staring at the scratches on Freddie's back.

Many were faint, but she could tell that two, now scarred over, had been deep enough to draw blood. They formed a perfect 'T'. *That T, I scratched in his back!* Tina's voice echoed in her head. Simone had wanted to plunge the knife deep into his back and leave scars of her own. She envisioned herself stabbing him for every scratch. But when she held the knife above her head, she froze and couldn't do it. She couldn't bring herself to hurt him, couldn't bring herself to cause him pain, even though her heart was filled with pain he had caused. She thought of the I-95 North sign and knew she could never leave him either. Simone felt trapped. While Freddie was running to escape prison, she had run into one. Her love had become her prison.

Chapter Twenty-Six

Slug returned from his honeymoon feeling refreshed and relaxed. Cancun and Hawaii had been lovely. He had never seen water so clear, so beautifully blue. The only water he was used to were pissy public pools or the polluted saline of Myrtle or Atlantic Beach. He had heard on TV about the soothing sounds of the waves, but thought that was just TV shit until he and Kiki sat on the beaches, watching the sunset, their bodies wrapped around each other intimately.

"What you thinkin' about, Slug?" Kiki asked, snuggled in his arms and feeling the tide coming up to her knees, caressing her warmly.

"Goldsboro Junior High."

"Huh?" She chuckled. "Why junior high?"

"That's when I read that shit about Columbus tellin' muh-fuckas the world wasn't flat and they ain't believe him."

"So?"

"I woulda been one of them muhfuckas," he chuckled, making her laugh. "Bein' in the hood all your life make you think that's all there is sometimes."

"For real."

He stayed silent for a few. "We gotta get outta there."

Kiki rose up on her elbows. "For real, Slug?" she asked, her excitement building.

He nodded. "That ain't no place for lil' Chris to grow up, or any other kids we have. Muhfuckas either end up dead, in jail, strung out on crack, or stay fucked up and broke. Fuck that, yo. I'll hustle blood to come up, but after that...we out."

Kiki threw her arms around him. "Thank you, baby."

"I ain't makin' no promises when, but my word, shawtie, we gettin' out the hood." Kiki said a prayer that they would make it out.

That was the mentality Slug came back with; not necessarily trying to get out of the game, but knowing he needed to. As soon as he hit town, the serenity melted away under the scorching ghetto sun. He was back to the alert street niggah that the streets had molded him into.

Slug cruised the 'Boro in his restored '72 Cadillac Eldorado convertible. It was pearl white, an exact duplicate of Boss Hogg's Caddy from *The Dukes of Hazzard* except for the gold Daytons. He'd had it restored while he was on his honeymoon, and he picked it up when he returned. Everything was normal. Money was straight and he was on his way to see Freddie, to have the talk with him that he had been putting off.

They agreed to meet in Herman Park where cats congregated and played ball. By the time Slug arrived, Freddie was already there running on a 3-on-3 pickup game. Slug didn't come to ball, he came to chill. He got out of the big Yak with his white Kangol cap tilted, ace deuce wearing a Carolina blue wifebeater, white shorts, and a pair of Carolina blue And Ones with no laces. He leaned against the gleaming Caddy, shaking hands and smacking asses that came within range.

"You better stop, Slug," flirted one delectable, cinnamon sister in a pair of coochie cutters, "before I tell Kiki." She smiled.

"Shit, you don't even believe that," Slug replied. "She might whoop your ass just for tellin' her." He chuckled and watched her ass wiggle away.

Freddie finished his game and approached Slug dripping with sweat. "What the deal, cuz?" Slug dapped him.

"Ain't nuttin'. You?"

"I'm chillin'," Freddie replied.

"Yeah?" Slug smirked like he knew something.

"Yeah," Freddie repeated, a little defensive. "'Fuck so funny?"

"What's this I hear about Tina being pregnant and telling Simone it's yours?"

Freddie wiped his face with his shirt. "Bullshit, yo. Ain't nothin' to it."

"You sure?"

Freddie felt like Slug was interrogating him. "What the fuck, yo? Yeah, I'm sure."

Slug lit up a Newport, took a drag, and exhaled smoke through his nose. "Look cuz, you need to check yourself. Shit—"

"Check myself? What—"

Slug cut in, "Listen to me. I been meaning to holla at you on the real. Ain't nothin' like a woman if she get it in her mind to get you fucked up. And Simone know too much about you, too much about what's poppin' wit' us, for you to be lettin' these chickenheads blow up your spot, cuz."

Freddie nodded. "I know and I feel you. But like I said, it's straight," he assured him.

"Naw it ain't, 'cause you still fuckin' wit' Tina. And I'm tellin' you, cuz, that bitch is conniving. Her M-O is settin' niggahs up."

"'Fuck I look like, Slug. A lame? You think I'ma let a bitch rock me to sleep?"

Freddie prided himself on how he handled women, and he felt like Slug was questioning his expertise.

Slug blew a stream of smoke into the air. "Niggah, you ain't gotta be a lame. A woman can rock any niggah to sleep if he slip."

"You sayin' I'm slippin'?"

Slug took a step closer to Freddie and softened his tone. "Freddie, look around you. You don't see it, but you makin' enemies. Broads ain't the only ones that catch feelins', niggahs do, too. And you runnin' up in niggahs' girls and baby mamas...You settin' us up for some ol' circus drama we don't need."

"Man, fuck that! Let these bitch-ass niggahs catch feelins' son! They want it, they can get it." Freddie's voice boomed and caused a few heads to turn in their direction. "You worry about yours—let me worry about mine! Matter of fact, you need to handle your muthafuckin' business and remember your position!"

Slug was taken aback by the word. "Position?" he echoed.

"Position. Honeymoon or no honeymoon, the grind is your responsibility. I don't touch shit. Don't forget the hand that feeds you, niggah! Wit'out me, you'd still be a nickel-ass niggah!"

By now, the attention of half the park was on Slug and Freddie so they were locked in. And neither of their egos would let them back down. Slug tossed his cigarette aside and pulled his shorts out of the sag he wore them in. "First off, youngin', you talkin' to a grown-ass man so lower your muhfuckin' tone. Second, don't try to shine on me cause you can't check yo' bitch, niggah." Slug spoke with force but didn't raise his voice.

Freddie threw a quick left hook that caught Slug behind his right ear. He dazed him but didn't drop him, and Slug threw up his southpaw. He shot Freddie a furious flurry that used all of his boxing skills, dipping and dodging, and throwing a straight right that busted Freddie's lip. A crowd had gathered around the two cousins going blow for blow, toe to toe, until Slug got up under Freddie, scooped him, and slammed him onto the hood of Shak's 500 series Benz.

"Ay, yo, hold the fuck up!" Shak protested as he and A.B. rushed to break up the fight because they were on his car. They struggled to pull them apart, A.B. grabbing Slug and Shak restraining Freddie. "Y'all niggahs chill! Y'all family!" A.B. barked.

They finally got the two men apart; they had been locked tighter than two red-nosed pitbulls. They huffed and puffed, glaring at each other, Freddie with a busted lip and Slug with a bleeding nose.

"Niggah, we can do this all night," Slug said, winded, with his hands on his knees. "That still won't change the fact that you slippin', cuz. If you gonna play, play. Just don't let these tricks play you." Slug stood up, dropped his shorts back in his sag, got in his car, and drove off.

Chapter Twenty-Seven

✝ "Freddie...Freddie, you sleep?" Simone asked, shaking him. He thought to himself, *If I wasn't, would you have to ask?* "Not now," he said gruffly. "What time is it?"

"Two o'clock," Simone answered, sitting on the edge of the bed, smiling at him. Her glow was back and she seemed to be getting bigger by the minute. Things between them had been rocky at first, but she had come around and returned to her old loving self. The only thing different was that all she seemed to say lately was "Freddie, I need some money."

Freddie sighed. "For what now, Simone?"

"To get some baby stuff," she replied.

"What happened to all that dough I gave you two days ago?"

"I went shopping," she lied. She was getting good at it, almost as good as Freddie.

"And bought what?" Freddie probed.

"Come on, boo." She smiled and wrinkled up her nose in the cute way that she did. "Don't be like that. Kiki is waiting for me."

Freddie just studied his smiling fiancée. Something wasn't quite right. Her smile didn't reach her eyes, but Freddie didn't see that. "Take what I got in my pants, aiight? Just let me get some sleep, yo," he said and rolled over on his side. He hadn't gotten in until close to four.

Simone kissed him on the cheek and grabbed his pants. She emptied both pockets like a professional pickpocket, then said, "That's all?"

"Simone!" Freddie barked.

"Okay, okay." She stuck her tongue in his ear. "I love you, daddy. Sweet dreams." She said it like she was rocking him to sleep and he nodded off.

Since his fight with Slug, things hadn't quite gotten back to normal. To the non-discriminating eye, it was all good—they still hustled together and could still laugh and joke. But deep down, something had been lost that couldn't be retrieved.

While Simone was hitting up his pockets, he was hitting up everybody else's. He tightened down on the chicks he was dealing with. He didn't really need the money but neither did they, in his book. He also didn't need to do what he did to Slug.

"Ay, yo, I hollered at my peeps. They said shit is hot up top so they gotta go up to eighteen five," Freddie informed Slug as they drove back from Raleigh. "So, yo...instead of 50/50, I gotta see 60/40, yo. Feel me?"

Slug smiled knowingly, "Yeah, cuz, I feel you...I feel you."

It seemed as if everything in Freddie's life was changing for the worst, everything and everyone except for one person—Gina. Freddie had begun to rely on her more and more, to get away from all the bullshit and stress he himself had created. They spent every other weekend together. One weekend was for business, the next was always just because.

This weekend was just because. Gina flew into Douglas International Airport in Charlotte where Freddie was waiting for her. They checked into the Hyatt and spent the day at Carowinds, an amusement park on the outskirts of Charlotte. It was a blazing southern day, so the water rides and breathtakingly exhilarating roller coasters were greatly appreciated. Gina felt like a young girl again, eating cotton candy, getting it stuck on her nose, and letting Freddie lick it off. Freddie even won her a large, stuffed toucan with a rainbow beak. It was so big, she had to hold it in both arms.

Being with Gina was like being free for Freddie. There weren't any games, there weren't any lies, so he could just be himself. It was like a breath of fresh air. They went back to the hotel to shower off the perspiration of the day, and then relaxed in the well-air-conditioned room, skin to skin while sipping on cognac: Grand Cru for him and Remy Red for Gina.

"I gotta give it to you, Freddie. You surprised me this time. I didn't expect that," Gina admitted, rubbing his nose with hers. "I haven't been to an amusement park in years. I had a lot of fun."

"Yeah, me, too," Freddie agreed. "And I ain't had fun in a long time."

"You okay?"

Freddie shrugged. "Mo' money, mo' problems." He sipped his drink.

"So I guess the life of a drug dealer ain't as easy as you thought it would be, huh?" Gina asked, but it was more like a statement.

"Naw G, it ain't that. Shit couldn't be sweeter."

"Then it must be Simone," she surmised.

"Something like that."

"Well," she began, kissing him softly on the forehead, "I hope you don't think I'ma lay here with you naked," she kissed both eyelids, "and listen to you talk about Simone," she kissed him on the nose, "when I'm trying to make you forget about her." She finished with her tongue massaging the inside of his mouth.

"And if you succeed?" he asked.

"Then you'll be all mine like you're supposed to be. Haven't you figured it out by now, Freddie? I'm the only woman who can handle you because I'm the only woman who truly knows you."

Freddie smiled. "Then if you know me, you know that 'only woman' ain't even in my vocab."

"Well, that's Simone's problem. As long as you wit' her, I'm her problem. But once you're mine, any other woman is my problem. So if you cheat on me, I'll kill you." She chuckled, but her eyes narrowed like a panther's. Freddie caressed her cheek and Gina kissed his palm.

"Be careful what you ask for, yo."

Gina was becoming Freddie's refuge and he felt attracted to her in ways he never had before. He leaned over and kissed her. "But tonight, it's just me and you, and I want to treat you like a queen."

"Like a queen," she teased with one eyebrow raised. "I am a queen."

Freddie started with her right foot, massaging it along the arch, rolling his thumb down and across the ball of her heel. She had been on her feet all day, so his gentle touch relaxed her. He ran his tongue along the bottom of her foot; tickling her and making her squirm with sensual delight. He worked his way up, gently brushing the tips of her toes with his tongue, ever so slowly finding his way to her ankle and inner calf. Gina gripped the covers and let a soft moan escape from her throat. Freddie parted her thighs, slid a pillow under the small of her back, and began nibbling his way closer and closer to her sex. Freddie had never eaten her out before, so when she felt his tongue licking and sucking on her extremely swollen clit, her eyes widened and all her breath was taken away.

"Fr... Freddie, what..." was all she got out before she found herself trying to squirm away from his wickedly delicious tongue. She scooted back until she was pinned against the headboard, and then she clawed the walls. Freddie's tongue explored her inner sweetness so deeply that it made her knees weak, and then he brought her down on his face. Gina was in another world.

"Oh, Freddie. Okay, okay, I give. Oh, baby, I give."

Freddie didn't know what she had given, but Gina knew. Deeper and deeper his tongue went until he felt her leg lock and spasm. She screamed his name as her stomach jumped and she heaved and hollered from the intensity of her orgasm.

Freddie rolled her over onto her back, spread her legs, and rubbed his hardness against her softness before penetrating her. Gina screamed like a virgin, "Oh, Freddie, I love you. Oh, I love you."

His slow grind and nipple tongue tease had Gina under his control; he took her rhythm and made it his own. She wrapped her legs around his back and cried into his chest. He licked her tears away only making her cry more. "I'm yours, Freddie. I'm all yours. Whatever you ask, I'll do. Whatever you want, I'll be," she whispered, sucking on his ear lobe. "I'm all yours."

Chapter Twenty-Eight

"Welcome to McDonald's. May I take your order?" the crackling voice asked through the loud speaker.

Simone leaned out of her car window a little and said, "Yes, give me two number ones with a Sprite, no ice, and a strawberry milkshake...and one number three with a Diet Coke."

The cashier repeated the order, informed her of the price, and told her to drive around. Simone turned to Kiki in the passenger seat and asked, "Girl, do me a favor and pay for our orders. I ain't bring no money out with me."

Simone and Kiki had gotten to be good friends. Marriage had mellowed Kiki out somewhat. She was still ghetto and she still loved to fight, especially Slug, but her demeanor was more serene. She was coaching Simone on the dos and don'ts of being pregnant.

"Sure, boo," Kiki said, going into her purse and handing Simone a twenty before adding jokingly, "Girl, you don't never have no money. Let me find out Freddie got you on a budget." Simone pulled up to the window and paid.

"Naw, I just went and paid the bills. I guess I just forgot," Simone lied smoothly as the man at the window handed her the food. She handed the bags to Kiki and drove off.

"How is Freddie anyway? I hardly ever see him since we moved out to the country," Kiki said, nibbling on a bouquet of fries.

"You never see him? I ain't seen him since Friday morning," Simone confessed sourly. It was Sunday afternoon.

"Friday?" Kiki asked, looking away on purpose and focusing her attention out of the window. "Is everything okay wit' y'all?"

Simone glanced at her with a reassuring smile. "Yeah, girl. Why'd you ask?"

"I was just, you know, checking. 'Cause, shit, if I hadn't seen Slug since Friday, Roy Jones wouldn't have nothing on me." The girls laughed.

"Naw, Ki, it's all good. Me and Freddie...we got an understanding."

Kiki let it go but she knew there was more to it. Every smiling face isn't a happy face, and something was different about Simone. What Kiki didn't know was what was different. She didn't know that her friend was only a shell of her former self, but she had learned a valuable lesson from Freddie—how to be a player.

Chapter Twenty-Nine

✝ Gina walked through the terminal of Newark International and all she could think of was Freddie. Everything she saw seemed to remind her of him. It was like the song by Luther Vandross: *Every time I think about you...*

She had just arrived back in Newark and she could hardly wait to return to North Carolina in fourteen days. Gina glided with a confident stride and a satisfied air, heading to the reserved parking area where she'd left her black Benz G wagon over the weekend. The traffic on I-9 was terrible, but she was too preoccupied with her thoughts to mind. She thought about the long drive out to Wayne but decided to go see her Uncle Lou on Clinton Avenue.

She pulled up in front of Lou's deli and spotted her Uncle's Lincoln LS parked down the block. She went inside to find Stephanie, Lou's lady friend of the last thirty years, behind the counter.

"Hey, Step," Gina greeted her and kissed her on the cheek. "Lou in the back?"

"Ain't he always," Stephanie retorted sarcastically. "Him, Woody, and the damn checkers. Can't you hear 'em?"

Now that she had mentioned it, Gina could make out the gruff voices of grumpy, older men and giggled as she went into the back.

"Woody, don't start that bullshit! Now we been playin' checkers for damn near 50 years, and we ain't never played jumpin' backwards!" Lou huffed, sitting on an up-ended milk crate.

"Bullshit! I ain't jump backwards, you blind motherfucka! Put yo' glasses on! I double jumped, and you can jump backwards when you double!" Woody exclaimed, rocking on his crate.

The two sixty year olds were lifelong friends and constant companions. Although Woody wasn't in Lou's profession, he benefited from it greatly because he owned a construction company. Lou made sure he stayed flooded with contracts. The two men sitting in the back of the small deli were a case study in microeconomics. They represented the fueling force behind the national GNP—crime and construction.

Gina walked in and kissed Lou on the cheek.

"Hey, baby girl! How are you doing?" Lou asked sweetly. Gina was his dead brother's child, but he had raised her as his own.

Gina looked down at the heavyset man. He was extremely short and extremely wide, with the frame and temper of a bulldog. Despite the weight he held in the streets, he was usually dressed as he was now, in a pair of Dickie work pants, a shirt, and a pair of black work boots. The only telltale sign of his wealth was his huge, diamond pinkie ring, gold Rolex watch, and diamond-encrusted gold tooth.

"I'm good, Uncle Lou. And what are you two arguing over checkers for?" she asked, totally amused.

"It ain't the checkers, sweet thang, it's your blind-ass uncle," Woody informed her. "If he knew how to play, we wouldn't be arguing."

"And hello to you, too, Mr. Woody. How are you?" she asked, giving him a kiss, too.

"Better now." He grinned like a sly, old fox, eyeing Gina's wide hips filling out her Apple Bottom jeans. "All that brown sugar! Lord, I love you woman! You can have all my money, just let me smell it!" He cackled.

"Watch yo' mouth, dirty-ass niggah," Lou warned playfully. "That's my niece you talkin' to. Besides, old as you is, just the smell'll give you a heart attack." Lou and Gina laughed.

"Then I'll die happy," Woody said, folding his arms across his chest like he was in a coffin, a satisfied grin covering his face.

"You too much, Mr. Woody," Gina blushed.

Lou was studying the checkerboard. "I guess you got my message."

"No. I just got back in town," Gina replied.

Lou looked up at her. "So you don't know?"

"Don't know what?"

Lou slowly eased himself off the crate. "I'll be right back, Woody. Lemme talk to Gina a minute...And don't cheat."

Sshhit! Woody thought as uncle and niece walked out the back door.

The door led out onto a large vacant lot that was filled with the usual ghetto debris. Lou looked around casually, but Gina knew her uncle, and his observations were never just casual.

He glanced at her. "You look good, baby girl. I take it that niggah takin' care of you, huh?"

At the thought of Freddie, she couldn't help but blush, "He's doin' alright."

"Hm-mmmm," Lou hummed skeptically, "I bet he is."

Gina knew what he meant but she let it go. She knew he didn't want to be giving Freddie weight. It had taken a lot to convince him so she knew to leave it alone.

"You said you sent me a message?"

Lou put his hands in his pockets and spit onto the ground. "The feds."

"The feds?" Gina repeated, looking around at the cars and visible windows. "Here?"

"Naw, not here…yet." He turned to face her. "Some people out in Elizabeth I deal wit' been dealin' wit' some people down in Willingboro, and a couple of them jokers caught a case. They don't know me and I don't know them, but you know the feds play domino rules: One fall and lean…the next fall and lean."

"They say anything yet?" Gina inquired.

"No, but they will. It's one in every bunch. Everybody wanna join the help yourself program. So listen…I'ma be shuttin' down for a while. I ain't takin' no calls and I ain't makin' none. So I can't do nothin' for ol' boy anymore."

Gina had figured as much when he began explaining the situation. She knew there wouldn't be anymore deliveries. Her heart sank when she thought about Freddie, what he was going to do, and how he would take the news.

Lou saw the concern on her face. "Babygirl, I know you wasn't expecting this, but there's nothing I can do about it."

"I understand, unc. It's just that Freddie's depending on me, so…" her voice trailed off.

Lou studied her for a while, then asked, "You really love this joker, don't you?"

Gina looked him in the eyes and answered, "I do, unc."

He sighed hard. "Well, what about the girl he down there wit'? Didn't you tell me he got a girl wit' him? What about her?"

Gina lowered her eyes. "I can't make him choose."

"It seems to me he already chose," Lou surmised, but Gina didn't respond, so he continued. "Baby girl, I raised you, so I know that when you got your heart set on something you're determined to get it. And you know I don't approve of this joker. He ain't got nothin' but larceny in his heart, but you gonna have to learn for yourself. But listen, if this niggah really worth your heart, then he gonna have to choose. And if he choose right..."

Lou looked out over the lot again like he was planning his next move. "If he choose right, I know some good peoples in Jamaica. I got some interest in a sugar company down there. Let me see what I can do about getting y'all down there."

Gina's spirits jumped into her eyes and she hugged her uncle. "Thank you, Uncle Lou! Thank you!"

"Hold on before you thank me. I said let me see what I can do. Besides," Lou said, holding her gently by the sides of her face, "the trip is for two. You and he, baby girl. You may not be able to make him choose, but I can. Let me know okay?"

Gina knew her uncle's offer was the answer to Freddie's problem. He'd be free from Dante, the police, and the game. With the money she had put away and her uncle's connection, they could grow old in Jamaica together without a worry in the world. It was the chance of a lifetime and she prayed that Freddie would see it that way, too.

Chapter Thirty

✝ Simone pushed her shopping cart through the Winn Dixie supermarket absentmindedly. She shopped by rote, grabbing the things she knew they needed without thinking about it. Her mind was on the mess her life had become, the mess she had let it become. She told herself at JFK that she was making a mistake, but she ignored her mind and followed her heart. Now she was trapped. She glided along to the checkout counter and waited as the extremely slow, new employee rang up the person in front of her.

"Excuse me, miss," the older brother in front of Simone asked the checkout girl politely, "but since when is Tide detergent $20.35?" He smiled, being patient with her obvious inexperience.

"I'm so sorry. I'm...oh, okay. Let me start over," the cashier said. But she was a little flustered, so the manager came over.

"Vickie, you okay?" he asked.

Simone saw that this might take a while, so she looked at the other lines. This was definitely the shortest. She rubbed her swollen belly and leaned on the cart. The manager helped the girl ring out the older man, who departed with a "God bless you" and left. His departing comment made Simone smile. That's what she liked about the South. Everyone was so friendly—at least at first they tried to be. Had this been Jersey, the cashier and the customer would probably be fighting right now.

The thought made her giggle as she moved to be rung up

and the manager looked up at her and smiled. "I'm glad to see somebody is having a good day."

Up until then, Simone really hadn't looked at the manager, but when he spoke, she got a better view of him. He was around 6'1" with a caramel complexion and a short, close cut full of waves. He wasn't heart stoppingly gorgeous, but his bright, white smile was warm and inviting.

"Oh, no...I just...was thinking about something," she stuttered in reply.

"Well, that smile just made my day," he flirted. He saw her swollen condition, but she was alone, and beautiful. Simone was well aware of his advance, so she busied herself unloading the cart. The checkout girl began to grab the groceries, but the manager stopped her and said, "I'll take care of this for you, Vickie," and she stepped aside, feeling like a third wheel.

"I can tell by your accent that you aren't from around here," he said, scanning groceries.

"Umm, no," Simone said, brushing the hair out of her face. "I have coupons," she continued, trying to keep the encounter professional.

He took the coupons and the hint. "That'll be $73.89," he told her, and Simone took out her wallet. Two twenties and a five were all she had. She cussed herself mentally, and tried to figure out what to keep and what to put back.

"Is there a problem?" he asked, still trying to use his megawatt smile.

"No...no problem," she answered. Reflexively, she grabbed her Visa and handed it to him. "I'm a little short on cash. Could you just charge it?"

"Sure," he said, taking the card.

Now that he wasn't looking at her, she looked at him. Simone watched his hands, and noticed his clean fingernails. She noticed his wristwatch and his choice of color. She studied his profile. He was definitely cute. Very cute. And she liked his personality, the way he flirted—not pressing, but persistent.

He turned back to her with a quiet expression. "I'm sorry, but your Visa won't go through."

Simone felt a little embarrassed, remembering that she hadn't paid her bill since she had left New Jersey. She had no choice now but to put some things back.

"I'm sorry to be so much trouble, but I'm going to have to put a few things back."

"Oh, it's no trouble. It's my job."

She finally got her bill down to under fifty dollars and got ready to push the buggy out, when the manager came around the counter and said, "Please, let me." He smiled.

"Oh. Thank you," Simone replied. She felt funny letting him push the cart for her and being in a man's company, but she was tired, so...

"So you go to Essex County College? What are you taking?" he asked, pushing the cart through the parking lot slowly. Simone started to ask him how he knew and he read it in her expression. "I saw it on your keychain."

She glanced down at her keys. She still had all of her old keys from Newark, she had merely added her new car and house keys to them.

"Oh, right...umm, accounting."

"Oh, you like to count other people's money, huh?" he joked, making her laugh, something she hadn't done in a while. "I'm in school myself. I'm going to Wayne Community College for filmmaking. I'm hoping to transfer to the NC School of the Arts in another year or so."

Dreams, Simone thought to herself, also thinking of her own, and what had happened to them.

"Well, I wish you luck."

"I appreciate that. And hey, maybe I'll look you up. As

beautiful as you are, you deserve to be up in lights."

Simone was sincerely flattered by his comments. She definitely didn't feel beautiful, she just felt heavy, physically and emotionally. She hadn't been much into fashion lately, either. She just kept her hair up in a ponytail. So often that Freddie had the nerve to say one day, "Why don't you do something wit' your hair, ma?" So she kept it like that, more out of spite than convenience.

She didn't know how to respond to the manager's comment, so she was glad that they were close enough to the Benz to chirp the alarm.

"Is this your car?" he asked, a little surprised. After the rejected Visa and the short money, he expected anything but a CLK.

"No," she said and he looked confused. "I mean, yes, it's my car, but no..."

It felt like her whole life could be summed up in that unfinished statement. Nothing she had felt like hers anymore.

He could tell she was a hustler's girl. The car was probably some drug dealer's and she was just driving it. He was probably her baby's daddy, too. But he could sense in Simone that everything at home wasn't all roses.

"Are you okay?"

Simone nodded, avoiding eye contact, trying to fight back tears of confusion.

"Look, I know this is none of my business, but...I can see you have a lot on your mind, and maybe...sometime...you may need someone to talk to, so..." he reached into his pocket, took out a pen, and wrote his name and number on her receipt, "if you do," he shrugged, "I'm a real good listener."

Simone looked at the paper and could read it in his hand: Mike. She was no stranger to flirtatious brothers. Every day she caught smiles and comments, but she always brushed them off and kept it moving. She truly saw no one but Freddie. But she had never let it go this far before. No other man had gotten two sentences out of her. She had never hesitated before, but now she had.

She took her receipt from Mike's hand and slipped it into her pocket.

Chapter Thirty-One

Gina bounced her crossed right leg on her left knee and checked her watch for the thousandth time in the last ten minutes. She was waiting for Freddie in the Hampton Inn in Rocky Mount. It was the drop-off weekend and Freddie was on his way, expecting the drop.

She had talked to him several times since she had spoken with her uncle, but she hadn't said anything about the cut-off. She didn't like talking over the phone, but that wasn't the only reason she hadn't said anything. Gina wanted to tell him in person, to use everything she had to convince him to come away with her and leave the States. She felt that the only thing that would stop him were his feelings for Simone. She tried to convince herself that he didn't love her, and she imagined him accepting her offer of freedom openheartedly, without reservation.

"I love you, Gina. You've always been there for me. And I know now that I wanna be with you," she imagined him saying, then taking her in his arms, and holding her so tight she could hardly breathe.

Gina stood up and nervously smoothed the front of her multicolored sundress, checking her reflection in the mirror. The knock at the door made her jump. She took a deep breath and crossed the room to the door. She peeked out of the curtain and saw Freddie standing there, smiling back at her.

"Hey, sweetness," he beamed. "You gonna let me in or what?"

Gina unlatched the chain lock and opened the door. Freddie stepped in and wrapped his arms around her, palming her ass, slapping it to feel it shake. "It's like candayyy!" he sang playfully. "What the deal, ma? You good?"

"Now I am," she replied, wrapping her arms around his neck and tonguing him down. "I missed you."

"I missed you, too, G," Freddie echoed. "You hungry? You wanna go get something to eat or just be something to eat?" Freddie teased with the tip of his tongue.

"No, no, I'm okay," she told him, but her tone told him otherwise.

"You aiight, G?" Freddie questioned.

"Uh-huh," she said and pulled away from him. "I, umm...just need to talk to you about something."

Freddie watched her pace to the far wall, then she turned around. "Freddie...how long do you plan on doing this?"

"Why, what happened? You ain't run into no trouble on 95, did you?"

"No, I...I just need to know. Freddie, you know you can't do this forever, and you can't run forever. As long as you are involved, anything can happen, and you need to think about that," Gina stated.

Freddie approached her. "Dig, ma, I feel you, but let me worry about that," he crooned, and tried to embrace her, but she evaded him again by stepping away.

"No, Freddie. I have to worry because I'm involved, too. Have you ever thought about that? What if something happens to me?"

He reached out and caressed her face. "Is that what this is about? You're right ma, and I'm sorry...And I have been thinkin' about it. I was thinkin' maybe we could get somebody to mule it. You wouldn't have to meet them or nothin', you could just leave—

Gina sighed and rubbed her forehead. "No, Freddie, that's not what I..." She sighed again. "It's my uncle."

"What about him?"

"Some people...they caught a case, and ...he doesn't know what they'll do, so he's gonna chill for a while." She finally got out.

"Chill?" Freddie asked, seeing the pieces but not the puzzle. "What do you mean, chill?"

"I mean—I can't bring you drops anymore," she informed him.

"Wait, wait, let me get this straight." Freddie paced back and forth. "You said some people caught a case. You mean his people?"

"No."

"So what that got to do wit' him?"

"He's just being careful, Freddie. You know everybody's snitching these days—"

"Can't he hit you once more? I know you said no more than five, but double-up just this once. We could mule it and—"

Gina could hear the hysteria building in Freddie's voice. He had become addicted to the paper chase. "I'm sorry, Freddie, I can't." It broke her heart to say it. "It's not my fault."

"Not your fault?! I gotta live, yo! I eat off this shit! 'Fuck I'm 'posed to do now?!" Freddie sat on the edge of the bed, rubbing his hands together.

"What about all the money you've made so far? I know you ain't spent it all. Don't you have enough to live on until we figure something else out?"

"A hundred thousand ain't shit!" he barked. He had been spending money like water and had only managed to squirrel away a nutshell. Freddie was used to the best and wouldn't settle for less.

Gina sat next to him on the bed and put her arm around his

161

On The Run With Love

neck. She ran her fingers through his curly hair. "Baby, listen...You didn't expect this to last, did you? I told you, anything can happen, but...I've got some money put up...a lot of money. The type of money we could retire off of...go away, leave the States, and leave this all behind. My uncle has friends in Jamaica—"

The laugh started low and built up until Freddie was laughing aloud. "You slippin', G," he said as he stood up. "Your game is gettin' weak, yo."

She stood up, too. "It's not a game, Freddie. Really. I'm serious. Leave with me. We can get away...before it's too late."

Freddie studied Gina with amusement. She had been reeling him in, slowly but surely; making him depend on her, not only financially but emotionally; and she almost had him. He had been feeling drawn to her, and now he could see why.

"You had this planned, didn't you?"

"No, Freddie, I—"

"You had this whole shit planned! Put me on, string me along, then freeze me out!" He chuckled menacingly. "I expected better from you, G."

Tears streamed down Gina's face. "I didn't have anything planned, Freddie. But I don't apologize for the way it turned out. You know how I feel about you and I just want the best for you."

"And that's supposed to be you, huh?"

"It's not Simone. She could never love you like I can."

"What about my unborn child, huh? Who's gonna love my son? You think you can buy me from my seed? Can you give me one? Can you?!"

Gina broke down into an all-out sob. "Please don't do this to me, Freddie. I just want to help you."

"Help me? Bitch, fuck you and your help!" Freddie roared. "You cuttin' me off! Naw, I'm cuttin' you off! Fuck you, you

162

barren bitch!" Freddie spat venomously and turned to the door.

The love in her heart wouldn't let him go. She couldn't stand the pain of seeing him turn away. After all she had done for him—for him to just turn his back. Her pride refused to accept his leaving, and each individual emotion combined in an explosive mix that launched her at Freddie's back.

"Niggah, you ain't never gonna leave me!"

Freddie had just opened the door when her body crashed into his, slamming him against the door. "Gina!"

But she was all over him like an enraged tigress. "I'll kill you if you walk out that door!" she vowed, swinging wildly.

Freddie's ire rose to boiling as he fought to get her hands off his neck. She was stronger than he had expected, so he had to fight fire with fire. He back-handed her hard enough to make her spit blood, then hit her with a merciless blow to the stomach, which instantly took the wind out of her and made her crumple to the floor at his feet.

"Freddie, why?...Why, Freddie?" she groaned and coughed, and balled up into a fetal position. "Why'd you do this to me?"

"Bitch, you did it to yourself," he coldly replied. "You did it to yourself."

Freddie opened the door and slammed it behind him, leaving Gina balled up on the floor.

She laid there crying tears of pain, which became tears of anguish, and finally tears of rage and revenge.

Chapter Thirty-Two

✝ "Hey, Ben," Detective Woods called, sticking his head into Det. Wilson's office. "Got a minute? I think I may have some good news for you."

"Good news? I remember that concept vaguely. Come on in, Mike."

Woods entered the small, messy office carrying a few faxes in his hand. He proudly handed them to Wilson.

"It's about the cop shooting and homicide a few months back," Woods informed.

"Believe me, son, I haven't forgotten. Every time I see Officer Williamson in that wheelchair, I'm reminded of this Holmes bastard," Wilson sneered.

Freddie had managed to elude Wilson for close to a year, and that infuriated him. He was used to making arrests within days.

"What am I looking at? All these funny codes and numbers. I'm in no mood for riddles, son."

"It's not a riddle, it's a Visa print-out," Woods informed him. "Remember the girl? You asked me to keep track of all her credit cards."

"Yeah?" Wilson answered sourly. "Didn't they go bad months ago?" He was wondering what Woods was getting at chasing dead credit cards.

"Well, it turns out that, for whatever reason, Ms. Simmons tried to run the card. It was rejected, naturally, but it still registered with the credit bureaus." Woods smiled and Wilson's whole demeanor changed as he got up on his feet.

"Son of a bitch! Goldsboro, North Carolina! There it is in black and white! Son of a bitch!" His eyes went to the words Winn Dixie. "Winn Dixie? What is that? Sounds like a supermarket or something."

"Exactly."

Wilson couldn't have been happier. "Do you know what that means, Mike? That she tried to use her card at a supermarket?"

Woods' brow furled up. "No."

"Think! When people go food shopping, they usually do it close to home. Had this been in Raleigh at a clothing store, it would have been like trying to find a needle in a haystack. But this tells us he's definitely in Goldsboro, probably in that very area."

Wilson grabbed his suit jacket off the back of the chair. "Get on the phone to Goldsboro PD and fax 'em a shot of our man, Freddie Holmes," Wilson ordered.

"Where are you going?"

"Home." Wilson smiled. "To pack for the trip to the dirty south." Then he was out the door.

Chapter Thirty-Four

✝ Slug sat in the back of the Soul Bowl, a famous soul food joint that boasted the best southern cuisine. He ate there every afternoon and this afternoon was no different. He was enjoying his meal of fried catfish, turnip greens, yams, and cornbread, with a side of coleslaw and french fries. He hadn't seen Freddie in days, since Freddie told him they had been cut off.

"What you mean cut off, cuz? Just like that? 'Fuck you do?" Slug asked.

"I ain't do shit!" Freddie exclaimed. "They on some ol' bull-shit, son!"

Slug knew there was more to it than Freddie was letting on, but he decided to let it play out. Then a few days ago, he got word that dudes in Wilson were moving major weight. Slug didn't put it past Freddie to cross him out, but he didn't expect it. He hoped he hadn't. Family or no family, if Freddie had cut him out, then it was Freddie who had violated, so no one could blame Slug when he served justice.

Then again—his mental channel changed—maybe it was all for the best. Slug was sharper than Freddie was, and he understood the game's tide. It rolled in and you got wet. The trick was not to get washed away when it rolled back out. Slug understood this, so he had been stacking. And now that he was married, it was time to make a power move to the 'burbs, mow lawns, and parlay. The feds were everywhere, and it was just a matter of time before his name came up, on a humble, and he

166

couldn't see doing a fed bid. He knew Kiki couldn't handle it. She loved him, but she wasn't cut out to bid a stretch. She was the type of woman who needed constant attention, and he planned on being around to give it to her. If Freddie had cut him off, he could make it on his own.

While he was filling his mind with thought and his belly with Ms. Jones' good cooking, he heard the bell attached to the front door jingle. He looked up and filled his eyes with the full figure of a woman who looked like she had been raised on a steady diet of grits and cornbread, but she wasn't fat by a long shot. She wasn't from around here, either. Her Coogi dress hugged her curves and the split up her left side revealed a succulent, mahogany-toned thigh. Her Manolo Blahnik boots had a four-inch heel sharp enough to stab someone with, and they were clicking in his direction.

She wore a pair of dark Chanel sunglasses that hid her eyes, like Aaliyah used to, and her layered bob accentuated her features.

"Slug." She said his name like she knew him well enough to be comfortable speaking it.

"You askin' me or tellin' me?" he drawled smoothly, wiping chicken grease from his mouth.

She smirked. "May I?" she asked, referring to the chair to his left. Slug nodded and she sat down, taking off her sunglasses, revealing the eyes of a woman with an agenda.

"You don't know me. But I know you, and we both know Freddie."

"Freddie?" Slug questioned as if he'd never heard the name before.

"Freddie...the five-a-month Freddie. Ring any bells?"

Slug now knew whom he was talking to—the connect.

He should've figured it was a woman. Now Freddie's attitude about getting cut off made all the sense in the world.

Freddie had fucked up, and Slug was about to find out just how bad.

"Don't you mean used-to-be-five-a-month Freddie? That river done run dry, lil' mama," Slug said, taking a bite of turnip greens.

"Well, that depends."

"On what?"

"On you," she stated, making iron-clad eye contact.

"I'm not sure I'm following you, lil' mama," Slug replied, wanting the picture made clearer. She understood perfectly.

"As they say, one monkey don't stop no show. What Freddie lost could be your gain," she explained. "But for you, Slug—whatever the quantity, I'll guarantee it, as long as you traffic it. And I'll give it to you for the same thing Freddie was getting it for—fifteen."

Slug chuckled. "Son of a bitch...Ol' boy said you was chargin' eighteen, and then you went up to twenty." Freddie had been playing him the whole time.

"Looks like Freddie was playing us both," she replied, with an undeniable bitterness that Slug had to question.

"Both?"

She hesitated before she answered. "Ever been in love, Slug?"

He held up his left hand, showing Gina his wedding ring. "Either that or rooted."

She leaned in closer. "Be good to her, Slug. Because there really is a thin line between love and hate."

"I'll keep that in mind, but, uh...what's the catch to what you throwin'?"

"Kidnap Simone," she stated firmly, catching Slug off guard. His mind thought she would say something about Freddie, but shorty wasn't playing fair. She was hitting where it hurt.

"I'm not asking for her to be hurt, but if she is that's not my problem. I just want that bitch snatched up, and I want you to ask for a hundred thousand dollars," she demanded, remembering the amount Freddie told her he had saved. "I want every dime he's got, every dime he made off me." Her voice trembled slightly with a rage that made Slug glad he wasn't in Freddie's shoes.

"You sho' know how to hurt a niggah, don't you, lil' mama?" Slug commented, sucking the meat out of his teeth and pulling out a Newport.

She smiled seductively and narrowed her eyes in an aphrodisiac-like gaze. "I know how to hurt a man," she cooed, then reached out to touch Slug's face, "but I know how to please one even better." Then she licked her lips slowly.

Slug moved her hand away from his face. "Dig, shawtie. I damn sho' wish I could find out, but uhhh—no offense—but I see what dick do to you, so I ain't even tryin' to put myself in that position."

She smiled, appreciating the weight of his statement. "I like you, Slug."

Chapter Thirty-Three

✝ Gina was working both ends of the East Coast. While she was working out the deal with Slug to kidnap Simone and take all of Freddie's paper, she had a plan working in New Jersey for Freddie.

"I'm comin' yo! Damn!" Cream yelled as he rolled lazily out of bed. He rubbed his face and checked his Cartier watch on the dresser: It was well past noon. He looked around for his wife as the door buzzer rang again. "Kandi, get the fuckin' door!" He got no reply. "Where that bitch at?" he asked out loud as he went down the steps to the front door of his two-story house.

"Kandi, you down here?" Still no reply. He opened the door to the foyer and glanced out the peephole, but he didn't see anyone. "Who da fuck playin' games, yo?" he asked, irritated that he had gotten up to answer the door, but whoever had come was now gone.

Cream opened the door to see if he could catch whoever it was before they left, but he saw no one. All he saw was a car turn the corner. He peeped down the street, but still saw no one.

That's when he looked down at his feet and saw an envelope. He bent over and picked it up. It was sealed but there was no address, no writing on it period. Cream ripped it open and found a picture inside.

It was Freddie.

His blood pressure went through the roof and he scanned

the streets again, thinking somebody was playing with him. He looked at the picture again, and then he turned it over. Some handwriting caught his eye: *Goldsboro, NC. You owe me ten grand.*

Cream couldn't believe it. They had been looking for him for months, and now, out of the blue, someone had delivered Freddie to Cream's doorstep, literally. Cream ran inside to call Dante.

Chapter Thirty-Four

✟ Dante was at his crib with a thick, topless redbone in a purple thong. He was taking pictures.

"Come on, ma. This is for my dudes in the feds. Bend over that chair and let 'em see that ass," he ordered.

She bent over and stuck her ass out real far, as if to kiss the camera with it. "You like this?" she flirted, mimicking fuck faces for the camera.

"Word. Hold up. One more. Aiight, spread that pussy and stick your finger in it," Dante said.

"Tay, you nasty," she responded, but did as she was told.

Dante was hard as a rock. "Aiight, take one wit' my dick in your mouth, yo." He grinned.

"No, Tay! I'm not taking any pictures like that." She pouted and sat down on the couch.

"Chill, yo," he said, approaching her and pulling out his dick. "I ain't gonna take it of your face, just of your mouth."

She looked up at Dante's dick in front of her face. "Just my mouth, Tay!"

"That's what I said, ain't it?" he answered as she slipped her juicy lips around his shaft.

"Luk diz?" she asked, with half her mouth full of Dante's male member.

"Naw, the whole thing," Dante said, making her deep throat him while he took pictures of her whole face.

His Blackberry rang.

"Damn," he cussed, dropping the camera while the red-

172

bone continued to brain him. "Yo," he barked into the phone, upset at the interruption. "Who this?"

"Cream, yo! Ay, Tay, you ain't gonna believe this shit! I know where that dude Freddie at!"

"Word!? Where?!" Dante asked, almost ready to cum.

"He down south, son. Down in the dirty, slippin'!"

"Ay, yo, word to Manny! We goin' down there today, yo, today! Be ready!" Dante yelled and hung up.

"Who was that?" the redbone asked, now licking around the head of his dick.

"Your clown-ass husband. Hurry up, Kandi, yo. I got a trip to make."

Chapter Thirty-Five

✝ Simone had long since stopped caring about who Freddie was fucking. She disregarded the hickies, the nights he didn't come home, and the mornings he returned. She even ignored the numbers she found in his pockets, which, instead of throwing away she laid on his nightstand. The only change was that she made him wear condoms whenever they had sex, which was more and more infrequent. The only thing they had in common was the joyful anticipation of their coming child. She and Freddie would share the experience of their unborn kicking inside her. She would beam proudly, and Freddie would beam equally proud. Simone didn't carry her grudge with an attitude, she just accepted the situation. If women were stupid enough to give him money, she was cool with spending it.

That morning she had been lying back on the couch, watching *Brown Sugar* on DVD. *So when did you first fall in love with hip-hop?* She loved that movie. While lying there, she heard a knock at the door. She struggled up from the couch thinking Freddie had lost his key again or that maybe it was Kiki. She looked out the peephole and saw a man dressed in brown and a UPS truck in the parking lot.

"Yes?" she said through the door.

"Delivery for Simone Simmons," he replied dryly.

Delivery? She thought. She hadn't ordered anything to be delivered. Then she thought that maybe it was a surprise from Freddie. He did still pamper her. She opened the door.

174

"I'm Simone. Where do I sign?"

"Right there" was the last thing she heard before the delivery man held a rag up to her face. She felt herself struggle momentarily. Then there was total darkness as she faded out of consciousness.

Chapter Thirty-Six

✝ Detective Wilson and Woods had been in Goldsboro for two days, held up in the Goldsboro Police Department. Little sleep and two-day stubble told the story of the endless cups of coffee and fast food they'd been through. The Goldsboro Police had been extremely helpful, but so far the detectives had been unsuccessful in tracking Freddie down. The only picture they had of him was five years old. At that time he was sixteen with cornrows and no facial hair, so he couldn't be identified by any of the detectives.

The closest they came was when the narcotics squad got involved.

"I swear I've seen this guy before," Jakes, the redneck who had taken Freddie's money, swore. "I just can't place where," he stressed.

"It's an old picture," Wilson explained, studying the large white man. Wilson had grown up in the South, and he could remember when men like these used to call his father, boy. *He probably thinks we all look alike, redneck cracker,* Wilson thought.

"He's probably cut his hair, maybe even grown some facial hair."

Timmons took the picture. "Can we get a copy of this? I'd like to show it around to a few of our informants."

"Sure."

Wilson thought they'd hit the jackpot when one of the informants turned out to be one of the crackheads that helped move Freddie's furniture. They rushed the apartment the crackhead had told them about, only to find it empty and abandoned.

Another dead end.

Wilson and Woods had already been by the Winn Dixie and surrounding stores showing Freddie and Simone's picture, but to no avail. The only hint of a lead they got was from Mike, the Winn Dixie manager.

"Sorry, Detective. I can't say that I've seen him before," Mike replied.

"Well what about her?" Woods asked, holding up Simone's picture again. "She tried to use her Visa in here about a week ago."

Mike was rigid, struggling not to let it show. He recognized Simone's face as soon as he saw it, and his heart sank. He hoped she wasn't wanted, just affiliated with a wanted man. He hadn't heard from her, and now he knew her situation. The police wouldn't get anything out of him...or so he thought.

"No offense, Detective...Woods, is it? But this is a huge store and I see a lot of faces. I'm just here to do my job and go home," Mike said with a slight edge in his voice that Woods missed, but Wilson didn't.

Wilson knew he knew the girl. It was written all over his face the minute he laid eyes on the picture. But he didn't know Freddie, which meant Freddie didn't know he knew Simone.

"Okay, sir. I understand. But if you see her, I ask that you give us a call at the Goldsboro Police Department," Woods instructed.

"Sure," Mike said. He was turning away when his eyes met Detective Wilson's momentarily. Wilson hadn't said a word the whole time, but Mike didn't like the way he was looking at him. He was happy to get away from his gaze.

"He knows her," Wilson told Woods while they walked

back to the rental car. "I'll bet my pension on it. I don't know how or why, but he's more than a casual acquaintance."

"Maybe he's a family member," Woods shrugged. He, too, had gotten the same impression now that Wilson mentioned it.

Wilson shook his head. "No, because he doesn't know Holmes."

Woods looked at him. "You think?"

Wilson shrugged. "Who knows. Maybe Miss Simone is into a lot of extracurricular activity. Whatever the case, we need a list of all his calls for the past six months, and hopefully we'll get a tap for any future ones, too."

The dragnet was slowly tightening around Freddie.

Chapter Thirty-Seven

✟ Dante and Cream had reached Goldsboro as well. Their crew arrived in town in two rentals. Dante and Cream were in an Explorer, and two shooters were in a Ford Focus filled with a mini arsenal. Both shooters were Puerto Rican females who were known to get down. They were heroin addicts, but you couldn't tell by looking at them because they were Angie Martinez/Jennifer Lopez-type dimes. But make no mistake, their guns did go off—loudly and often.

They rode around to all the hot spots, dropping Freddie's name, trying to find him.

"Yeah, yo. I told son I was comin' through," Dante told one cat in a green Range Rover, acting like they were friends, "but I ain't know when I was gettin' out, so I decided to surprise him."

But no one gave Freddie up. Those who didn't know him, couldn't tell, and those who did, wouldn't. Eventually, word got back to Slug.

"Two niggahs in a Explorer?" Slug asked.

"And two bad-ass Spanish mamis," the Range Rover cat informed Slug.

Slug thought it might be connected to Gina in some way, but with Freddie, you couldn't tell. Maybe they really were looking for him. Slug had no idea because he no longer trusted his cousin. But since he had already made the first move, he felt he had the upper hand. So if Freddie had exported an army, he was ready to go to war, chess move for chess move. Because he already had his queen.

Chapter Thirty-Eight

Simone awoke in a darkened apartment with a splitting headache. She found herself lying on a couch while two men with black bandanas tied around their faces watched her. She stiffened with fright, remembering what had transpired.

"Just be cool, lil' mama. If your man act right, this'll all be over in a minute," one of them said, then turned to the other, "Call your folk."

The second man grabbed the phone and dialed. After a moment, he spoke into the phone, "It's done." Then he hung up.

Simone looked from face to face, scared to death. "Please let me go. Whatever Freddie did, I didn't have anything to do with it. Please..." she begged.

"Just like a bitch," the second cat hissed. "As long as shit is sweet and the money is comin', it's all good. But soon as shit get gangsta, they all fo' self!"

The first man laughed. "Be cool, folk. Just make the call to Freddie."

Freddie was on his way back from Wilson, when his cell phone rang. He turned down his Sam Scarfo CD and answered it. "What da deal?"

"Yo' girl, niggah." The voice cackled.

Freddie sat up straight in the seat. "My what?"

"Listen."

Freddie heard muffled sounds. Then it felt like a hand

squeezed the blood out of his heart when he heard, "Freddie!"

"Simone?!"

A thud hit his stomach and he had to pull over to keep from wrecking his car, a sudden dizziness filling his head.

"Freddie, they came to the house! They..."

"Simone!" he hollered into the phone, but the only reply was a menacing laugh.

"Damn, dog! This pussy that good, it got you hollerin' like that? Shit, you don't act right, I might just have to see for myself."

"Muthafucka! You touch her and I'll kill you! I'll kill you!" Freddie screamed and pulled out his gun like they were right in front of him.

The second man laughed again, eying Simone's chocolate thighs. When they kidnapped her, she only had on a tee shirt, a bra, and no shoes. "Damn. Lil' mama got some pretty feet, dog," he said as he ran his gun up Simone's thigh.

"Please...don't," Simone begged, seeing the lust build in his eyes.

He pulled her shirt up and saw that she wasn't wearing any panties. "Damn! And no panties!" He cackled.

Freddie was sick to his stomach. "I'ma kill you, niggah! I'ma kill you!" He kept repeating it, tears welling up in his eyes.

"Niggah, you ain't gonna do shit but come off that hundred grand, ya dig?" he demanded.

"I...I hear you," Freddie replied. "Just don't touch my fuckin' girl!"

"Niggah, I already did," he boasted, and jabbed a finger inside Simone's sex. Then he held the phone to her screaming mouth.

"Freddie, please!!!"

Freddie opened the car door and vomited.

"You still think it's a game, dog? Huh?" the kidnapper

181

taunted.

"Naw, man." Freddie broke down. "It ain't a game."

"A hundred gees, partner. I'ma call you at the phone booth outside Darnell's in one hour. Have my scrilla and you get yo' bitch back." Click.

Freddie laid his head against the steering wheel, mind racing, trying to figure out who could have done this. They had kidnapped Simone, and it was killing him. He straightened himself up for the drive. They could have the money even though it was all he had. But he swore on his unborn that these fools would pay for this with their lives, whoever was involved.

Freddie drove straight to the crib, running red lights with complete disregard. He was in kill mode. He would gladly trade his soul in exchange for the people responsible. To have them on their knees, begging for their lives, which he lusted to take...

Inside the apartment, he busted the safe and emptied it. He knew he had a little over a hundred grand—by a thousand or two—but he had no time to count it. Besides, he had twenty-five hundred in his pocket, and three gees stashed in the CLK. He was going to give it all up without hesitation. Simone and his unborn child were worth that and more. Simone alone was worth that. No matter how grimy he was or how bad things had gotten between them, he truly loved Simone with all his heart, and he'd do anything to make sure she was safe. Until she was safe, nothing else mattered to him.

Freddie stuffed the money into a shopping bag, balled it up, jumped back into his car and jetted out to Darnell's gas station.

When he arrived, he checked his watch nervously. He had ten minutes. He looked around for any shady faces or out-of-place sights, but besides the usual crowd of bums, drunks, and nickel hustlers, Darnell's was normal.

All kinds of things went through his mind about what they had done to Simone. The thought crossed his mind that if he paid them, they might deliver her dead body. In a kidnapping, there were no guarantees, Freddie knew. Maybe she had seen something she shouldn't have seen, or heard something she shouldn't have heard, and they wanted to make sure they weren't going to be identified.

Suppose they had…Freddie hated imagining that someone was raping his heart, taking what was his without permission. He envisioned Simone screaming out his name, and him being unable to hear her, help her, or save her.

He knew it was all his fault. The life he had led, the enemies he had made—all of it contributed to the present situation. He vowed that if he got Simone back safe and sound, they would leave Goldsboro. Go where, he didn't know, but as long as they were together…

The pay phone rang and he answered before it had finished the rattle of the first ring. "Let me speak to my girl," Freddie demanded.

"Easy, dog. You'll get yo' pussy back in the same shape if, and only if, you got my scrilla," the voice taunted.

"I got it, muthafucka! Now put her on the phone! I ain't givin' you shit 'til I hear—"

"Freddie," Simone sobbed, "why is this happening to me?"

"Baby, it's gonna be okay. Did they…hurt you?"

"You mean, did we fuck yo' bitch?" the man asked, taking the phone from Simone, "Not yet, niggah. But if you don't put the money inside that green dumpster on the side of the store and leave, we gonna bust this pussy wide open, and then kill her. Ya smell me?"

"Bitch-ass niggah, why you ain't come at me? Come see me! Come see me, you fuckin' bitch-ass niggah!" Freddie barked uncontrollably, but the kidnapper hung up. Freddie made the drop, then jumped back into his car and skidded off.

Chapter Thirty-Nine

Slug was playing pool at William Alston's poolroom when he got the call.

"Yeah."

"We got the scrilla."

Slug didn't respond.

"What you want us to do wit' lil' mama?"

"'Fuck you mean 'do'?" I told y'all niggahs to leave her alone. You got the scrilla, cut her loose." Slug ordered and hung up.

He felt bad that Simone had gotten caught up in Freddie's bullshit, but he didn't regret it for two reasons, or at least that's what he tried to convince himself of. One, he did it for the money. With his cut of the ransom and what he had already put up, he had enough to kiss the game goodbye and get out the 'Boro. Second, from the look in Gina's eyes when she propositioned him with her scheme, if he had said no, she still would have gotten it done. And ain't no tellin' what total strangers would've done to Simone at Gina's request.

Slug studied the spread on the table and thought about the irony of life. Everybody wanted to be a shot caller.

"Nine in the corner," he told his opponent before he sank the shot, cross table.

And once a shot was set in motion...

"Combination, ten into the twelve, twelve side pocket."

The only thing that controlled it was finesse, the amount of force behind it.

184

The twelve ball teetered, then dropped.

Too much force and you could scratch yourself out of the game. Too little, and you could miss the shot that could win the game.

"Eight ball, bank," Slug announced, a Newport hanging out of his mouth, his eyes squinting against the smoke. The clack of the cue ball hitting the eight rang out across the pool hall. It careened and tumbled off the bank, then rolled as if magnetized into the winning pocket. Slug smiled.

"Bank, niggah."

Chapter Forty

✝ Simone sat in downtown Goldsboro on an old bus stop bench. The sun had set so the streets were all but deserted and all the stores were closed. Her face was outlined with salt from all the tears she had shed.

There were no more illusions or facades to hide behind. Freddie's actions had cost her more than love, they had almost cost her her life. They had waved guns in her face, snatched her out of her own house, off her own doorstep, and taken her prisoner. She could still feel the man's finger inside her, violating her womanhood while he laughed at her pleas. He taunted her with threats of doing worse and she was helpless to stop him. It seemed as if her unborn child had sensed the danger and was laying dormant, not kicking or moving, so out of character.

Simone was all cried out. There would be no more tears. She sat stone-faced and half-naked at a public bus stop, like she had been abandoned and discarded. This is how Freddie found her when he skidded up to the corner and jumped out, gun drawn. When they got the money, they told Freddie where he could find his Simone. He went there, holding his breath, not knowing exactly what he would find.

"Simone! Are you okay, baby?" he inquired intently, checking her from head to toe. She stood and Freddie tried to embrace her, but she didn't hug him back. She just stood there like a lifeless doll baby wrapped in his arms.

She pushed him away firmly, but calmly, and said, "Just

186

take me to the apartment, Freddie."

He was so happy to have her back, he failed to realize she called it the apartment and not home.

Chapter Forty-One

✝ Dante and his crew of shooters sat up in the Motel 6 plotting their next move.

"Man, this country-ass hicktown ain't but so big. Where the fuck is this joker at?" Dante wanted to know, pacing the floor. He had waited a long time to avenge his brother's death, and now that he was this close, he wasn't about to give up. He was growing impatient.

"At least we know what kind of car he's drivin', papi," the brunette hit-woman offered as consolation. They found that out from a local hustler whose baby mama had been letting Freddie juice her on the regular for all she had or could get her hands on. He had seen through Dante's game, and he had nothing but hate in his heart for Freddie.

"And who the fuck is this Slug mufucka?" Cream asked, mouth full of pizza. "We find him, we beat Freddie's whereabouts the fuck outta him!"

"Whoever Slug is, these bamas damn sure ain't tryin' to point him out," Dante commented.

"Fuck it, let's ride out some more. We bound to see this CLK Freddie pushin'," Cream suggested.

"'Fuck, yo," Dante spit, "I ain't leavin' 'til this cocksucka bleed. That's my word on everything I love!"

Chapter Forty-Two

✝ Detective Wilson had the same thing on his mind. Nobody shoots a cop and gets away with it in his book.

"Look man, I done told you all I know," the skinny, damn near toothless crackhead said, sitting in an interrogation room with Wilson and Timmons.

He was the same crackhead that had moved Freddie's furniture, but he had caught a felony larceny charge, and he was trying to duck the habitual offender category looming over his head by giving them Freddie's.

"I don't know where he live no more. All I know is, him and Slug makin' paper. A lot of paper. And he push a Benz."

"What about hangouts? Where's he pushin' the stuff?" Wilson asked eagerly.

"He don't. Neither one of 'em do. The only place I can tell you he might be is Pop Bogan's or the Midnight Lounge. All the major dealers be out there on Saturdays."

Wilson looked at Timmons, who shrugged and said, "It's worth a try."

"So...if y'all catch him, y'all ain't gonna forget about me, is you Timmons?"

Timmons looked at the dirty crackhead with disgust. He hated a black man on drugs, but he hated a snitch even more. "Take yo' ass back to the cell."

Chapter Forty-Three

✝ Simone and Freddie rode home in silence. Freddie wanted to ask her if she recognized anything, heard any names, and most importantly, ask what they had done to her. But her facial expression was one he hadn't seen before. He knew the ordeal had been traumatic, but he prayed she'd be okay.

When they reached the apartment, Simone went straight to the bedroom and slammed the door. Freddie started to go to her but decided not to. She was home safe. He could hear the bath water running from behind the closed door and thought it best to leave Simone to herself.

He turned his attention to payback and picked up the phone to call Slug. Things hadn't been good with them at all since the fight, but they were blood, and he knew Slug would ride out with him.

"Hello?" Kiki answered the phone.

"Ki, this Freddie. Where Slug at?"

"He ain't here, Freddie. Call him on his cell. How you doin'?" she asked.

"I'm cool."

"Simone there?"

Before he could answer, Simone walked out of the bedroom fully dressed and carrying a small suitcase. Freddie didn't even bother to answer Kiki and hung up.

Simone dropped her keys onto the coffee table. "Let me go, Freddie," she stated firmly, a look of resignation in her eyes.

"Go where? What you mean, boo?" Freddie asked, know-

190

ing full well what she meant. He tried to take her hand but she stepped away from him. "Baby, I know that what happened—"

"No, Freddie, you don't know. You couldn't know. They didn't have a gun in your face, you didn't—" she sighed. "I don't want to talk about it, I just want you to let me go."

Freddie was beside himself with fear. Any man who's been confronted with the loss of everything, the only thing he's ever cared about, can understand. Those who haven't, couldn't understand until they had.

His mind raced and his tongue stuttered, "Y-you right, ma, I don't know. But I do know that whoever did this is gonna pay. I swear to God, they're gonna pay for what they did to you."

Simone laughed without smiling. "You just don't get it, do you, Freddie? There's nothing you can do to pay them back for what they did to me. Ever!"

Freddie grabbed both of her hands and said, "Then let's get away. You wanna leave? Cool, I'm feelin' you, but let's leave together. Let's go somewhere and start all over, get away from all—"

Simone walked away from him. "So you can do the same thing all over again, Freddie? So I can lay in another bed, alone? In another strange place, hearing your lies and your apologies? I can't do this anymore, Freddie. I don't love you anymore."

"Please, boo, don't say that," he whispered, trying not to cry, "I know I fucked up…I know there's nothing I can do to make this all go away, but please don't take your love from me. It's all I got." Tears welled up in his eyes and Simone had to turn away to keep from being magnetized by his open display of emotions.

"I can't do this, Freddie. Can't you see? It's over, Freddie. Just let—me—go," she repeated her demand.

"How could you leave me, baby? How? I gave up every-thing I have for you, to get you back, Simone," he begged.

"And I gave up everything I am for you! How dare you ever say that, Freddie! I gave up my life, my dreams...my body! They were going to rape me, Freddie!" Simone cried.

Freddie went to her and embraced her, and she found her-self hugging him back. "I'm sorry, Simone, I'm so sorry...Please, boo, I'll make it better. I will, I promise."

At the word promise, Simone cringed and pushed him away. "No, Freddie, no! I don't love you, I hate you! Do you hear me? I hate you! Just let me go!"

To hear his heart turn on him was too much for Freddie's pride to bear. "You wanna go? Go! I ain't stoppin' you!" He paced the floor, realizing his love was leaving, but he had to salvage his manhood to survive. "You wanna leave? Leave! 'Fuck you waitin' for? Huh?"

"Yes, Freddie...let me go," she whispered to herself.

"I gave them everything! Everything! And now you wanna leave?! Bitch, breeze. I can make another baby. Can you make another Freddie?"

He was purposely trying to hurt her, not knowing that's what she meant by let her go. Freddie's words stung her, but she knew it was what she needed to break free.

She reached down and picked up her suitcase. "I...I need a ride to the bus station."

Freddie tossed the phone at her feet. "Call a cab," he hissed dryly and turned his back to her.

"Thank you," she whispered and turned for the door. The first step was the hardest, but she forced herself, step-by-step, until she was halfway down the street.

Freddie stood in the middle of the living room, cold and alone. Simone had walked out the front door with his heart. So he had no choice but to be heartless. He wanted to go after her, beg her to stay, and he knew she would. He knew the power he had over her, but without the love, it wouldn't be the same. Simone was right. It was over.

He grabbed the half pint bottle of Grand Cru Remy Martin cognac he had left on the kitchen counter days ago, cracked it open, and tossed it up. The smooth elixir slid down his throat, burning his chest. He didn't take the bottle down until it was half empty. His head was spinning as he tossed it up again, and drained it this time. Then he dropped it on the floor. He staggered over to the full-length mirror on the wall and looked at his reflection.

"I shoulda let 'em have that ungrateful bitch," he said, trying to remain cold because it was the only way he could remain numb to the pain he was running full-speed from. "I'm muh...fuckin' Freddie," he staggered and slurred. "Naw, Simone!" he yelled, "I ain't fucked up, you fucked up. 'Cause you'll never find a muhfucka like me. But you a dime a dozen!"

He wished she was still there so he could cuss her, humiliate her, and demean her. Then he smelled her Gucci fragrance and it sent him for the Crown Royal.

Simone was gone. There was nothing he could do about it. And his money was gone, too. He had to do something about that. Fifty-five hundred dollars wouldn't last him the weekend. He had to make a power move, and he knew just where he needed to start.

He stumbled over to his cell phone laying on the floor and went through his contacts until he reached the Cs. Cynthia, the white broad he had coned out of three gees a few months back. He hadn't called her since, but he was glad he'd kept her number.

"Hello?" she chimed.

"Cynthia," Freddie slurred, and she knew exactly who it was. She was standing in her bedroom in her slip, getting ready for a white-tie event. She glanced into the bathroom where her husband was busy at the sink.

"Freddie," she whispered with nervous excitement, "is that you? Why haven't you—?"

Freddie cut her off sharply. "Check this—I ain't in the mood for no muthafuckin' questions 'cause I'm a grown-ass man, aiight?"

"I know that, Freddie, I just thought—"

"Didn't I just tell yo' dumb ass I'm a grown-ass man? I don't need anybody to think for me. You can either listen or hang the fuck up!"

Cynthia swiftly left the bedroom, closing the door behind her. "I'm listening, Freddie, but you don't have to talk to me like that," she said, trying to sound firm, but Freddie already knew he had broken her. If he hadn't, she would've hung up.

"Then understand where I'm coming from and I won't have to. Look, Cynthia, there's some things I need to share with you, some secrets I need you to keep. But I gotta know I can trust you...that I can count on you. I ain't sayin' jump when I say leap, I'm sayin' come when I call. Can you do that? Can I count on you for that?" By the time Freddie finished, Cynthia was a wrap.

"Oh, of course, Freddie. You can count on me. What do you need me to do?"

"I need to see you tonight," Freddie told her.

Cynthia thought about the thousand-dollar-a-plate charity banquet she was supposed to attend, and then she thought about the golden dick she had been fiending for. The decision made itself. "Where?"

"Get a room somewhere...Wilson; get a room at the Marriott. I'll call you in an hour, aiight?"

"O-okay, Freddie. Whatever you say," she responded eager-ly.

"And bring some money."

"How much?"

"Surprise me." He smiled and hung up. He purposely left the amount up in the air to determine what level they were on, and how he needed to put it down to elevate it. To Freddie, Cynthia was just the beginning, his door to that country club, jet-set pussy. It was time to step his game all the way up.

Freddie went and got dressed in his beige, white, and brown velour Coogi, a matching beanie, and a pair of brown and beige Gators. He threw on his jewels, earring to pinkie, not forgetting his Gucci frames.

He stepped in front of the mirror to admire himself. "Damn, you a pretty muthafucka!" he told himself. "What? Them niggahs thought they could break me? A hundred grand ain't shit. As long as bitches got pussies, I'ma get paper."

He wanted to shine on whoever had kidnapped Simone. He wanted all of them to know who they were dealing with. Freddie decided to stop through the Midnight Lounge on his way to Wilson, so all of them would know he couldn't be broken, that he was unbreakable. He jumped into the BMW M3 and headed for the club.

Freddie pulled up to Midnight and hopped out of his M3. He was so drunk, it was a miracle he'd made it that far. Normally, he would be on point coming to the hot spot, checking his surroundings as he and Slug cruised through the parking area. But because of the liquor and Slug's absence, he hadn't noticed that he had just passed two detectives. Fortunately for Freddie they hadn't noticed him either. They were looking for the platinum CLK. His inadvertent choice of whips had gotten him past the police surveillance.

He entered the crowded club staggering noticeably. He looked around, knowing that whoever had played him was at the club and probably watching him, and they were. Slug and the kidnappers, J-dog and Bruno, were all together in the body-infested establishment.

"There go that pretty muhfucka now, folk," Bruno said, watching Freddie move through the crowd.

"What up, folk?" J-dog asked Slug, ready to set it.

"Ain't shit up, folk. He still family. Ain't no need in pressing the issue. Y'all cats take that twenty grand and be out."

J-dog gave Slug a pound. "We gonna miss you, baby boy. Holler at your manz and 'em sometime, dog."

"Fo' sho'," Slug told them, and then they walked off.

Freddie spotted Slug and smiled at him. He came over to the table and sat down. "What the deal, cuz?"

"You," Slug replied and they shook hands. "You aiight, cuz?"

"If I ain't, I'm gonna be, yo," Freddie boasted. "Why you ask?"

Slug shrugged his shoulders. "Look like you got a lot on your mind, folk."

"Simone left me, duke," was all Freddie said. He started to tell Slug about the kidnapping, but decided against it. What's done is done, and he was now ready to move on.

"What you gonna do now?"

"Relocate," he stated simply. "And step the game up."

"I feel you, cuz," Slug said, pulling on his Newport. "I was thinkin' the same thang. 'Cept I'm leaving the game where it stands, yo."

"The game's all I got, son," Freddie replied.

Slug nodded and looked away. He felt sorry for Freddie. He was trapped, but he had trapped himself. Family was family, but at the end of the day, a man's gotta stand on his own.

"Be easy, cuz, I'll be right back," Slug told him and got up, headed for the bathroom.

About that time, Dante and Cream walked up in the club

looking around.

"Yo, duke, spread out. If you see that lame, don't do shit. The guns are in the car, but these his people, so we know somebody's strapped. We spot him, we lay until he bounce, and work him then, aiight?" Dante laid it down and Cream nodded in understanding. They split up and began looking for Freddie.

Cream bumped into Tina, who was heading the other way carrying a bottle of Grand Cru. She saw Freddie laying low in the corner and went over to him instinctively. She slid into the booth next to him, kissing him on the neck, and caressing his thigh. "What's poppin', stranger? What's the matter, you ain't got time for Tina no more?" She pouted with her sexy bottom lip poked out.

"Naw, I just ain't got time for no games, yo," Freddie answered.

Look who's talking, she thought, but instead she said, "What's that supposed to mean, Freddie? You think I'm playing games with you?"

"It means shit's fucked up right now and my paper ain't straight. So until it is, I'm keeping everything official and everyone around me official, yo." Freddie shot back at her, grabbing the Grand Cru and turning it up.

"And I ain't?"

"Are you?"

Tina smiled. "Freddie, I'm about the same thing that you about. But you got the game fucked up lettin' that square bitch carry you when a real boss bitch, like me, was born to take care of you." She ran it down, checking game with science.

Freddie just stared straight ahead, his thoughts a blur. Tina stuck her hand in his pants, grabbed his dick, pulled it out, and began pumping along the whole shaft.

"Let Tina take care of you, baby," she purred, and lowered her head, taking him into her mouth. Freddie put his head back and did something he hadn't done in years. He cried from the heart. He cried for his mother, knowing all she had put up with from his father; he cried for his father because he couldn't be a real father or a real man. He cried for everything he had put Simone through, and he cried for his unborn child that he now feared he'd never know. He also cried for how he had treated Gina and played Slug. But most of all, he cried for himself.

Cream saw Tina's head bobbing, sucking someone off over at one of the booths. "Damn, these country broads are some freaks!" he mumbled in disbelief, but his attitude changed when he saw who she was going down on. "Oh shit!" he exclaimed, pushing through the crowd looking for Dante.

Chapter Forty-Four

✝ Dante was in the bathroom taking a piss at the urinal and, right next to him, Slug was taking a piss, too. The two men acknowledged each other's presence then went on with their business.

Slug finished first, washed his hands, and headed out. As he was leaving, a guy walking in said, "What up, Slug?"

"What up," Slug replied.

Dante almost pissed on his shoes trying to get his pants up. He didn't even wash his hands as he rushed out, trying to follow Slug. Cream ran up to him.

"I found Freddie!"

"Where?" Dante asked, forgetting all about Slug.

"In the back wit' some bitch blowin' him!" Cream snarled, imagining that Freddie had had his wife doing the same thing. "Come on. When he come out, we'll be waiting for him."

Timmons checked his watch and looked at Wilson. "You ready to call it a night?" Before Wilson could answer, he saw Cream and Dante hurry out of the club and walk over to two women in an SUV.

"I know that ain't..." Wilson began, then he looked over at Timmons. "I don't know how he got past us, but Holmes is inside!"

He and Timmons got out of the car and headed for the door.

Chapter Forty-Five

✝ "What's the matter, boo?" Tina was looking up with a wet mouth. Freddie had gone limp, but he hadn't cum. That's when she saw his tears. "Freddie, what's wrong?"

Freddie brought his head down and shook it. He started to push Tina away, to push it all away, but his eyes froze.

The first bullet whizzed through the air, shattering the bottle of Grand Cru Remy Martin on the table and piercing the soft flesh of Freddie's upper left side, separating two of his ribs. The burning sensation ignited his insides letting his intoxicated mind know he had been shot. But he wasn't surprised. How could he be when he saw it coming—saw them coming—from across the crowded club.

The second shot caught him in the neck. His blood splattered all over a screaming female beside him who was scrambling to get away.

Yes, he saw the bullets coming. He could see them in his eyes before he saw the glint of the cold steel in the shooter's hand. When their eyes first met, his instincts went into survival mode. He saw murder and knew he was the victim. As he reached for his pistol, something happened. Something just made him stop, and he accepted what was taking place. He was tired.

Even the fourth bullet, the last shot he felt, seemed to move in slow motion. From the barrel of the gun, he followed its matrix-like trajectory as it zeroed in on him. He watched the bullet come dangerously close to a woman's ducking head, break a glass in a man's hand, and finally lodge itself deep inside his own flesh. Simultaneously, Freddie's mind was sent to that place where pain can no longer reach.

His last sight was of those eyes and the determination in them. He knew it was coming, no one can run forever. His last thought was "Damn, why did it have to be me?"

Chapter Forty-Six

✟ Simone trekked along the busy thoroughfare of Wayne Memorial Drive, carrying her small suitcase. She was finally free. The things Freddie had said made her feel used and depressed, but she had needed to hear them, had needed to hear him say them to her to let her go.

She had lied to Freddie—she did love him. And she knew in her heart that she always would. Deep down, she wished Freddie would pull up beside her, beg her not to leave, embrace her tightly, and declare his undying love. But it didn't happen.

Simone was in no condition to be walking, so when she reached the corner gas station, she called a cab from the pay phone. While waiting for it, she saw Freddie drive by in the BMW he had bought for her. She could hear Jay Z's *In My Lifetime, Vol. 1* pumping out of the open windows. He didn't look in her direction, just kept his attention straight ahead, bopping his head to the music. He looked like he didn't have a care in the world, like he could care less about her leaving him. She noticed that he had changed clothes. She couldn't tell what he was wearing, but she knew it was different from what she had just seen him in.

Simone guessed at where he might be going—Tina. That made her blood boil. She imagined Tina in her apartment, in her bed, maybe even in her clothes, taking her place. The cab pulled up and Simone got in. Her mind was set to go to the bus station, but she heard herself say "the Midnight Lounge." She had to see for herself, confirm what she already knew to be true and see Freddie with her.

Simone arrived at the club, asked the cab driver to wait for her, and then disappeared inside. The club was packed, as usual, and the thump of the music hurt her ears. It made her grab her stomach in a motherly embrace. Recognition flashed across the faces that knew her and, in her condition, they wondered what she was doing there. Simone even started to wonder herself. Freddie had obviously gone on with his life, and it was time to get on with hers.

That was her thought before she saw Freddie in the corner booth, and he wasn't alone. Tina was with him. Seeing her hugged up under Freddie and whispering in his ear brought back all of her anger, frustration, and grief. For six years, she had made Freddie her world, and to see him hugged up not even an hour after she left made her forget everything. All she felt was hate.

That is, until she saw Tina's head lower and begin to bob slowly up and down in Freddie's lap. *I can make another baby. Can you make another Freddie?* he'd said. Simone just snapped.

Quietly and calmly, she began her approach. She only had the gun because of the kidnapping. She saw the small .380 on the dresser and grabbed it out of fear. Now, here in the club, she felt the weight of the steel in her hand.

Simone took aim and it was like Freddie could feel her from across the room, feel her pain. He lowered his head and looked directly at her, and she fired.

She had aimed for Tina's bobbing head, but instead hit Freddie. Tina screamed and scrambled to get up. She fired again and watched the blood from Freddie's neck splatter all over Tina's back. Tina fled for safety and the club erupted into a frenzy. She fired the last two shots in rapid succession, each one tearing away a piece of flesh from the man she loved.

The pushing and shoving of the escaping clubgoers brought Simone back to reality and she knew she had to get out. She made her way toward the door amongst the other clubbers, then stepped outside and into the waiting cab.

"What the hell!" Wilson exclaimed, watching people run, screaming, from the lounge.

"They shootin', yo!" somebody shouted.

Wilson and Timmons pulled their pistols and aggressively pushed their way inside. "Police! Out of the way! Move!" They looked around, scanning the place for the shooter and listening for more shots. All they heard was a girl crying over a body slumped in a corner booth. "Oh my God! Oh my God! Freddie, please don't die!" Tina begged hysterically.

Detective Wilson and Timmons ran up on the scene. Wilson saw the man he had been looking for. "Get an ambulance!" he directed.

Chapter Forty-Seven

✝ Dante and Cream were sitting in the Explorer, hecklers on
their laps, eyes glued to the door, when people came burst-
ing out.

"'Fuck is goin' on?" Dante asked, getting out of the car,
scanning the faces, and making sure Freddie wasn't one of the
people running away.

Cream got out and stood beside him, gun in hand. A girl
ran by and Cream grabbed her arm, "What the fuck goin' on?"

"Somebody got shot!" she said, then snatched her arm
away and continued running.

"Yo, Cream, go see what's good," Dante said, sending his
boy to gather information.

They didn't have long to wait. The ambulance arrived along
with several squad cars, and they cordoned off the front of the
club. But that didn't stop the curious from huddling around.
The EMTs, along with Timmons, Wilson, and Tina, walked out
of the club, and then came Freddie on a stretcher, oxygen mask
affixed to his face. Tina clung to his side. Cream looked into
Freddie's face and felt mixed emotions. He was glad that
Freddie was the one who had been hit, but he hated the fact
that he hadn't been the one that hit him.

"No, Miss, you can't—" The paramedic tried to stop Tina
and she flipped.

"No! I'm going! I'm his wife! I'm going motherfucka!!" she
ranted and raved as Miller silently nodded an okay. They all
piled into the back of the ambulance and the door shut.

205

Slug stood outside in shock. He had heard the shots, but didn't know who got hit until now. He looked around the crowd and his eyes found Cream. Slug never forgot a face. He remembered Cream from the shootout in Plainfield, and he knew instantly that these had been the cats asking about Freddie.

His mind told him that these were the dudes that had gunned his cousin down. Regardless of everything that had happened, Slug wasn't about to let this violation go unpunished.

Cream ran back to the SUV and got in. "Son, they fuckin' shot Freddie!" he exclaimed, disgusted.

"Who?"

"Fuck, I don't know. But that was him in the ambulance." Cream hit the dashboard in frustration.

"He dead?"

"They ain't have a sheet over his face."

That was all Dante needed to hear. He started the truck up. "Then he ain't dead." He signaled for the two girls to follow. "Let's go find this fuckin' hospital." Dante pulled out onto Ash Street with the Ford Focus behind him.

"Yo, Tay, what are we gonna do when we get to the hospital?" Cream asked. He wanted Freddie, too, but he wasn't down for no wild cowboy shit.

"'Fuck you mean? We ain't leavin' 'til this niggah's dead, fo' sho. I ain't come all this way for nothing. Word to—"

Dante never got a chance to finish his sentence. As he sat at the light, he didn't see the two CBR 900s that pulled up on both sides of the Explorer. J-dog and Bruno simultaneously raised their guns and let off a barrage of shots into the SUV. Dante and Cream never even had a chance to react. They jerked and twitched violently as the bullets filled their already dead bodies.

But Cream and Dante weren't the only ones caught off guard. J-dog and Bruno didn't know that the two girls in the Focus behind them were with the cats in the Explorer.

"Mira, aqui!" the J-Lo look-a-like yelled and opened fire with a Mac. Her partner in crime was synchronized perfectly with her, twin 40s blazing. Their shots hit metal and flesh, sending sparks and soft tissue flying in all directions. J-dog and Bruno lay tangled in their motorcycles.

The blonde Boricua walked up on a half-dead Bruno and stood over him. "Muerte, punto!" she sneered, and emptied the rest of her clip. Then she checked on Dante and Cream. They had both met their maker.

"Mami, vamanos!" the other Latina yelled, hearing the sirens in the distance. They both jumped into the Focus and disappeared into the shadows.

Chapter Forty-Eight

✝ The first thing Freddie saw when he opened his eyes in the hospital was a bright, white light, and two blurry faces. As his vision returned and his pupils focused, he saw that the two faces belonged to two smiling men he had never seen before but recognized instantly—cops.

"Welcome back, Mr. Holmes," Wilson announced triumphantly. "You almost got away from us...for good. But thank God for the miracle of modern medicine. Wouldn't you agree?"

Freddie just looked at Wilson, stone-faced.

"I didn't think you would. But I can't say that I blame you, because where I'm sending you, you're going to wish you were dead." Wilson taunted, then began with the all-too-familiar-words, "You have the right to remain silent..."

Epilogue...

ONE YEAR LATER

✝ Trenton State Prison was the end of the road for anybody in the New Jersey prison system with twenty-five years or more. Nothing but concrete and steel, it was where dreams died and inmates prayed for miracles. This was where Freddie was expected to serve out his twenty-eight year sentence. He had been charged with three murders and one attempted murder. Three murders because the gun he killed Manny with had two previous bodies on it. He easily beat the first two bodies, but copped to one count of second-degree murder and attempted murder for the cop he shot.

He lay back on his bunk, looking at the letter in his hands. The return address read:

Simone Simmons
54 Renner Ave.
Newark, NJ 07102.

He smiled. He had been down for almost 9 months and Simone hadn't written him one letter. She had sent numerous pictures of his daughter, Nadirah, and had sent the beautiful bundle of joy up to see him with his mother, but she had never written him prior to the letter he held in his hand.

Freddie was almost afraid to read the letter, satisfied with the daydream of what he wanted it to say but knew in his heart it didn't. He had written her countless letters, and this was her first reply. There was a scent to it.

On The Run With Love

Hello Freddie,

How have you been? I received all of your letters, and to answer your question, Nadirah and I are doing fine. Did you get the last pictures I sent you? She is growing so fast, it's amazing! Every day I thank God for her little fat-faced self. Everyone says she looks like I spit her out. I must admit, she does look a lot like me, but those are definitely your dimples and your eyes. Every time I look into her eyes, I think of you, the good times that we shared, and it makes me smile.

I am also glad that you are doing well with your college courses. I always knew you had it in you. Remember I used to try to get you to go back to school? I'm glad you're doing it now. Never stop learning, regardless of where you are.

After all the times you wrote me, I guess you're surprised to finally hear from me. But I felt there were some things that I needed to say to you, for you and for myself to have closure. You said in one of your letters that you're sorry for everything you did to hurt me and that you don't blame me for what I did to you. Believe it or not, Freddie, I don't blame me either. I'm not trying to rub it in or be an evil bitch, but you owed me at least that. Do you remember what you said at the airport? What you vowed to me? You pledged on your soul to give me your life. Do you remember, or were those just sweet words you're so good at talking?

You say you don't hate me and I don't hate you. I feel sorry for you because I don't think you deserve all that time. It was a no-win situation for you, and you did what you had to do. But ask yourself this. If you hadn't had sex with that girl, would you have even been in that position? Think about that, because until you change that part of yourself, you haven't changed at all, like you claim.

As for money, I'm okay. I'm working in Elizabeth and going to school at night. Plus, I have some money put up, which I have you to thank for. All that money you were giving me I was saving, saving for us, until us became our daughter and I. With what I saved, plus the twenty-five thousand Slug and Kiki gave me, I bought the house that you now have the address to. It's hard but I'm making it.

And lastly, as to my personal life, you need not be concerned about that and I don't need any advice from you as to what kind of man I need. There will never be another you, because no one will ever hurt me like you did. No one will be playing daddy, as you put it, either. I will continue to send you pictures of our daughter, and I'll send her to see you with your mother at least twice a month. But please don't think you can use Nadirah to set things right between you and I. They are as they are meant to be.

I'm praying for you, for your strength and wisdom, and I pray you can get out because our daughter deserves that. She deserves to have her father in her life. Stay strong, Freddie.

Sincerely,
Simone

Freddie sat up on the bunk and laid Simone's letter beside him on the pillow. She was right and there was nothing he could say. He had made many promises to her, promises she had bet her life on, and he had let her down. He must have been a fool to think that after all that, she'd do twenty-eight years with him. Freddie didn't even know how he could do twenty-eight years. One day at a time, he guessed.

Slug hadn't written him once since his incarceration and that angered him. But knowing Slug had hit Simone off with the amount of money he had made him grateful to Slug in his heart. He had no way of knowing it was his own money, the money he had paid Simone's ransom with, nor would he ever.

Freddie thought about what Simone said about the time he got. He didn't feel he deserved it either, but looking back on all the people he had used, abused or manipulated, he realized that justice had truly been served, and he had to accept it.

His thoughts turned to Gina. He hadn't written her or heard from her at all. He really didn't have anything to say. Until now.

Freddie crossed his small cell to his desk and took out his notepad and pen. His attention was caught by the series of pictures of Tina on his desk. Tina had hopped the fence months ago, after she learned what he had been on the run for. She wrote for a few months, then the letters just stopped. The only reason he kept the pictures was because she was naked or in a thong in all seven of them. He chuckled to himself as he grabbed his pen.

G,

I don't know if you'll ever read this or if you even want to hear from me. I'm sure you know where I'm at and the bid I got. You've always got your ear to the streets (smile).

I'm not gonna stress this scribe with all kind of

apologies or whatever because I know you know I am sorry for how I treated you, but you probably don't want to hear it. It's all good, though. I just wanted to tell you that I finally learned the measure of a man. The measure of a man is taking responsibility for your own actions, good and bad. When you do something good, it's only the result of the lessons from doing bad. And when you do bad, you accept the consequences. I ain't doing this time for murder, but for the life I led that led me to that. I understand that now.

I just wanted you to know that I truly appreciate all that you mean to me, and I'll forever value the time we spent together. I don't expect to hear back from you, but I just wanted you to know at least this.

Peace and happiness,
Freddie

Freddie sat back and tilted the chair until he was looking at the ceiling. Twenty-eight years. He was 22 and would be 50 when he got out. He sat the chair down on all four legs and looked at the notepad. He felt he had a story to tell, and he definitely had the time to tell it. He took up his pen, and this is how it began:

The first bullet whizzed through the air, shattering the bottle of Grand Cru Remy Martin on the table, piercing the soft flesh of my upper left side, breaking two ribs. The burning sensation ignited my insides, telling my intoxicated mind that I had been shot...

Other Hot Titles by J.M.Benjamin

Down In The Dirty
My Manz And 'Em
Ride Or Die Chick
Ride Or Die Chick 2
Menace II Society (anthology)
Christmas In The Hood (anthology)
Changin' Your Game Plan (non-fiction motivational)

**Other Upcoming and Hot Titles from
A New Quality Publishing**

Back Stabbers by Nyema (Summer 2008)
Have You Ever...? by FiFi Cureton (Summer 2008)
Belly Of The Beast by Caleb Alexander (Fall 2008)
Heaven & Earth by J.M.Benjamin (Winter 2008)

HEAVEN & EARTH

By J. M. Benjamin

As Chill turned onto Walnut Avenue in his silver Dodge Charger RT and parked, his eyes immediately zeroed in and locked on Kwan. Hail Mary's track off the classic "All Eyes On Me" Tupac CD was cut short as Chill shut his vehicle off and hopped out. Chill took a quick glance down at his Ed Hardy hooded sweatshirt, making sure the chrome 45 concealed underneath tucked in his waistband was not bulging. Thinking that he had noticed a slight detection of his weapons presence, Chill smoothened out his hoodie before making a bee-line over to where Kwan was standing.

"Ayo K, lem'me holla at you for a minute kid," Chill called out walking up on Kwan.

Kwan was in the midst of puffing on a blunt of goodness when Chill rolled up and instantly he became agitated by Chill's sudden presence. He was not surprise to see Chill having a good idea as to why Chill wanted to speak to him, but he was not in the mood and he intended to make it known.

"What'chu wanna holla at me about?" Kwan retorted aggressively. "Can't you see I'm busy," he added holding up the blunt to his mouth indicating that Chill was disturbing his weed smoking session. Chill disregarded Kwan's words. A grin appeared across his face as he sighed. He knew confronting Kwan was not going to be an easy task, but nonetheless knew that it was long over due.

"Ayo Kwan, why you keep stepping on my lil' mans toes out here dawg?" Chill blurted out catching the attention of everyone within ear distance. "I know it's enough paper out here for everybody sun, you ain't gotta be on no cut throat shit," Chill continued.

After receiving the disturbing phone call that had interrupted him in the middle of something important, it was Chill's intention's to maintain his composure when he confronted Kwan, but as Chill spoke he could feel his adrenaline stirring up inside of himself. And Kwan's reaction did little to minimize it.

"Leek, you see this shit? This lil' bitch ass nigga gonna go run and call his daddy," Kwan chimed in disgusted, directing his words to one of his street colleagues by the name of Malik he had just been sharing the blunt of Purple Haze with. Malik made no reaction or gave no indication that he condoned or entertained Kwan's remarks. He was cool with both Chill and Kwan and remained neutral in the potential altercation, as he continued to puff on the blunt Kwan had passed him.

"Ain't nobody cut that lil' nigga throat B," Kwan barked in a DMX tone taking offense to Chill's accusation. "I told that ma'fucka that was one of my regulars," he continued in his defense, claiming the drug addict the dispute was over was a personal customer of his.

This was not the first time Chill and Kwan had exchanged words over a drug sale. And Chill was not the only one whose workers had a problem with Kwan's tactics in regards to how he hustled on the block, known as Walnut Ave either. He was just the only one who had stepped to Kwan about it. Everyone else was either too afraid of the ending result of a confrontation with Kwan or felt that his antics were not affecting their pockets. But Chill did not fall into either category. For him, it was merely the principle of the matter. It was about respect. Something he'd felt had diminished a long time ago in the game, but because he was old school, he still gave it, so in return he demanded it.

"Come on dawg. He told me how shit went down," Chill stated firmly, trying to hide his annoyance with Kwan. He had believed all that was relayed to him by one of his workers over the phone prior to his arrival, despite the fact that he had known Kwan longer. The only thing knowing Kwan longer than his little man accounted for was the fact that Chill knew how Kwan got down. He knew that Kwan was as guilty as sin and had done exactly what he was being accused of doing. "Yo he said that fiend nigga didn't even know you son," Chill revealed now getting fed up with all the word play between he and Kwan.

Kwan's facial expression grew cold. "I don't give a fuck what that lil bitch nigga told you," Kwan quickly snapped back. "That was one of my ma'fuckin cuttys and he wanted to cop from me like I said," he added with emphasizes.

"Yeah aight" Chill replied dryly.

"I know its aight nigga", Kwan said in attempts to chump off Chill.

Chill caught the sly remark but didn't feed into Kwan's attempt; instead he began to step off seeing that he was actually fighting a lost cause. That is until Kwan's next words caused him to pause in his tracks.

"What you need to do is find you some real ma'fuckas who can hold their own out here to hustle for you and get rid of them three pussies you got on your team," Kwan spit. Chill caught the combination of blatant and humor at his expense in Kwan's tone and it had instantly caught his vein. For the life of him he could not understand why his childhood friend was trying to provoke and force his hand. Chill had been in the game for a long time and had been through his share of trials and tribulations in the process and in his opinion had made it through just fine on his own.

No one had ever dictated or schooled him on how to move or conduct his business in the streets, or anywhere else for that matter, he simply learned and taught himself, which is why Kwan's words had bothered him so much. He did not take too kindly to someone trying to tell him how to run his operation or handle his B.I., especially someone who nothing about running or being a team player.

Chill spun back around. He was now an arm's length away from Kwan.

"Don't worry about who the fuck I got on my team or what I'm doin'", said Chill with emphasis, gritting his teeth through clinched jaws.

"Well nigga then don't be worry about what the fuck I'm doin' then", Kwan spit back. "And back the fuck up anyway unless you try'nna see me fo' somethin," Kwan added.

"It's whatever yo," Chill replied with no intentions of backing down.

"Whoa,whoa, yo both you niggas chill the fuck out", a next kid named Troy intervened. "Niggas trynna eat, fuck all that other shit, Kwan go 'head with that man."

If looks could kill Troy's family would all be dressed in black sobbing over his casket the way Kwan had shot him a rock stare.

"Mind ya ma'fuckin business, this don't have nothing to do with you", Kwan ordered.

Troy started to respond but thought it best not to comment on Kwan's remark. Not while he was without the 40 cal. he normally kept on him. His only intent was to try and defuse the arising altercation between his two street colleagues, but he knew that Chill was capable of handling himself in any situation. Troy knew also that both men were just alike and neither would back down, which is why he was not surprised when Chill began to speak.

"Yo, ever since you came home from Rahway you think you run shit around here dawg, but yo, you ain't Debo kid and this ain't Friday. You can't keep tryna muscle jokers and think that shit gonna fly, Chill stated sternly. "Them days is over, this is '08 baby".

Chill's words only fueled Kwan's fire that had been slowly igniting inside him.

"You say that to say what dawg? You threatening me or something?" asked Kwan, with a distorted expression on his face, chest swelling up as his right hand grazed the butt of his gun. He could feel his own adrenaline beginning to kick into overdrive at the thought of what could possibly happen next.

Despite him being aware of how everyone viewed him around his hood, Kwan knew that not everyone on his block feared him and Chill was one of the ones amongst that small percentage. And like himself, Kwan knew that Chill too had a reputation for being strapped at all times, not to mention a rep. for busting his gun when necessary.

As Kwan towered over Chills' 5 foot 5 inches, 150 pound frame there was no doubt in his mind that Chill was packing heat. There was no way that Chill would have ever rolled up on him. Not unless he was just plain stupid, had a death wish, or both, thought Kwan. No matter what the case, Kwan was growing tiresome of Chill's cockiness ready to put an end to the verbal sparing match. In the past he had put hot slugs in dudes for less, but Chill was an exception because they had a history. A good one. Before the drug game. But as the situation progressed Kwan was beginning to block all of that out. He was on a mission and Chill was trying to come in between he and his plight.

"Yo kid, I don't threaten. All I'm sayin is—".

"Fuck what you sayin nigga", Kwan interrupted in a baritone voice cutting Chill's words short." I helped pioneer this mafukin block and damn near raised most of you niggas in the game out here. You niggas got drop tops and all types of trucks and shit while I'm pushin' a old ass Beamer. Bottom line, I'm doin what the fuck I wanna do out here until I feel my paper right and if a bitch wanna test me then that's their ma'fuckin' funeral, feel me," Kwan growled adjusting his hammer in his waistband.

Kwan's words drew attention in his direction. Every hustler on the "Ave" had heard what he had just said and felt some type of way about his statement, but no one dared step up and voice their feelings on the matter. But in their minds, each man plotted and anticipated on the day they or someone caught Kwan slipping. Troy was the only one who was tempted to intervene for a second time but thought better of it, seeing the visual daggers between Kwan and Chill being thrown at each other.

Kwan's words tore into Chill like hot slugs. He knew that this day would someday come. He had tried his hardest to avoid him and his childhood friend's clash. The fact that their was not a person within ears distance that wasn't paying attention to what Chill and Kwan were saying to each other only heightened the situation because now reputations were at stake. Most of the other hustlers were glad that Chill had enough heart to say what they had felt but kept to themselves, while others feared the worse. It was no secret that Kwan had come home from East Jersey State Prison, which was one of the roughest prisons in New Jersey six months ago, after serving six years and had been on a paper chase from day one home since then. Originally, he had only supposed to have served four years for the shooting case he went to prison for, but while doing his bid, he stabbed a kid from Camden in the neck in the mess hall over a verbal dispute about a basketball game. Luckily, for Kwan, the kid survived but the incident landed him in solitary confinement for two years and lost of 2 years good time, causing him to serve an additional 2 years. The word had spread throughout the entire Trenton how Kwan from "Walnut" put "work in" in the joint and those from his hood knew that when he came home he would be the same, If not worse, then before. And they were right. Coming home 6 inches taller an nearly 100lbs heavier, at 5'10, 240 lbs, Kwan tried to flex his muscles, literally, in attempts to intimidate other hustlers who he felt stood in his way of fattening his pockets. He even toted a snub-nosed 44 in his waist band in plain view to let everyone know that he stayed strapped at all times. That is why everyone knew that he would not let Chill's words ride. His rep depended on it.

Judging by the situation at hand, Chill felt there was no way of getting around it today.

Feeling the tension and knowing both mans caliber, everyone began to fade into the background in attempts to stand clear of the potential harm and danger that existed. What started out as a minor confrontation was steadily erupting into something major. All eyes were locked on Kwan and Chill from a safe distance. Everyone was in fact so focused on the two that no one ever noticed the un-identified SUV parked a short distant up the street. . .

~ ~ ~ ~

The navy blue stolen 2007 Cherokee pulled along side of the curb on Walnut Ave and parked.

"That's him right there", the backseat passenger of the Cherokee pointed out.

"Which one?" the driver asked.

"The big tall dark skinned one with the velour sweat suit on."

"It don't even matter which one he is", the front seat passenger interjected.

"It ain't like these niggas out here gonna just let us walk up on their man and do something to him, then just walk up outta here."

"I was thinking the same thing", said the driver.

"So what are we gonna do?" asked the backseat passenger.

"You ain't gonna do shit, you gonna stay ya ass in the truck while we handle this shit. If he see ya ass he gonna remember you."

"Look", the driver said to the front seat passenger. "Something about to go down."

The front seat driver immediately drew attention to the commotion.

"Not without us it ain't," the front seat passenger said, snatching open door, just before pulling the black mask over their face.

"Get behind the wheel and be on point", the driver instructed the backseat passenger doing the same with their mask before exiting the SUV to back-up their partner.

"Yo Kwan, you must think shit sweet dawg", said Chill, standing his ground. "Ain't nothing pussy about me kid so all that shit you poppin is extra. Ain't nobody try'nna test you big homie. Niggas know how you get down, but just like I know you not gonna let a bitch carry you like a sucka you gots to know that neither am I. So, what are we gonna do? Huh? Shoot each other over a punk ass $100.00 sale, cause I got my strap on me too daddy," Chill informed Kwan lifting the Ed Hardy hoodie up enough to reveal his 45 automatic. "And if you reach for ya joint that's exactly what's gonna happen my nigga" Chill added giving fair warning. Chill had hoped that Kwan used what little sense he had given him the benefit of doubt for having and saw the bigger picture causing Kwan to make the right decision. The last thing Chill wanted was to catch a body or get bodied over a petty drug dispute. But he knew that in the streets people had killed and died for less so he was prepared for whatever.

Kwan grilled Chill intensively while pondering over his words. Kwan knew himself all too well and knew without a doubt in his mind that if he pulled his gun he wouldn't hesitate to use it, but the two things that weighed on his mental the most were 1. Was he ready to go back to the one place he despised the most and 2. Would he actually be able to beat Chill to the draw? It was those two reasons and them alone that caused Kwan to make his decision to let sleeping dog's lie. For the moment anyway, but made a mental note and a promise to himself that he would finish what Chill had started some other time.

"Fuck that $100.00", Kwan spit, reaching into his pocket.

A small load had been lifted off of Chill's shoulders. At first, Chill thought Kwan was reaching for his gun and was about to reach for his own until he saw that was not the case. Instead, Kwan pulled out a knot of cash. "Here take this shit", Kwan then said tossing a hundred dollar bill in Chill's direction.

Insulted by the gesture, Chill instantly replied, "Man, I don't want ya money kid." In all honesty it wasn't about the money at all with Chill but Kwan did not get it. He now also felt insulted by Chill's decline.

"Oh, my paper ain't good e———"

"Boc! Boc! Boc! Boc!,"

"Brrrgah! Brrrgah! Brrgah!"

"What the——- Boom! Boom! Boom!"

"Aaah!"

"Brrrgah! Brrgah!"

"Oh shit!"

"Boc! Boc! Boc! Boc!"

"Brraap! Brrraap!"

"Screeeech "Get In!"

"Boom! Boom! Boom! Click! Click!"

"Somebody call a mafuckin ambulance!" shouted Troy.

The sound of Troy's voice caused Chill to end his pursuit.

"Yo, who the fuck was that?" an out of breath Chill asked making his way back to where shots had moments ago erupted, with 45 still in hand. He had just chased and unloaded his clip on the navy blue Cherokee in the middle of his block the two masked gunmen jumped in and sped off in. He watched as the Cherokee's tail lights vanished up the street.

"I don't know, but Kwan's hit", yelled a bewildered Troy.

By now, everyone had come out of their hiding places and surrounded Kwan.

Kwan's body laid helplessly on the ground as blood spilled out of his mouth and seeped out of his bullet riddled body. Countless shots ripped into his flesh before he even had the chance to pull his own weapon.

Kwan could hear the voices surrounding him asking the questions amongst one another of "who" and "why," with no avail. The only one that was able to provide them with answers was Kwan himself but the blood that began to clog his throat passage prevented him from speaking out as he lay there fighting for his life. He made an attempt to speak but had only managed to grunt inaudibly. Kwan could not believe or rather, didn't want to believe that this was his final fate. During his time in prison, he had heard so many stories about other brothers getting out after serving years and years on lock down, going home in search of their ghetto 40 acres and a government mule only to have their lives cut short from making the mistake of underestimating a person capabilities. Now here it was, Kwan was faced with the same type of statistical situation from making that same fatal error.

As his life began to flash before his very eyes, Kwan couldn't help but to think about how he had gone around the drug block the other day, smacking up and robbing the young pretty girl who had bruised his ego by rejecting him. He would have let the matter ride until the girl had added insult to injury by pulling more money out of her own pocket then Kwan had possessed in his own, after he'd tried to impress her with a "Baller" demeanor. And now, it was because of his egotistical way of thinking that Kwan had gotten more than what he'd bargained for. And because he'd reacted first without thinking he had now felt the unfortunate wrath of Heaven & Earth.

That being his last thought on his mind, Kwan's eyes began to dilate in the back of his head as his body began to go into convulsion. Death had opened its door and embraced him before the ambulance arrived.

Chapter 2

"Le-Le, slow the fuck down", Earth commanded from the backseat of the Cherokee pulling off her mask. "You gonna get us knocked the fuck off." Glancing at the speedometer, Le-Le did as she was told. She hadn't realized she was doing 80 mph up Walnut Avenue. Her only concern at that time was getting her two girlfriends out of harms way after the gun battle jumped off on Walnut and Chambers. There was no way she would have been able to live with herself if something was to have happened to either of them. After all, it was because of her that they had gone around the drug block in the first place.

"Are ya'll alright?" Le-le asked looking back at them through the rearview mirror

Yeah, we good", Heaven assured her. "But I can't say the same for that nigga", she added.

"So ya'll got 'em then?"

"Fuck you mean did we get 'em? Of course we did", Earth stated irritably.

"Cool out", Heaven said. She knew where her friend's hostility was coming from and didn't blame her, but now was not the time for either of them to lose a level head. Still, Earth would not let it go.

"Nah, fuck that", Earth retorted. "We wouldn't even be in this predicament if it weren't for this bitch. I told ya dumb ass before about showing off for mu'fuckas", she spit directing her words at Le-le.

"I wasn't try'nna—-."

"Just shut the fuck up and drive", Earth said cutting her off.

Heaven knew better than to intervene when Earth was reprimanding one of their workers. Not only were her and Earth partners in crime, but more so they had been friends even longer, so Heaven knew her girl all too well. There was no doubt in Heaven's mind that if she attempted to aid Le-le in any type of way, specifically trying to calm her road dawg, it would only add fuel to Earths fire. Earth had been that way for as long as Heaven could remember, extending back to their days when the two had first met at Edna Mahan Correctional Facility for women in Clinton, New Jersey. As Earth continued to scold and verbally chastise

Le-le, Heaven could not help but to reflect on her and the partner's first encounter.

2000...

It had been six long and stressful months in Mercer County's jail and now Heavenly Devine Jacobs was finally being shipped out to prison. She was more than ecstatic. First time ever being locked up, Heavenly had copped out to a plea agreement of 7 years with a 3 _ stipulation; all for the sake of love. At least that's what she had thought at the time.

Growing up in North Trenton, raised by her father, who was known to be one of the biggest heroin dealers in town from a notorious drug block named Brunswick Avenue, and a mother who was deemed on of the baddest females in all of Trenton, Heavenly's childhood, was that of a ghetto fairy tale. At birth, she had inherited her mothers God given beauty but as she grew older she gravitated and inherited her father's taste for the streets and money. By the time she was 15, Heavenly, who had shortened her name to Heaven, had every baller, young and old alike, that laid eyes on her wanting her for them selves. But only those who had paper and plenty of it could afford the luxury and even then Heaven made it hard for them because her father saw to it that she wanted for nothing. That is until an uneventful day occurred, changing Heaven's life forever. When she was 18, Heaven's parents were murdered during a home invasion over money and drugs, while Heaven was away partying in Cancun with friends.

Having practically been left with nothing, Heaven instantly switched into survival mode, using her knowledge of the game and her most valuable assets to get ahead in life. In no time, Heaven had secured the position of wifey / ride or die chick, with a known "money getter" named Screw from a major drug block out in East Trenton from Bruning Avenue. Initially Heaven's intent was to "Do what she had to do" to survive, but as time progress she found herself falling in love with Screw. It was that same love that caused her to take the weight for 250 grams of coke and 100 grams of dope that was found during a raid in an apartment under her name. Heaven was convinced that Screw had loved her just the same if not more, which is why she didn't hesitate to step up to the plate and wear the drugs when Screw had asked her to. Screw had constantly and continuously showed his love and support to Heaven, making sure her commissary was strapped accepting her collect calls, never missing a visit or court date and sending letters and cards daily. Screw had done everything any woman in Heaven's position would want a man to do for them all the way up to the time Heaven had signed and was sentenced on her plea. The entire time Heaven assumed that her man was keeping it real with her like she was with him, but the entire time. Screw was keeping it real fake.

The first day Heaven had arrived at the Clinton Women's Prison and entered the housing unit that would be her place of residence for the next three years or so, she know she was going to have a problem. Women of all shades of color, weight and heights filled the dayroom area. Heaven heard someone cat call "Fresh Meat," as she and five other women carefully walked down the tier with bedrolls in hand in search of their assigned cells. Other women began to pour out into the day-room from their cells hearing the "Fresh Meat" call. It was apparent that two of the females that had been shipped with Heaven had been to the facility before. Heaven noticed that they were giving handshakes and hugs to a few of the women and over heard one of them ask what had they done this time to return? While she continued down the tier in search of her cell, Heaven also peeped three roughly looking females eyeing her from afar, but did her best to pretend as if she hadn't noticed.

After only a week at the facility, the same trio, who Heaven now realized were female studs, tried to run up in her cell with the intentions of conducting a gang rape. Heaven was no slouch when it came to throwing her hands, but she was not sure if she could fight off the three braulic butch chicks. Ready to defend her womanhood or die trying, Heaven positioned her back against the cells wall, threw her hands up and got in a fighting stance. The three would be rapers all smiled. "Bitch we can do this the easy way or the hard way," the biggest of the three said in a deep tone, unfazed by Heaven's attempt to fend for herself. The other two manly looking females barricaded the entrance of the cell with their huge and grotesque bodies, while their partner prepared to make her move. Just as the gorilla of a woman was about to launch her attack towards Heaven, a shadow over swept the six by nine cell from behind them all. Heaven had also noticed the sudden dimness but couldn't see the cause through the women.

When the three would be rapers all turned and directed their attention towards the cells entrance, their eyes widened at the sight of Earth. Earth stood just outside of the cells doorway in her white wife beater, gray sweatpants and beige state boots tightly tied, twirling two razor blades around in her mouth with her tongue. Earth had watched from day one when the pretty long haired voluptuously shaped red-bone had come into the institution and Teresa and her clique immediately began scoping her out. Normally Earth didn't get involved in other people's affairs, but there was something about the new girl that drew Earth in, beside the fact that she had a weakness for light skinned women.

Well aware of Earth's reputation with the two infamous blades she always kept in her mouth, Teresa and her two girls stood down. No one wanted any problems with "Big Earth." The last female who had made the mistake of going against her had received more zippers on her face than Edward Scissor hands, resulting in Earth serving nine months in lock-up. Without uttering so much as one word, the three disappointed females bailed out of the cell like a row of ducks, not even attempting to glance over at Earth out of fear of triggering her off.

Not knowing her motives at the time, Heaven said, "Thanks, but I could've handled that."

"I'm sure you could've," was all Earth replied before walking off.

Two days had gone by before either of the two said anything else to one another. It was actually Heaven who had broken the ice by thanking Earth again, this time introducing herself. From that day forward Heaven and Earth became close, forming a bond as thick as thieves. Three months later Earth had beaten a female from New Brunswick unconscious just for commenting to someone that she felt Heaven thought she was all of that. She ended up serving another six months in lock-up for that. That incident lead everyone, including the officers, to believe that Heaven and Earth were lovers, being as though Earth was a lesbian and so over-protective of Heaven, but that was far from being the case. They were more like sisters than anything and whenever Earth was not in the hole their discussions and plans extended far beyond sexuality. And even then, they managed stay in touch, plot, and plan through letters and messages passed on by cool officers and trustees who frequented and worked the ad-seg unit. As beautiful as Heaven was and despite the fact that Earth had a thing for thick red bones, she had the utmost respect for Heaven and never came at her on that order. It was that same respect that had spilled over into the streets when the two had been released from prison.

coming soon!

Ride or Die Chick 2

Closure

"All rise for the Honorable Judge William H. Braswell of the District of Virginia."

Teflon sighed in frustration as she struggled to lift herself up out of the wooden courtroom chair. She was sick and tired of being lugged back and forth to court month after month for something she already knew the final outcome of. It had been a long and drawn out case she felt. When she first laid eyes on the jurors who would determine her fate there was no doubt in her mind what type of verdict would be handed down. Seeing them over to her far right now, and the way they stared and murmured amongst themselves only confirmed Teflon's thoughts. The only reason she had actually taken her case to trial was because she knew it was what Treacherous would have wanted her to do." We fighters babe, we go hard or go home," he would always say to her, Teflon recalled. She fought to suppress her emotions at the thought of her other half as a sharp pain jolted through the small of her back. Between the spasms she had been having since the gun shot wound she was recovering from and the nine month old life growing inside of her, her movement was turtle like and painful. As tough as she was, she was no match for the battle she had been going through with the life inside of her. Noticing her facial expressions, her attorney made an attempt to aid her. It was apparent to him that she was in pain, but he was stopped in his tracks by her sudden expression that spoke volumes, making it perfectly clear to him that his services were not welcomed nor needed. After representing her for the last eight months, he had grown accustomed to her non-chalant and cold demeanor so he was not at all surprised that she had declined his help. Teflon stood in front of the table with her hair pulled back in a pony tail sporting her grey county sweat-suit and county issued tennis shoes. She used the table to brace herself as the judge entered the courtroom. The additional twenty one pounds she put on between the baby and jail made it that much more difficult for her to stand. The weight was un- comfortable for her and she couldn't wait to shed both it and the baby and get back to her normal size nine/ten.

"Please be seated," the judge instructed

"Umph" Teflon grunted as another spasm shot through her lower back.

"This is the trial of the United States of America versus Teflon Jackson, counsels state your names for the record."

"Your honor, Mark Stanford of the public defenders office of Norfolk for the defense," announced Teflon attorney

"Christopher Malloy District Attorney of Norfolk for the prosecution your Honor."

" If I'm correct, today is the final day of this trial," the judge stated skimming through the paper-work before him. "Counsels will deliver their closing arguments and remarks and the jury will render a verdict based on the information and evidence that has been presented to them throughout this trial. Counsels are you ready to proceed?"

" Yes your honor, " both counsels replied.

"Mr. Stanford."

This was the moment of the truth, thought Mark Stanford. He took one look back at Teflon and slightly shook his head in disbelief as he sighed to himself. In exchanged, Teflon stared him right in the eyes, unfazed by his sympathetic eyes. He couldn't believe how hard core Teflon was and had been throughout the entire time of his representation. In his thirteen years of practice as a public defender, he had never encountered a client more difficult and rebellious then Teflon Jackson. In the eight months he had been her lawyer, from day one she was un- cooperative. It had been like pulling teeth trying to get her to open up in order to assist him in trying to soften the blow of what he knew was her inevitable fate according to what he had read and discovered about the case. There were a few angles and approaches he would have liked to have taken for her defense but Teflon refused to talk with him after stating she wanted to go to trial. She wouldn't budge even when he tried to appeal to her maternal side still, she rejected the notion of helping him help her, so his only defense was based on the lack of evidence they actually had against her. Attorney Stanford sympathized with the pregnant young woman, but due to his heavy work load and promising cases of clients who were willing to help themselves as well as the government in exchange for leniency, he was all too happy to be bringing this particular case to a close. Mark Stanford took a sip of the ice water that sat before him and cleared his throat. "Members of the jury," he started as he walked from behind the courts table and adjusted his tri- color neck tie. "In the past few months you have heard allegations from the prosecution against my client that literally makes her out to look like not only this modern day Bonnie from the historical Bonnie & Clyde, but also this stoned -cold killer. As you know Ms. Jackson is being charged with multiple counts of conspiracy to commit armed robbery in the first degree and conspiracy to commit murder in the first." He let the accusations of the charges linger before he continued. "But what she is being accused of and charged with is not the case here today. No," he paused.

"The case here is what evidence has been presented to substantiate these allegations against my client." He paused again then pivoted.

"The prosecution would like you to be convinced that my client, Ms. Teflon Jackson conspired to connect armed robbery, but yet he failed to produce any surveillance video clearly showing my clients direct involvement in the allegation. Nor was he able to produce a witness from inside the bank that could testify to the fact of whether or not my client was held against her own free will by the diseased Mr. Treacherous Freeman."

His words and the mentioning of Treacherous name instantly gained her attention and rubbed Teflon the wrong way. She had no idea or clue as to her attorney's closing arguments and really didn't care up until the time he had just tried to portray her as the victim and her other half as the villain. She was tempted to jump up and set the record straight, but Treacherous words danced in her head as if he were right beside her in her ear. "Using emotions over intellect is never justifiable," she heard him repeating.

Why the fuck you leave me like this, Teflon questioned in her mind staring up to the ceiling as if Treacherous were up there looking down at her. She grabbed a napkin off the table to wipe her left nostril. It began to run. She sat up and became attentive as her lawyer continued. "The prosecution states that my client is guilty of conspiracy to commit MURDER," attorney Stanford said with emphasis's turning to face Teflon pointing in her direction. He could tell she was not too pleased by the comment he had made about her deceased boyfriend. He knew he would be treading on thin ice with her by painting the picture he just had, but it was the only way he felt he could help spare her life. He was fully aware of the bond the couple shared. He had found out first hand a few months back, when he had made the fatal mistake of merely referring to Treacherous as

this guy and making mention of him being deceased. At forty-three years old, standing at five feet ten inches, tipping the scales at two hundred- fifteen pounds, he had never been so afraid of someone who he outweighed and felt he'd out matched in his life that day. And to top it off, it had been a woman that had instilled this fear within him. It wasn't anything she had done - but what she had said, and how she had said it, that sent chills throughout Mark Stanford's entire body. He couldn't help but replay the words that invaded his sleep many of nights in his head." If you ever speak of my deceased loved one in vein in my presence ever again you're gonna meet him."

The calm manner in which she spoke convinced him that she meant every word of it. His first instinct was to report the incident and abandon the case, but his curiousness overpowered his decision. He wanted to see how this particular case unfolded and wanted to be the one who played a part in its unfold.

"But yet instill, none of the murder weapons retrieved from the crime scene possessed my clients finger prints."

His words caused Teflon to peer over towards the juror's direction. She noticed a few puzzled and quizzical expressions on a few of their faces. She knew that key element of her case would stir up some if not a great deal of confusion amongst them. That was something she herself was confused about initially, knowing her involvement like she knew the back of her own hand. As she played the tapes back to the event, there was no a doubt in her mind that she had hit at least one of the officers when they came out of Bank of America before she herself took one in the side. The only explanation possible she could come up with was that Treacherous had wiped her prints off the gun she used, but why? That was something she would not get the answer to until the two of them met up in the future she reasoned. Teflon listened as her attorney continued. "Yes, my client is guilty. But not guilty of the charges she sits here with child being accused of." Attorney Stanford paused for a second time to let the statement about Teflon being with child marinate. "The only thing my client is guilty of here today is loving a man too much and too hard," he said. He really wanted to say, "Loving the wrong man," but he didn't want to go over-board with offending his client. Teflon's threat months ago sat at the forefront of his mind and he thought better of it. "And that ladies and gentleman is not why my client is on trial here today. I hope you take all that I've said into account when making your ruling." Attorney Stanford ended with a bow and walked back around the table where Teflon sat. The two exchanged quick glances. Teflon gave her attorney no indication that she approved of his argument and he wasn't looking for one. After all, it was his job. District Attorney Christopher Malloy skimmed through his notes one last time before he stood. He then looked over at Teflon who felt his eyes on her.

"What the fuck you lookin' at?" She mumbled under her breath just enough for him to   hear and read her lips. The DA smiled and pushed his glasses up on his face. He had no sympathy what so ever for the female criminal who sat across from him. According to the evidence there was no doubt in his mind or heart that Teflon Jackson deserved all that she would receive and then some after a verdict was handed down. Despite what he was able to produce to build a strong case against her, he was confident the jury would render the right decision and continue to keep the female menace to society off the streets. It was DA Malloy's intent to push for the maximum penalties once providing the verdict was what he believed it would be. " Ladies and gentlemen the jury despite what counsel says the prosecution failed to produce. There has been evidence presented to you that clearly shows that the accused is in fact guilty if the charges she stands trial for. Evidence showed that Ms. Teflon Jackson and Mr. Treacherous Freeman exited the Norfolk Virginia branch of Bank of America with weapons and were involved in gun battle with police. Evidence clearly showed that their was a high speed pursuit for Ms. Jackson and the deceased, endangered the welfare of other pedestrians and law enforcement Evidence showed that the vehicle used as the get a way car was in fact the same car that was car jacked at a local McDonalds resulted in two murders. Evidence also shows that during this crime spree six state police officers and four federal agents were killed in the line of duty, which five others were wounded. I'm not standing before you trying to convince you to speculate or even try to figure out what I didn't or why I didn't present the evidence council said I failed to produce. All I ask is that you look at the evidence that was presented to you by the counts and based on that and that alone render the decision that you feels fit. Thank you," DA Malloy clasped his hands together and ended with a slight bow to the jury. He then prevented and returned to the table opposite of Teflon and her attorney. She rolled her eyes at the District Attorney as he flashed her before. When he sat down, he looked over at Teflon again, who now had a gun of her own plastered across her face. He had no way of knowing that Teflon was visualizing Treacherous pistol whipping him with the butt of his gun while she stood there and watched. "Members of the jury. You have heard both arguments in the case of The United States of America verses Teflon Jackson. It is your duty after hearing both parties and based on the evidence presented before you that beyond a reasonable doubt a decision is made. It's now 10:45 am the court will recess for an hour while the jury returns to chambers. Bailiff please escort the jury back to chambers. " The judge ordered with gavel and hearing that, the two the front marshals setting tow rows behind Teflon and her attorney stood and approached the front of the courtroom "Ms. Jackson, please stand and turn around," the female marshal requested with hand cuffs in hand. Teflon exhaled and complied, the cuffs were then placed around her waists. " Too tight?" the marshal asked Teflon answered with a nod. I'll be back there to see you shortly." Her attorney announced as Teflon was escorted through the court and to the federal holding cell. She didn't bother to acknowledge that she had heard his words. Attorney Stanford and the male federal marshal exchanged mutual lunches. In their line of work they were all too use to detainees acting the way Teflon was. "Okay, let me get these cuffs off you " the federal marshal said. "I'll be back to check on you periodically and I'll see if I can get you a pillow or blanket, the female marshal added as she locked Teflon in the bull pin. Being a mother herself, she empathized for Teflon. She recognized labor symptoms when she saw them. She knew Teflon would deliver her child any day now. The female marshal shook her head in sadness at Teflon's present condition and situation as she and her parties exited the holding quarters. Teflon hold on the bullpen's bench slowly made her way to the floor. The bench was too small and uncomfortable for her so she chose the floor instead, using the edge of the bench for support. In just under an hour she would receive closure on this chapter of her life. Despite her attorney's best attempt to defend her, Teflon knew she would not be walking up out of her situation scot free not now, not later or if at all. And she had come to terms with herself with that. And when she felt she could no longer take it, she'd meet up with Treacherous again. She lifted up her sweatshirt and white tee underneath and began rubbing her stomach in a circular motion as images of her last moments with her other half flashed through her mind. "Treach," yelled Teflon as she pointed her 380 and nine millimeter beretta in the direction of the police and began squeezing the triggers. " Babe get in!" Treacherous yelled over to Teflon attempting to cover her as police returned fire. Treach I'm losing a lot of blood," cried Teflon as she applied pressure to the right side of her hip in attempt to minimized the bleeding. "Just hold on Boo I got you, You gonna be aight We gonna make it up outta this shit, and I'ma get you to a hospital. "Tef? Tef?"

"Huh."

"Wake up baby. Don't fall asleep. Stay awake you hear me ?" Teflon could feel him rubbing her hair. "Daddy I'm weak and it's cold."

"Tef! Man the fuck up you aight . Shake that shit off. Stop all that mufuckin whinnin and shit and man the fuck up!"

"Who the fuck you yellin at boy?"

"Boo my bad Don't talk save your strength," Treacherous said moving Teflon's hair from out of her face.

"Don't start bitchin up now , mufucka ," despite her condition she managed to smile. " "Fuck you." Treacherous smiled back. "Boo hold on, we almost there." Teflon heard Treacherous words but could not respond. She was slipping in and out of consciousness. "Tef," she heard her lover call out again but still she was unable to respond again, Treacherous voice was muffled and his words because inaudible. "Teflon!" was the last word she heard before she lost full consciousness.

"Ms. Jackson." Hearing her name snapped Teflon out of her daze. When she looked up her lawyer was standing outside the holding cell. She raised her sweatshirt and wiped her entire face. Her trip down memory lane made her emotional. She was mad at herself for allowing her attorney to witness her in that state. Out of respect, Mark Stanford pretended not to notice by going thru his cellular phone for no particular reason. Teflon made an effort to stand up. "No please, don't get up," her attorney advised. "I was just coming to let you know that the juries should be returning in about twenty more minutes. The marshal will be to get you in about ten. Honestly, I have to say Ms. Jackson, I have a good feeling bout this case. I think the juries may possibly rule in your favor," attorney Stanford made failed attempt to council his client. His words were more so for himself. This was his fourth trial case and so far he was three for three, hoping to add a fourth one to win the case and claimed he felt they would, but in the back of his mind he was not totally convinced of the final outcome, And his clients uncaring facial expressions did nothing to his confidence level. " I'll see you back in the courtroom, "Teflon's attorney dryly remarked, again shaking his head in disbelief about how nonchalantly she was acting. "Has the jury reached a verdict?"

"Yes we have your honor," the middle age white female juror replied

"Ms. Jackson, please face the jury." Teflon slightly turned her head toward the jury. The judge shot her a look of disgust.

"Ms. Jackson, please turn and face the jury," he repeated. He had just about enough of the pregnant woman's court antics. "Tsk!" Teflon sucked her teeth and shifted her direction towards the jury. "Juror number one, please stand and read your verdict." The juror did she was told and stood and unfolded the white piece of paper she held in hand, faced the judge, then began to read. "We the jurors, in the case of the United States of America verses Teflon Jackson find that on the charges of conspiracy to commit armed robbery in the first degree on counts one three sixteen, we find the defendant," she paused, turning her attention to Teflon. "Guilty on all counts." Teflon's lawyer dropped his head and placed his head in the palm of his hand. Teflon only smirked with a slight snicker. She was not at all surprised at the verdict as far as she was concerned the juror did not have to finish. "On the charges of conspiracy to commit murder in the first degree, on counts one three thirteen, we find the defendant Guilty as charged." Just as the first, the second conviction did not faze Teflon. She had already mentally prepared for the verdicts, after all, she was guilty of the charges she stood trial for. Life as she knew it was literally over for her the day they had taken Treacherous from her. Besides the life she carried inside her, she had no other reason to live for. Mentally and emotionally she was already dead, no there was nothing more they could do to her she felt. The DA had the look of victory plastered across his face as he stood. "Bitch ass nigga," Teflon murmured just loud enough for the DA to hear as the two made eye contact.

"Your honor, the prosecution is moving to impose the maximum penalties under the federal guide lines against M. Jackson," The DA burst out, breaking his stare with Teflon. " I object your honor," Teflon's attorney hopes up and rebut. "My client."

"Your client is an un- remorseful menace to society and threat to our community," the DA quickly snapped back, cutting Teflon's attorney short of his words "Fuck you you gay ass muthafucka !" Teflon lashed out insulted by the District Attorney's statement. "Order!" The judge demands, repeatedly banging his gavel. The marshals were now out of their seats, rushing towards the potential altercation, seeing Teflon attempting to raise up out of her chair. "Ms. Jackson, we will not"

"I don't give a fuck I don't give a fuck!" Teflon screamed before the judge could complete his sentence. By now the marshals had reached Teflon. "Calm down Ms. Jackson." the female marshal advised as she took hold of Teflon's left arm. The other marshal said nothing. He grabbed her by her right one. "Fuck that kill me now." The DA put distance between he and Teflon fearful of what could possibly happen next. The jurors were bewildered at Teflon's sudden out burst and become afraid of the wild woman. They were imme- diately escorted out of the courtroom. "I don't give a fuck, kill, ugh!" Teflon belled over and grabbed hold of her stomach. "Ms Jackson are you okay?" her attorney was the first to ask. "Demitri, call a EMT , I think she's going into labor, the female marshal instructed. Teflon continued to scream in agony. Her cries shook the courtroom walls. "Holy cow," Teflon's attorney shouted. Everyone attention was immediately drawn to her lawyer wanting to know what had stifled him. "She's bleeding." When they looked down they saw the burgundy stained between her legs. "Where's that EMT, She's hemorrhaging," the female marshal yelling seeing her partner reentered the courtroom. "On their way. Be here in five," he replied.

"Tell em to make it two," she retorted. Teflon was uttering something to herself. The female marshal assumed she was trying to say something and moved in closer.

"Ms. Jackson, I don't understand you, I need you to speak clearer." Teflon paid her mind. She was somewhere else. The female marshal continued to try to make out her words with no avail .Just as the EMT burst through the courtroom door, The female marshal was almost curtain she had figured out what Teflon had been chanting. To be sure, she moved in closer until Teflon's lips were nearly touching her lobe, " Treacherous I love you," was what she had heard right before Teflon Jackson had passed out.... Teflon awake to a handcuffed wrist to a hospital gurney and take running from her body to machines her body was sore. The scenery was like Dejavu to her as she recalled the last time she landed herself in the hospital. Only how she came about being transported to the faculty and why. Teflon remembered going into labor and losing consciousness inside the courtroom as she reflected back, the thought of her and Treacherous child came to light in her mind where was her baby she wondered? Then it dawned on her. The last words she had heard before she blacked out was that she was hemorrhaging. Her chest began to tighten and her mouth became dry. There was no doubt in her mind she had lost the one thing that would have kept her and Treacherous connected for life. Teflon could not believe she had a miscarried as she felt her stomach with her free hand. Something didn't feel right to her. She slid the hospital sheet to the side and hiked the hospital dress up over her waist. When she looked down, Teflon saw that her stomach possessed staples. They had cut her open she instantly became enraged. Not only had she lost her child, but was left with a scar that would remind her for the rest of her life. In the nine months she had the little life growing inside of her, Teflon had grown to love her expected arrival despite Knowing she would have to detach herself from it. Now there was no need to. Teflon became emotional bothered by the thought. There had only been three living creatures in the world that Teflon had ever love, One, her mother, Treacherous being the second, and their un-born child being the third. And none of the three existed any longer. With that in mind just as the last time she wind up in the hospital, Teflon thought to end her own life. The only reason she had lasted this long was for the baby's sake. But now there was no real reason for her to live any longer. Her eyes searched around the room looking for something within reaching distance to aid her in her departure. For the second time, Teflon began snatching the tubes out of herself with her free hand, only to be interrupted by a loud cry. "Sssh, don't," the young white nurse said to the little infant wrapped up in the powder blue blanket. She was so engulfed with trying to quiet the baby that she never noticed that Teflon was awake let alone her pulling the tubes out. Teflon's heart skipped a beat seeing the nurse holding the screaming baby. "Ooh," the nurse said startled. By the time she had looked up, Teflon had ceased her behavior. "Didn't know you were awake," she remarked over the babies cries, while rocking and putting the infant on the back. "I've been bringing him in here everyday for the past few days to see you. "Him," Teflon heard the young nurse say. A boy that made her smile on the inside. She was hoping to have a son to carry on his father's legacy. "Look, mommies woke, "she said child like to Teflon's son.

"He's very handsome," she added bringing the baby closer to Teflon. One look at her son and Teflon's heart melted like fried ice cream. For that brief moment, her black heart was replaced with a pin cushion. She didn't feel like the gang stress she always portrayed. She felt like a woman a mother. "You wanna hold em?" the nurse asked already handing the infant over to Teflon. She cuddled her son with her free hand and looked at him and could see he was the spitting image of Treacherous. "Little Treach," she whispered. Just as she was about to lift her son up and embraced him with a kiss, her room door flew up and two federal agents appeared. "Mam. Please take the child from the detained, " one of the agents instructed. His words snapped Teflon back to reality. The nurse took hold of Teflon's son. " Sorry she whispered with a genuinely sympathetic smile right before she hurried out the room. Teflon knew that would be the last time she would see or hold her son again. On the day she was sentenced to 480 months in a West Virginia federal prison, she also signed her son, who she named Treacherous Antwan Freeman Junior over to the state of Virginia.....

coming soon